I0760281

THE Corpse WITH THE Emerald Thumb

CATHY ACE

FOUR TAILS PUBLISHING LTD.

Second Edition

The Corpse with the Emerald Thumb

ISBN: 978-1-990550-37-9 (hardcover)
ISBN: 978-1-990550-36-2 (paperback)
ISBN: 978-1-990550-38-6 (electronic book)

PRAISE FOR THE CAIT MORGAN MYSTERIES

"In the finest tradition of Agatha Christie…Ace brings us the closed-room drama, with a dollop of romantic suspense and historical intrigue." – *Library Journal*

"…touches of Christie or Marsh but with a bouquet of Kinsey Millhone." – *The Globe and Mail*

"…a sparkling, well-plotted and quite devious mystery in the cozy tradition…" – *Hamilton Spectator*

"…If all of this suggests the school of Agatha Christie, it's no doubt what Cathy Ace intended. She is, as it fortunately happens, more than adept at the Christie thing." – *Toronto Star*

"Cait unravels the…mystery using her eidetic memory and her powers of deduction, which are worthy of Hercule Poirot."
– *The Jury Box, Ellery Queen Mystery Magazine*

"This author always takes us on an adventure. She always makes us think. She always brings the setting to life. For those reasons this is one of my favorite series."
– *Escape With Dollycas Into A Good Book*

"…a testament to an author who knows how to tell a story and deliver it with great aplomb." – *Dru's Musings*

"…perfect for those that love travel, food, and/or murder (reading it, not committing it)." – *BOLO Books*

"…Ace is, well, an ace when it comes to plot and description." – *The Globe and Mail*

Other works by the same author
(Information for all works here: **www.cathyace.com**)

The Cait Morgan Mysteries
The Corpse with the Silver Tongue
The Corpse with the Golden Nose
The Corpse with the Emerald Thumb
The Corpse with the Platinum Hair
The Corpse with the Sapphire Eyes
The Corpse with the Diamond Hand
The Corpse with the Garnet Face
The Corpse with the Ruby Lips
The Corpse with the Crystal Skull
The Corpse with the Iron Will
The Corpse with the Granite Heart
The Corpse with the Turquoise Toes
The Corpse with the Opal Fingers
The Corpse with the Pearly Smile

The WISE Enquiries Agency Mysteries
The Case of the Dotty Dowager
The Case of the Missing Morris Dancer
The Case of the Curious Cook
The Case of the Unsuitable Suitor
The Case of the Disgraced Duke
The Case of the Absent Heirs
The Case of the Cursed Cottage
The Case of the Uninvited Undertaker
The Case of the Bereaved Butler
The Case of the Secretive Secretary

Standalone novels
The Wrong Boy

Short Stories/Novellas
Murder Keeps No Calendar: a collection of 12 short stories/novellas
Murder Knows No Season: a collection of four novellas
Steve's Story in "The Whole She-Bang 3"
The Trouble with the Turkey in "Cooked to Death Vol. 3: Hell for the Holidays"

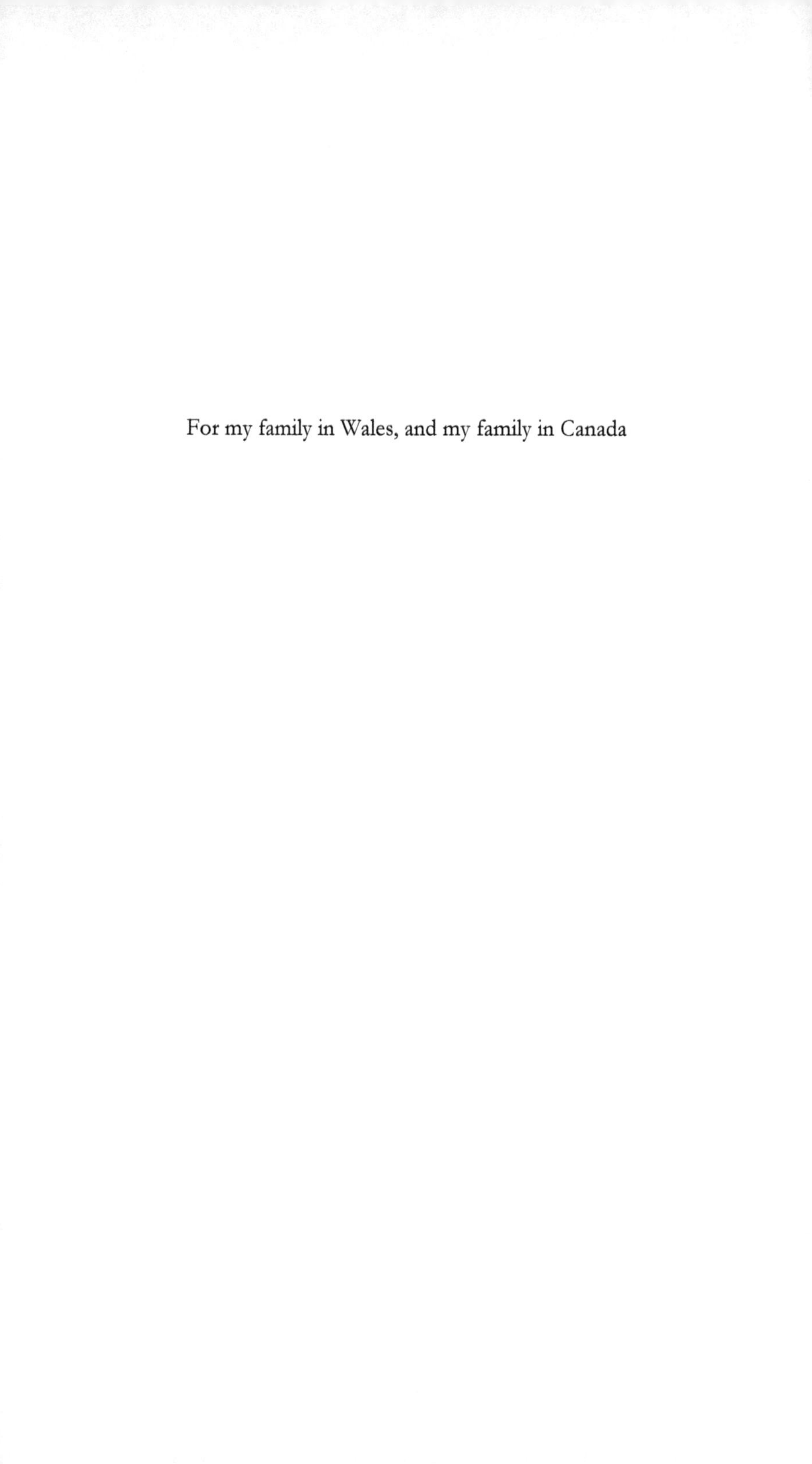

For my family in Wales, and my family in Canada

Foreword to the Second Edition

In February 2024 the original publisher of the first eight Cait Morgan Mysteries reverted the publishing rights to me, the author. Years have passed since I wrote this, the third book in the series, so I suppose it's only natural that, given this opportunity, I'd want to revisit it.

Just so you know…the story hasn't changed, though the telling of it has. Think of this as you'd think of a "Director's Cut" of a movie: this second edition is the "Author's Cut".

I always strive my hardest to write the best book I can, and hope I write books that are – as far as possible – timeless, in that they're contemporary, and reflect and rely upon aspects of humanity that do not alter.

I constantly hope to become more certain of my writing voice, and I've worked to develop my skills and my craft over time, through experience.

For those reading this tale for the first time, I truly hope you enjoy it. If you've treated yourself to this second edition, having already read the previous one, I trust you're not disappointed that the story hasn't changed, and hope you enjoy the re-telling, which I daren't say is "better", but it's certainly been crafted by an author who's learned (hopefully) a thing or two over the years.

Cathy Ace
February 2025

1

Seven Days

Bud dumped an impressive mound of personal items out of his pockets and onto the breakfast bar of our Mexican vacation condo.

I said – lovingly of course, "You could do with a manbag."

"I think the correct term is 'murse'," replied Bud. He looked endearingly smug.

"Fashion-speak from a retired cop who owns just three jackets?" I gave him a friendly poke.

He grinned. "Now all that dead weight's gone, I'm off to get supplies. I saw a bodega across the road when we drove in, and I need a beer, or three. You'll let me back in, right?" He grabbed a handful of cash as he made for the door, grinning.

"As long as there are treats for me too."

It had been a long day already: we'd arrived at Vancouver airport at a ludicrously early hour, and I was still recovering from being squashed into an unreasonably narrow seat on our flight to Puerto Vallarta, followed by a sweaty drive to the actual resort in a car where the only air conditioning had been courtesy of opening the windows.

Treats are definitely in order.

Bud's parting shot was, "Okay. I'll see what I can find to make you smile. Back soon."

I decided to make myself useful, so grappled with the shutters at the windows in the main room, which eventually flew open to reveal a narrow road and a row of white stucco buildings below, beyond which glittered the magnificent Bay of Banderas.

A whole week of just me and Bud being us. Wonderful.

As I repeated the successful shutter-wrestling process in the bedroom, I hoped that the ominous clouds gathering on the horizon wouldn't spoil our exploration of the resort's supposedly lush gardens…then spotted Bud leaving the bodega holding a promisingly bulky carrier bag. He popped into what was clearly a florist's store next door. I smiled as I began to unpack my suitcase, daring to picture Bud presenting me with a lovely bunch of flowers upon his return.

How romantic.

A distant bell chimed noon.

Idyllic.

It was the scream that drew me back to the bedroom window.

I looked out again to see a wailing woman holding open the door to the florist's store. Though the internal lighting provided only partial illumination, I could make out the shape of a figure kneeling, and its hands were…around the throat of someone who was flat on the floor. The figure looked up and mouthed something at the screaming woman. I couldn't hear what was said, because just then a pickup truck roared by, but in that instant I recognized the face of the figure who was throttling the person on the ground.

Bud!

Slack-jawed, I stood at the window as the scene below me played out. Two men in almost farcically elaborate blue and gold uniforms rushed out of the bodega next door to the flower shop: one was a short, portly guy, the other a tall, lean one. The short one attended to the still-screaming woman, who was swaying and clutching at the air, while the tall one pulled open the door she'd allowed to swing closed. A weapon had magically appeared in his hand, and he pointed it into the building as he held the door open with his foot.

In the gloom, I saw Bud raise his hands and clamber to his feet, then turn, ready to be handcuffed, which he was.

3

I felt as though I were watching a movie: transfixed, yet…disconnected.

The tall man – who was quite obviously a cop – dragged Bud out of the store into the midday sun. I could see that Bud's shirt, arms, and knees were covered in blood.

Please let that not be his.

The tall cop appeared to bark instructions at the short one, who propped the distraught woman to sit against the wall, then ran off and returned moments later in a police car; I guessed it must have been parked around the corner, at the end of the row of buildings.

As Bud was roughly manhandled toward the vehicle, he pushed out his bloodied chest, pulled himself up to his full height, turned his face skyward, and shouted with all his might, "Jack…Jack…Petrov…Cartagena…" Then he was gone – shoved unceremoniously through the back door of the sedan.

The tall cop spoke to his shorter colleague, waved his arms around a bit, then took off his hat and jacket, tossed them into the trunk, and jumped into the driver's seat. The car shot off along the road, throwing up dust and small stones in its wake. Its wailing siren sliced through the humid air.

I breathed in for what seemed like the first time in many moments. I found I still couldn't move.

What just happened?

None of it made any sense. Well, given the circumstances in which he'd been discovered, what had happened to Bud did make sense…but how had he managed to get himself into that position in the first place?

You've only been out of the apartment for about ten minutes.

I knew, instinctively, that the person on the floor inside the flower shop was dead, and it seemed to me that the tall cop had been pretty sure that Bud had killed them. A switch flipped somewhere in my brain, and I worked out that there'd probably be the arrival of a coroner – or the Mexican equivalent – then the body would be removed, and the crime scene secured. Then there would be an investigation into why Bud had done it...but there could never be any resolution to such an investigation, because Bud couldn't – *wouldn't* – have done it.

I sat down, hard, on the edge of the bed and wondered what to do. My instinct was to run to the short policeman, who was managing the gaggle of people milling about outside the florist shop, and tell him who I was, who Bud was, and that Bud couldn't possibly have killed anyone.

I realized that my own background as a professor of criminal psychology at the University of Vancouver might not give much weight to such assertions, but was sure that Bud's long career in law enforcement would speak volumes. We'd worked together for quite a while, when he'd hired me to consult as a victim profiler for his homicide investigation teams, and we've been dating for a few months short of a year – so I know him well both professionally, and personally...and also know that he couldn't possibly have killed a complete stranger just moments after arriving in town.

But...the cop who'd carted him off didn't know him from a hole in the ground. All he'd done was his job...so all I had to do was go down there and point out the mistake that had been made.

I can't get up off this bed because my legs are so wobbly.

What had Bud shouted? It must have been important. I didn't need my useful, but largely secret, eidetic memory to recall what he'd called out.

"Jack. Jack. Petrov. Cartagena."

I concentrated. No...I didn't know anyone called Jack Petrov. Nor, as far as I knew, did Bud. The only Jack I could think of was Jack White – Bud's old mentor and colleague. He and his wife, Sheila, owned the apartment where I was sitting, and it was also their little car that we'd used to drive from the airport. They were even looking after Marty, Bud's tubby black Labrador, on their acreage in Hatzic, back home in British Columbia. Jack and Bud had worked together for decades, and as I visualized Jack's kind, pale face and his tall, spare frame – which always seemed to be in motion – I decided that since I couldn't ask Bud himself what to do, speaking to Jack was the next best thing.

But how?

I dragged my cell phone out of my bag and checked the directory. No, of course I didn't have the Whites' numbers back home. I spotted Bud's phone on the counter, where he'd dumped it with all his other bits and pieces; I didn't like the thought of checking his phone, but it seemed the only option. Luckily, I knew his passcode, so punched it in, then scrolled through the names and acronyms in his contact list, most of which meant nothing to me. Finally, I reached "White Cell" and "White House". I dialed the house to start with. After several rings, I disconnected and punched the button to call the other number.

An instant later, I heard Jack's voice, echoing on speakerphone. "Jack here. I'm driving, and Sheila's in the truck with me, so be careful what you say, whoever you are."

I could hear giggling, and then Jack's adorable, if sometimes overly fussy, wife said, "Oh, you are wicked, Jack White. Don't say that; it could be anyone."

I could picture them both quite clearly: the perfectly paired couple, happily heading out somewhere in their truck on a Sunday afternoon. My mouth dried as the seriousness of Bud's situation jangled my nerves.

6

I managed to squeak out, "It's me, Cait. Cait Morgan."

"Ah, get there okay?" Jack sounded cheery.

I mumbled, "Yes, thanks."

"Everything alright with the car and the condo?" Jack sounded as though he were grinning.

"Um...yes. Everything's fine. Well...no, it's not really. Look, Jack, something terrible has happened and I don't know who else to turn to." As the words left my lips, I knew I sounded pathetic and useless. I hated myself for it.

Buck up, Cait.

"Hang on a minute," replied Jack. After a pause, "Okay, I've pulled over. It sounds like you need my attention. This can't be good news. Where's Bud? Is he okay?"

I took a deep breath. "No, Jack, he's not. He's been hauled off by the police. I think they believe he killed someone."

I heard Sheila gasp, and Jack curse.

Jack snapped, "Tell me exactly what happened, Cait."

I did. Briefly.

When I finished, Jack said, "And his exact words were 'Jack', 'Petrov', and 'Cartagena', right?"

"Yes. Does that mean something to you?" I hoped it did, though I couldn't imagine what.

"Sure does," said Jack. "It means you'll have to clear out everything, and I mean absolutely everything, that you and Bud brought to the condo, get it into the car, and drive back to the airport. The apartment must look as though neither you nor Bud has ever been there. Find a cloth, a towel – anything – and wipe down all the surfaces and objects you've touched. Lock up behind you. And do it fast. Now."

"Do what?" I couldn't fathom what Jack was saying.

The man's disembodied voice snapped, "Look, Cait, just do as I say. It's important. You did exactly the right thing calling me, because the message Bud shouted wouldn't make any sense to most people. But it makes sense to me. There must be no connection between you and Bud at all. Do you understand? Nothing to connect him – or you – to that apartment, either."

I snapped back, "Now wait a minute, Jack. I'm not leaving Bud here, alone, in the hands of the police, suspected of a crime he didn't – *couldn't* – commit. No way am I doing that."

Silence. Then I could hear Sheila quite clearly – despite the fact that she was trying to whisper. "Jack, she's not used to this. She might not even know. You should tell her."

I barked, "What don't I know, Jack? What should you tell me?" I knew I sounded angry; I was.

Jack sighed. "Did Bud have any ID on him when he was picked up?"

"Any ID? I don't think so." I spread out the mound that Bud had created on the counter. "No. His credit cards, his wallet, his passport, his phone – I'm using it now – they're all here. I think that all he had with him was some cash."

Jack asked, "Which of his passports is there?"

What?

"What do you mean 'which of his passports'? His Canadian passport, of course. How many has he got?" I must have sounded as puzzled as I felt.

Jack replied evenly, "Well, I don't know how many he's got now, or which ones he brought with him or traveled on, but he's often had several, and I'm guessing that, even though he's retired, he's still got his Swedish one."

I spluttered, "Why's Bud got a Swedish passport? He's Canadian, not Swedish."

"You've got a UK passport and a Canadian one, right?"

I tutted. "Yes, but I'm Welsh. I kept dual citizenship when I emigrated, so of course I have a UK passport as well as a

Canadian one. Bud was born in Canada; why would he have a Swedish passport?"

Jack hesitated. "You know that his parents are Swedish?"

"Yes."

A shoe's about to drop…

Sheila's stage whisper cut in again, "Tell her, Jack."

Jack sighed heavily. "Bud sometimes used a few used alternate Canadian IDs with different names on them for his CSIS work. I think one of them even used his real name. But…he was born in Sweden and brought to Canada as a baby, so sometimes he used his Swedish ID, too."

Okay, so not just a shoe dropping, but an entire collection of heavy boots.

I sat down on the corner of the sofa and felt my multi-purpose right eyebrow shoot toward my hairline. "CSIS? The Canadian Security Intelligence Service? Bud's a spy?"

"Don't be silly, Cait." Sheila's voice cooed at me. "It's just that, over the years, Jack and Bud have worked on some cases that needed CSIS clearance, that's all. Right, Jack?" I pictured Jack nodding at his wife, or else glowering at her. She continued calmly, "So they have all these special papers for when they travel doing stuff like that. Of course, Bud's last job heading up that international gang-busting task force meant he had to use them a lot, but maybe he's told you all about that?" She sounded hopeful.

"Not a word," was all I was able to say, though I suspected that my tone conveyed a great deal more.

How can Bud not have told me all this…if he really loves me?

Sheila and Jack cleared their throats. In unison.

Jack tried, "Well, we're not really supposed to talk about it. I guess Bud stuck to that. Better you don't know."

I snapped, "What? In case somebody arrests me, too, and points shiny lights at me until I talk?"

This was all sounding quite ridiculous.

Bud, and Jack, working for CSIS?

And Sheila knows all about it?

And me? Not a thing.

Jack paused, clearly trying to decide what to say next. "So, back to the question of passports. If one of his Canadian ones is there, the chances are that's the one he traveled on. So he's got no ID on him. And I know he won't say a word. Literally."

"How? How do you know that?" I was beginning to panic.

"He called out 'Petrov', and 'Cartagena', that's how I know," replied Jack. "It's a case we studied during a CSIS training course: how to deal with being picked up by the locals when you're in a highly compromising situation. Petrov was a Russian operative who was found on the roadside next to a dead street vendor in Cartagena, a port city in Colombia, back in the 1980s. He tried to talk his way out of it, then tried to bribe his way out. It's used as a case study of what not to do. Rule of thumb: say nothing. That's what Bud will do. If he hasn't got any ID on him, they won't know where to start. They won't be contacting any consulates, because they won't know which one to talk to. That gives us time. Where did they take him, by the way? I'm going to guess they started by dumping him into the cells at the local police station, but do you know if that's the case?"

I was grappling with everything that Jack was throwing at me. "Where did they take him? I don't know. They bundled him into a car and took off. How on earth would I know where they went? But…I'll find him somehow. I must. I have to save him."

Jack shouted, "Stop it, Cait!" His voice echoed in the cab of his distant truck.

"Jack...shh...don't speak to her like that," hissed Sheila.

Jack sighed. "Cait, listen. This is serious. Very serious. You must get out of there. Clear out. Completely. Do not connect with Bud – don't even try. Get yourself onto a flight and get back here as soon as you can."

Not happening.

"I'm not leaving him, Jack, and that's that. There's no way I'm running away from this. From Bud. I'm staying, and I'm going to help him. When it comes to fight or flight, you'd better realize that we Welsh do not run…we stand our ground, and fight it out if necessary – if we can't talk our way out of it, of course."

I was close to tears, but every molecule of my body was determined that I would stay in Mexico to help Bud.

Somehow.

Jack groaned. "Right. New plan. I still need you to clean up the apartment, and clear everything out, like I said. Then drive back to the airport, but just hang around until another flight comes in from Vancouver. Then get back in the car and drive to…grab a pen – I'll give you instructions."

"Hang on." I scrabbled in my purse, hunting for my always-disappearing reading-cheats, and ruing the fact that I needed them at all. Finally, I found them, shoved them onto my nose, and got ready to take notes: I might have an eidetic memory, but I didn't trust my emotional state to allow me to retain what was obviously going to be something important – maybe even critical – to Bud's safety…or my own.

Jack said, "When you eventually leave the airport, drive as though you're returning to the resort where you are now, but stay on the main road for about a mile beyond the turning you took to get there. You'll see a sign on the right for the *Hacienda Soleado*, got it?"

"Got it."

"Turn there. Once you drive off the main road, you'll have to get yourself along a pretty poor track, up into the hills, until you come to the place itself. It's an agave plantation where they make tequila. One of the owners is a buddy of mine and he's got a place there. All the owners have. I happen to know that he left for his home in the States last month. I'll make some calls…tell him a friend of mine wants to borrow his place for a week. When you get through the entrance, you'll see a big adobe building: that's the tasting room and restaurant. Go there. They'll have the keys and codes you'll need, and someone will tell you exactly where to go from there. Clear?"

"Clear."

"I'll get myself down there as fast as I can. In the meantime, just get to my friend's place at the ranch and lay low. His name is Henry Douglas, by the way. If anyone asks…you are who you are, he's a friend of a friend, and you're there for some sort of – I don't know – an academic retreat or something. Okay with you?"

"Yes, okay." I could hear my voice quiver. "Jack…what happened to Petrov…in Cartagena?"

Silence.

Eventually, Jack's annoyingly deflective reply was, "I'll get this sorted, Cait. The fact that Bud was covered in blood makes me think he was trying to help someone who'd been injured."

I blurted out, "Of course he was…Bud was trying to help someone. It was the victim's blood all over him, not his. Why didn't I think of that straight away?" I felt so relieved, but dim.

"Because you're not thinking clearly, dear," came Sheila's overly soothing tones. "Just do as Jack says, and he'll fly down and help straighten everything out. It doesn't need to become some huge international incident."

"No, it doesn't," agreed Jack. "That's exactly what we don't want. None of us. Down there, the municipal cops don't deal with murders, so they'll be looking to hand Bud off to their federal colleagues as soon as they can. As it's Sunday today, maybe I can get there before they pack him off to Tepic or Guadalajara, which is likely what they'll do. From your descriptions, Cait, it must have been Al and Miguel at the scene. I know them a little, from the time Sheila and I have spent there. Al's the tall one. Nice guy. Though why they were in their dress uniforms, and in Bob's Bodega next to Margarita's flower shop, is beyond me."

It had completely escaped me that, with Jack being a "local" in *Punta de las Rocas* whenever he and Shelia were able to get away to the sun, he would know all the people involved.

It also dawned on me that he might even know the victim. I asked as reasonably, and gently, as I could, "Who might it have been, Jack? On the floor of the flower shop."

Jack tutted. "I don't know. I can't be sure. It's Margarita's store. She's the florist, and a wonderful plantswoman…she can grow pretty much anything. She has a nursery up in the hills, not far from the plantation I'm sending you to. In fact, it's her father, Juan, who's the *jimador* at the *Hacienda Soleado*…the one who cares for the agaves there. He's also the mayor of the municipality, the *intendente.* Important guy, in his own way. If it's Margarita? Well, I can't imagine who would have wanted to harm her; I've always believed she's well respected in the area, and all she does is grow plants and sell flowers. Nothing…dangerous. It's puzzling. And worrying."

I was looking around the apartment and beginning to focus on my tasks as I replied, "Jack, look, I'll do as you asked, and maybe I can call you again when I get to the hacienda?"

This is better…there's something concrete I can do.

"Sure. By then I'll have made some calls, and should be able to tell you when I'll arrive."

The cavalry is coming…

I had a thought. "Hang on a minute, Jack – why would I have your car? I mean, if I'm not supposed to be connected to Bud, then should I be connected to you? Why would I be driving from the airport in your car? Wouldn't I just get a cab?"

Jack didn't answer immediately. "You make a good point, Cait. I'll need to think through whether or not it might be alright for us to 'know' each other...though why you'd be at Henry's place if we didn't could be...problematic. I'll tell you when we speak again. Meanwhile – let's err on the side of caution: park my car in the short-term parking lot and leave the ticket in the glovebox. I'll collect it from there when I fly in. I've got keys here; you've got the spares. You have the keys, right? Bud didn't have them in his pocket?"

I double-checked. "They're here. No worries."

No worries!

Jack continued, "Okay, Cait, when you're at the airport and you see a flight getting in from Vancouver, keep an eye open for when folks are leaving the baggage area, join the crowd, and jump in one of the government cabs that park right outside the terminal. There's no point dragging the luggage across the road to get a city cab, even though they're a bit cheaper. Have you got local cash?"

I checked in my purse. "Yes, I brought a fair amount with me, so I should be fine."

"Good. And how's your Spanish?"

"My reading comprehension's excellent, but I get easily tripped up by accents. Speaking it takes a bit of time, but I can manage." I allowed myself a wry smile as I thought about the book of conversational Spanish that Bud had given me when he'd told me about this vacation. He knows how lazy I am when it comes to languages, but he told me I had to learn Spanish before we left...which isn't as easy as it sounds, even for someone like me who has an eidetic memory. Language isn't just about remembering stuff; it's about putting all the right bits together in the right order…and then making it sound right. Now I was glad that I'd applied myself.

"Good," replied Jack, "you might need it with the cab driver. Use the details I've just given you. You'll be fine out at the *Hacienda Soleado*. Everyone speaks English there. You'll be a bit isolated at the plantation, of course, but that fits better with the idea that you're trying to get away from everything. Just lay low. You know, just be quiet and generally uncommunicative. Act like a brainbox taking a break."

I felt another wan smile creep up on me. "Okay. I'll keep a low profile. And I'll peer at people over my sunglasses to make myself appear more forbidding."

"I know you're a quick study, Cait. Bud's always boasting that you belong to Mensa. Which reminds me – there *is* something you can do that could help Bud: do that memory thing he's told me about…you know, when you recall the exact details of an event, or a place, or a person. You might have seen something that could help."

"Bud told you about that?" I was surprised; I'd thought that Bud would have respected my choice to keep my special skill set private. There again, the last fifteen minutes had been full of surprises about Bud, and none of them, so far, had been pleasant.

"Yes, he told us, but he also told us not to tell anyone else, and we won't, right, Sheila?"

Sheila sounded almost joyously conspiratorial when she said, "Oh, of course not. I know lots of things I don't really know."

Only too well aware that this cloak and dagger stuff was all new to me, and still reeling from what I'd seen happen to Bud, I asked, "Is there anything else I should, or shouldn't, do?"

15

Jack's voice sounded soothingly confident. "No. I think we've covered everything. Call me when you're settled at the hacienda. Go on, get going. We'll head back to our place right now, because it'll be a better base for me to get in touch with the people who can help Bud. Talk to you in a few hours or so. And Cait…don't panic. This will be sorted out. Bud will not be held, or charged, or incarcerated – for long – for something he didn't do. Right?"

"Okay. But, Jack…you never told me what happened to Petrov in Cartagena. Tell me. Please?"

"Cait, it was a case study of what not to do, so don't give it any more thought."

"Jack, please?"

Jack sighed. "Petrov was tried for murder, found guilty, and…umm…executed. But he did everything wrong, Cait. That won't happen to Bud. We won't let it. He won't let it. Now stop thinking about the idiot Petrov and get going."

"Yes, Jack. I'm on it."

We disconnected, and the silence closed about me.

I shoved toiletries into my suitcase – not an hour after I'd taken them out – and felt tremors in the foundation upon which I'd believed my relationship with Bud was built.

Bud's Swedish?

Cleared by CSIS?

Jack had said that one of Bud's passports bore his real name.

Is "Bud" not Bud's real name?

I wondered if this was how Alice had felt when she'd gone sliding down the rabbit hole.

16

No Time to Waste

Putting the apartment back exactly as we'd found it, and wiping down every surface I'd touched – and trying to guess those Bud might have come into contact with – seemed to take forever. Then I grappled, alone, with the luggage that Bud and I had hauled up to the condo together; as the cases thumped down the stone staircases, I realized that my bag weighed almost twice as much as Bud's.

I was pretty sure I'd managed to make my way about the resort unnoticed; the place appeared to be deserted. I guessed that was because the schools hadn't closed yet for the summer, but most of the snowbirds had already departed for their other homes, in more northern climes. I also reasoned that, with all the action that was taking place at the crime scene in the street – which was on the other side of the resort – the parking garage was hardly going to be the center of attention.

By the time I pushed the keys into the ignition of Jack's car, I was sweaty and breathless. Forcing myself to focus on the matter in hand, I reversed the route Bud had taken earlier in the day, but now – instead of joyfully heading toward a vacation promising togetherness and relaxing hours in the sun – I was running away from a crime scene at the behest of Jack White, a man I, frankly, hardly knew at all. I could feel my turmoil present itself as an acid tummy as I stuck to the speed limit, and let the idiots in the fast lane scream past. By the time I got back to the airport, parked the car, and hauled two suitcases plus my carry-on tote into the main terminal, I was a wreck – both physically, and mentally.

I checked the Arrivals board and noted that a flight from Vancouver was due to land in an hour or so, so I hunted down a small coffee shop where I could wait. Managing to avoid making eye contact with the hordes of salespeople trying to offload timeshare condos quickly became a priority, so I kept my head down, rolled the luggage along as best I could, and grabbed a couple of innocuous-looking wraps, a chocolate bar, a bottle of water, and a bucket-sized cup of coffee at the counter.

Finally, I plopped onto a plastic seat that faced a wall decorated with photographs of the seawall promenade, the *Malecón*, in Puerto Vallarta. One of them featured a whimsically surreal sculpture entitled "In Search of Reason", created by Sergio Bustamante. I stared at the triangular-headed figure at the base of a ladder that shot, unsupported, into the sky – upon which two smaller figures teetered – and thought I understood what the artist had been trying to say: When nothing makes sense, you'll do anything – however dangerous, reckless, or even hopeless it might seem – to find a way to reach the freedom that reason, and understanding, offers.

And yet, here I sit…trapped in a bubble of non-sense.

What I'd seen earlier in the day only made sense if Bud had been helping someone who'd been gravely injured.

Okay.

What I'd then been told about Bud, by someone who'd known him for a heck of a lot longer than I had – decades, in fact – only made sense if...if Bud didn't trust me enough to tell me about his work, or his true self.

Eat your chicken and salad wrap, Cait…and think.

The food might as well have been shredded paper wrapped in cardboard for all the pleasure I got from it, which, for me, is unusual…because, however bad food might be, I always at least notice it. Of course I was trying to manage the shock of seeing Bud in such a terrible situation, but my mind wasn't just reeling because of that; it was whirring and clicking because I was wondering if, once again, I'd chosen to open up to someone –

let someone into my heart – who was being less than truthful about himself.

I'd done it with Angus all those years ago in Cambridge, when I was studying for my master's degree in criminology. He'd been handsome and charming, but as soon as he knew I was his, he'd subjected me to the pain, and agonizing shame, of beatings and – possibly even worse – a complete undermining of my self-confidence. Getting hauled out of my own home by the local police and being accused of having killed him – after finding him dead on my bathroom floor a few weeks after I'd officially kicked him out – highlighted just how bad a choice I'd made…in more ways than one.

After that, I'd constructed walls around myself, defenses so secure that no one could get to me…until…Bud. Had I done it again? Picked a "wrong-un", as my mum had always referred to the boys I'd brought home. Of course, according to her, they'd all been "wrong-uns". Given that at forty-eight years of age I'm still single, maybe she'd been right. There was no question that Angus had been bad. Bad through and through. And most certainly bad for me.

But Bud? No. Whatever Jack might say, I know Bud.

Since Bud's wife, Jan, had died so tragically, we'd talked and talked…about nothing at all, and about all the important stuff. I believed I'd come to know the truth at the heart of Bud Anderson.

Yes…I do believe that. I know he's a good man.

Bud's a man who's dedicated his life to upholding the law, and bringing those who deserve it to justice. He's not a man who would harm, hurt, or deceive me.

But – if Jack White's telling the truth – Bud has deceived you, Cait.

He's warm, and funny, and loving. Okay, so he has pretty questionable taste in clothes…well, no taste at all really, because material things don't matter to him. Which isn't a bad thing. And Bud can be very sure of himself, in a quiet way. Years as a police officer will do that for a person: there's an air that never leaves ex-officers. I see it in all his retired colleagues. True, he sometimes doesn't agree with my point of view on certain matters, but everyone's entitled to their opinion, and we usually end up with a truce that holds...until the next time the topic comes up. My being a criminal psychologist and his being an ex-cop can lead to some juicy up and downers, usually concluding with us both having to agree that psychology might explain some activities, but it doesn't excuse them.

Crumbs from the wrap I was eating had landed on the shelf that is my more-than-ample bosom. As I wiped them off, I dragged myself to a more reasoned outlook of the current situation.

Focus, Cait.

Bud was being held by the Mexican police for a crime I knew he hadn't committed. As I stirred my coffee with my chocolate bar – *don't indulge too much, Cait* – I came to a decision: I would do as Jack had asked, and show up at the *Hacienda Soleado*, but, beyond that, if a chance presented itself for me to help Bud in any way, I'd take it.

The first comforting taste of melting chocolate spurred me to realize that I could use the time I was stuck at the airport to recall the exact events surrounding Bud's arrest, rather than dwell on my anxiety about not knowing his real name...or where he was born...or the fact that CSIS had issued him multiple passports over the years. I'd deal with all that stuff...at some point.

I took in my surroundings. The airport concourse was noisy and chaotic: groups of people jostled past each other, looking up, or back...anywhere but the direction in which they were moving; announcements were being made over a boing-ing loudspeaker system; and the shrieks of invisible children echoed off the marbled and tiled surfaces. I drained my coffee, pocketed the remaining wrap, shoved the bottle of water into my bulging carry-on tote, and headed toward one of those we-sell-everything stalls as I left, because I suspected – hoped – they'd have cigarettes there.

Stop it, Cait!

I'd promised Bud I'd give up smoking and I'd done really well on the nicotine gum lately; I'd packed a big stash of it to get me through our entire vacation. But…I could imagine lighting up, taking that first long draw, and rationalized that I was under tremendous stress…and that Bud wouldn't know.

My addiction is undermining my willpower. No…yes…no…

The young man behind the counter in the store warned me that the laws about not being able to smoke almost anywhere in Mexico meant that there weren't many places where cigarettes were on sale. I knew he was probably just angling for a bigger sale, but caved in and bought five packs of some light cigarettes of an unknown-to-me brand, just to be on the safe side; wasn't prepared to risk not being able to have another chance to stock up. Then I all but ran out of the building to find a spot where I could get my fix. I followed the signs that promised an area where I could indulge to an out-of-the-way corner, perched on a narrow bench that offered a least a little shade, and lit up.

Once the dizziness subsided, and I got used to the strangely bitter taste, I felt better just holding a cigarette. I smiled when I realized that I kept glancing around, fearing that Bud might materialize and give me at least a filthy look. I told myself to stop being stupid…that Bud was locked up…somewhere…and that's what finally allowed me to settle myself mentally and recall, in detail, everything I'd experienced that morning.

It's not a process I totally understand; it's just something I've always been able to do. If I close my eyes to the point where everything goes a bit fuzzy, and hum to myself, I'm able to recall, in every one of my senses, what I've experienced. Of course, the psychologist in me knows that it's not a perfect ability: sometimes I get things wrong, and sometimes I misinterpret what I've seen, smelled, felt, heard, or even tasted. We all do that, with every stimulus we perceive – we apply our own knowledge, attitudes, and expectations to everything, all the time. And then that's what we "remember".

I made the most of the shade being provided by the trunk of a towering palm, and a slight breeze cooled the sweat that the sun and humidity had squeezed out of my still-pale skin. Then I made sure I was touching every piece of luggage before I screwed up my eyes, and…I was back in Jack and Sheila's condo in the *Rocas Hermosas* Resort.

22

The Beginning?

I'm pulling and pushing at a red-painted wooden shutter at the tall casement window as the door of the condo closes behind Bud. He's heading to the store, humming to himself. He's happy. Content.

When the shutter creaks and flies outwards, the light dazzles me. My eyes adjust, and I immediately look out to the sea, which heaves and glints beneath the midday sun. I smell salt in the air; I feel the freshness of the breeze on my skin.

Delightful!

I don't like the look of the dark clouds in the distance; I've been anticipating my enjoyment of the "lush gardens and multi-level pools" promised by the resort's website, so hope the weather won't break. I've opened the casement windows inward to their full extent, and the shutters are now wide open, flat against the exterior wall. I can't look straight down, it makes me nauseous and dizzy, so I only glimpse the green, shrub-filled beds that surround our complex.

I can, however, look out…and I see the red-brown, dusty stone road that lies between our temporary home and the buildings that sit between us and the sea. Two low white stucco buildings with flat roofs sit back-to-back, parallel to each other, with a lane running between them. One faces the building I'm in, the other faces the sea.

The building facing our condo houses three establishments. On the left is BOB'S BODEGA – a massive sign covers the whole of the top of the store, which takes up about half of the building. It's almost totally glass-fronted, with large double doors and a clear view inside. I can see racks of groceries, toiletries, vegetables, and breads, as well as items of clothing, swimwear, and row after row of bottles of booze. The right-hand wall of the store houses the counter area, where I can see a cash register. I can't see anyone inside.

Next to the bodega, beyond a pillar of stucco, is a florist shop: MARGARITA FLORES is painted in vivid yellow on the sign. It's a very narrow store. Most of its frontage is comprised of a single glass door, with a glass panel on either side. The panels are covered in photographs of floral displays, all of which are faded; they look like complex arrangements, but – without color – they lack appeal. The door is lined with some sort of covering that makes it dark, impossible to see inside.

To prevent the sunlight from reaching the stock, and wilting the blooms?

On the far right of the building, filling the rest of its length, is SERENA SPA, announced by a gold and brown painted sign above a glass door. The glass walls, which are interspersed with stucco columns, are covered with photographs. Some show lurid, highly decorative manicures of the sort that suggest the person having them done would become completely non-functioning in the real world. Others display women with beatific expressions whose perfect, oily bodies are being massaged with glistening stones. There are also models with glamorous hair and alarmingly large white teeth, grinning inanely at passers-by. As I'm taking this all in, a woman comes out of the door of the spa and waves to someone inside.

She's the woman who screamed when she saw Bud.

She's wearing loose white capri pants, flip-flops, and a royal blue tee. The color looks good against her tanned skin. Her long, dark hair is pulled up, hanging loosely in a ponytail. She must be about thirty, is slim, and moves as though she's in good shape. Lithe. She's speaking to a person inside the spa, and she's holding…what is it? It's a cake box. I can't imagine this woman eats a lot of cake. She's too slim to indulge in that sort of thing often. Just as she turns away from the spa, I see Bud go into the bodega. The sunlight flashes on the glass door as he pulls it open. A seagull cries above me, and I glance up.

The woman in the capris calls to someone on the same side of the street as our complex. I can't see the person, because I don't look down, but the woman in the capris is beckoning to them with her free hand, and smiling. She's got a kind face, and I know I shouldn't judge her too harshly for having the willpower to stay slim. I see her start to cross the road toward our condo.

As I step back into the apartment to go into the bedroom, I catch a flash of something out of the corner of my right eye. It's a flash of white, and glinting gold, popping out from beyond the gleaming, white-painted end wall of the building nearest the bodega. It's human height, and moving; I didn't know what it was, at the time…now I know it must have been one of the policemen in their fancy outfits. Yes: gold braid, white feathers in their hats…that must be it. That's where the police car emerged from…they've just left their parked car.

Now I'm moving to the bedroom: I see my suitcase on the floor and I lift it, awkwardly, onto the bed. It's heavy. The bedroom and bathroom are small, as is the entire condo, but I don't care, because Bud and I are going to have a wonderful time. No students to corral, nor papers to grade for me, and a total break from familiar surroundings for Bud…all of which are saturated with memories of his dead wife. After nine months of dating, we're finally going to have some time alone together which is…a delightful prospect.

I'm opening my suitcase as I'm thinking this, and not really looking at what I am doing. When I do look down, I realize how dark the bedroom is with the shutters closed, and that it's stuffy, with a slightly unpleasant smell of aging potpourri. I leave the suitcase, pull open the second set of casement windows, and begin to wiggle at the fastenings on the wooden shutters, which are just as difficult to open as the others had been in the main room. As I fiddle, in my mind's eye I'm seeing Marty, Bud's gentle, amber-eyed black Lab, as he jumps and gambols when we run him on the beach.

Oh, but all that sand that sticks to him.

I smile at the thought, and wish we could have brought Marty on the trip. It's not just Bud I've fallen for, it's Marty, too…though both man and dog shower me with unconditional affection, so that's hardly surprising. But we knew we couldn't bring him with us, and we're happy that he's staying at a doggy version of paradise at Jack and Sheila White's place in Hatzic, where there's acreage to run around with their three dogs, and as many sticks to play with as…you can shake a stick at.

The bedroom shutters fly open, and I'm dazzled again. Once more I look across the road, and now I see Bud leaving the bodega, a red-and-white-striped carrier bag in one hand; it looks bulky. He holds open the glass door of the bodega for the woman in the capris who's carrying the cake; a man has joined her. The man is older, and taller, than Bud, so the older guy must be about six feet tall. He's thin and wiry, and is wearing cargo shorts – all the pockets are bulging – a striped golf shirt, socks with his sandals, and a sun hat.

It looks like a Tilley hat, so maybe he's Canadian?

Once the man and the woman have entered the bodega, Bud lets go of the glass door. He's smiling as he walks, and adjusts his baseball cap to shade his eyes from the sun. After just a few steps, he pulls open the door to the florist shop.

The romantic gesture wasn't lost on me then, and it's not lost on me now: not many men have ever bought me flowers.

The air feels more humid than it did mere moments ago. As I scan from the road toward the sea – to check on those clouds gathering on the horizon – I spot a man in the lane between the two parallel buildings; he's leaning against the back wall of the building that faces the sea. It, too, is long and low, and he's particularly noticeable because he's wearing a vivid red, double-breasted shirt with black pants which stand out against the snowy white stucco of the building. He's standing beside a door that's in two halves, like a stable door: the top half is open wide, the bottom half is ajar. Inside, the building is a black cavern, but I can see a glimpse of daylight on the floor.

The building must be open to the sea view at the front. Nice spot.

He's holding something: a glass of water and two sticks.

Why do I think they are chopsticks?

Ah, I understand…I can just make out a white chef's hat pushed back on his head; I almost didn't notice it against the brilliance of the stucco.

So…he's a chef. Maybe taking a break from a hot kitchen?

Did I smell any food on the sea breeze at the time? No.

I take one last look at the horizon, wishing the clouds away, then return my attention to my suitcase and my toiletries. As I pull out the carefully packed plastic bags, I hear a bell. Twelve distant, almost mournful, chimes. I imagine they are coming from the gold-coroneted tower of the Church of Our Lady of Guadalupe in Puerto Vallarta, but then reason it's probably too far away for me to hear across the bay…and that the bell must be sounding from a local clock…though I hadn't seen any obvious bell towers on our drive into the resort.

I feel the stress of having taught an intersessional semester – with all the work of a full-length semester squashed into half the time – lift from my shoulders. I had a particularly tough group for the Deviant Criminal Behavior: Background and Insights course, and there'd been a few temper tantrums when students had seen their grades. Now, with Bud buying beer and flowers, and me able to forget about students and grades, the next week will be wonderful.

I know it.

I've just balanced a can of hairspray on the edge of the bathroom counter when I hear a scream. It's a long howling scream. I rush the few steps out of the ensuite bathroom, past the bed to the window, and look to the street below. The woman in the capris and the blue tee is holding open the door to the florist shop with her left hand; her right is raised above her head, its fingers splayed wide, as though to catch a large ball. She's looking down and away from me, but the keening noise that she's making slices through the midday air.

At first, I can't see what she's looking at; my eyes are adjusting to the stark contrast between the sunlight and the comparative gloom inside the florist store. I have a clear line of vision, and I quickly make out one figure lying on the floor with its head nearest the door, its arms splayed-out…but I can't see the whole of their body, because there's a person kneeling over them. The kneeling figure has its hands at the throat of the one on the floor. Now the kneeling person raises their face to the screaming woman, and I see their mouth open: a big O, then teeth bared in an E shape.

I know that face.

It's Bud's face.

A truck roars along the road between the condo and the stores. It's a blue pickup, battered, old, with a horribly noisy exhaust; the driver's window is open, and I see…an elbow. That's it.

These two things happen simultaneously. My eyes are on the face of the man I love; the truck is in the periphery of my vision.

Have I missed something?

Is the truck important?

My eyes haven't left Bud's face…but then the screaming woman in the white capris loses her grip on the door and it swings shut, obliterating my view of the man I love. Just as the door to the florist's closes, the double doors to the bodega swing out into the street, one person pushing open each door. I know now – thanks to Jack's local knowledge – that these are local police officers, that the tall one is called Al – which strikes me as a pretty odd name for a Mexican policeman – and the short one's Miguel.

Miguel rushes to catch the woman in the capris just as she's about to collapse. She's flailing, grabbing at the air; he supports her as she falls, helping her to sit against the stucco wall. Simultaneously, the tall cop – Big Al, as I now think of him – draws his weapon and shouts at the closed door. He pulls the door open and points his gun down toward the body, then at Bud, who I can see once more.

Big Al holds the door open with his left foot; he has both hands on the gun. He's shouting – I can tell by the way his shoulders are heaving, though I can't hear what he's saying – and he's waggling the gun at Bud, indicating that Bud should stand.

Bud is shaking his head. His body language says…*defeat?*

He's giving up.

He removes his hands from the throat of the body on the floor and holds them above his head, showing Big Al he has nothing in them. First, he puts his right foot flat on the floor, then he pushes himself up from a kneeling position to a standing one. His hands are still above his head…and now I realize his hands aren't in shadow; they're dark with blood.

Big Al pulls a set of handcuffs from beneath the royal blue tunic bedecked with gold epaulets that's just a little too tight on him. The surreal vision of a blood-soaked Bud being handcuffed by a man with gold-tasseled shoulders, wearing a tall antique-style, white-feathered hat, will always be with me, of course – because of my special memory – but it will never be as bittersweet as it is at this moment...because it is now that I recall, for the first time, the look in Bud's eyes as he casts them upwards, toward our condo.

I realize now that he must have seen me standing in the window. For no more than a split second, he looks right into my eyes, and I can see his expression: love and dread.

Oh Bud!

Having checked the body on the floor, Big Al pushes Bud out of the store. Bud blinks in the sunlight. The tall cop speaks sharply to the short one, Miguel, who pats the capris woman on the hand and abandons her, leaving her propped against the wall. He heads toward the spa; he doesn't exactly run, but he walks smartly with an odd skip and a stuttering gallop thrown in...the way unfit people, like myself, move when they're trying to hurry along but can't really make that much of a sustained effort. I see him disappear around the far corner of the building out of the corner of my eye.

I only see him in this way because I'm still looking at Bud.

Now in broad daylight, I see that the front of Bud's blue and white squiggly-patterned shirt is covered in blood. I can just about see his bloodied forearms pulled behind his back, and I know his hands are in the same state. His knees below his khaki shorts are dripping with blood.

A white saloon car, marked clearly as a police vehicle, squeals around the building and pulls up in front of Bud and Big Al. Miguel jumps out of the driver's seat and draws his weapon – quite unnecessarily. Big Al – who's about six feet tall, with a spare, athletic frame – grabs Bud by the shoulders from behind, and begins to steer him toward the rear door of the car. Bud stands up straight, pushes out his chest – preventing Big Al from moving him forward – and lifts his head skywards.

Of course…Bud doesn't want the cops to know he's calling out to me.

"Jack…Jack…Petrov…Cartagena…" The effort of making his voice carry as far as possible means Bud's chest heaves with each word.

Big Al regains his momentum and shoves Bud, head first, into the back of the cop car; Miguel is holding the door open, his gun pointed at Bud's back.

That's my last glimpse of Bud. I can't see him inside the car.

Someone's switched off a light in my life.

Big Al moves to the driver's side of the vehicle, talking and waving his arms at Miguel, who's nodding and trying, somewhat unsuccessfully, to re-holster his weapon. I guess that he doesn't use that gun very often…he's not at all comfortable handling it. He's overweight, sweaty, and unfit; he's all dressed up like something out of a musical-comedy movie from the 1930s…and he's been pointing a weapon he's unfamiliar with at the man I love.

None of this is comforting.

Big Al throws his jacket and ridiculous hat into the trunk of the car, then slams it shut.

He's angry…very angry.

He's still shouting at Miguel and gesticulating as he jumps into the driver's seat, starts up the engine, and accelerates. Dust and small stones shoot from the tires. Miguel flaps his hands in front of his face, waving the dust away.

With Bud gone, I breathe out, even as my eyes follow the police car along the road, until it's out of sight. Its siren is piercing, without any musical tone.

It's a dead and mournful sound.

By the time I look down to the street below me again, more people are on the scene: the man with the Tilley hat is helping the woman in the capris to her feet, and he's being aided by another woman. This is the first time I've seen her: she's short and round, wearing a floor-length traditional Mexican dress. She's dark skinned, with black-but-graying hair pulled into a bun on top of her head. She's offering the woman in the capris a bottle of water, and I suspect she's something to do with Bob's Bodega, because, together with a dark-skinned, older man – also in what appears to be traditional dress – she's helping capri-woman into the bodega in a solicitous manner.

The skinny man in the Tilley hat is now approached by two other women, who are rushing from the direction of the spa. One is as tall as Tilley-man – so she must be about six feet tall – and I'm guessing she weighs about three hundred pounds, though it's difficult to tell because she's wearing a full-length bright orange, voluminous dress, topped with a matching broad-brimmed orange sunhat. I can't judge her age at all. Beside her is a shorter, trimmer woman, maybe in her fifties or sixties. She's blond and smartly dressed; preppy. She and Tilley-man display body language that screams "couple" when she greets him. The large orange-clad woman clearly knows them both.

Yes…everyone seems to know everyone else.

Just as the women reach Tilley-man, they are all joined by the chef I'd seen in the lane between the buildings. He comes from the end of the building that houses the bodega. It's clear that he knows cop-Miguel – who's waving everyone away from the florist's store and is, apparently, keen to share information. There's a great deal of breast clutching and head shaking exchanged between the cop and the chef; the women hold their hands to their mouths in horror. The chef shakes a fist at the heavens.

Now yet another woman rushes around the bodega end of the building: she's short, very thin, dressed as though for tennis,

Black, and might be in her fifties...or even her sixties. She makes for the short, blond woman; they embrace, then share shock and horror. The large woman in the orange robe waves her arms about, the chef in the red shirt beckons to everyone, and gradually – with cop-Miguel encouraging them – they all enter the bodega.

Just as I decide that I need to think about what it is that Bud had shouted out...I see a tall, heavy Black man wearing a vivid Hawaiian shirt, come barreling around the spa end of the building. He's smiling broadly and opens his arms toward Miguel – who's still holding open the door to the bodega, having ushered everyone else inside – in a jolly, welcoming manner. Miguel speaks to him rapidly, and the big man rushes into the bodega, a look of concern clouding his face.

That's when I call Jack, and – while we're on the phone – I hear a distant siren; I surmise it's the vehicle that's been dispatched to collect the corpse.

I opened my eyes, adjusted my sunglasses, and lit another cigarette. The shade had shifted, and I realized I'd managed to catch a bit of sun on my nose. I pushed the annoyingly uncooperative luggage along the gravelly ground, and moved along the bench a few feet, to get back into the shade.

So, other than getting sunburned, what have I achieved?

I gave my recollections some analytical thought: only about three minutes had elapsed between the time I saw Bud enter the flower shop and the moment I heard capri-woman scream.

Not long.

Had Bud fought with someone inside the store?

Had he had to kill...someone...to save his own life in there?

Who lay dead on the floor?

How had they died?

When had they died?

Was there maybe even more than one body in there?

Why did Bud have his hands around the person's throat?

What had he said to the screaming woman?

Would he really not say a word to the police?

Questions…more and more questions.

I looked at my watch. The flight from Vancouver was due to land at any minute, so I grappled with the luggage again and made my way toward the entrance of the airport. I managed to push my way inside, then hung about until I spotted the pale, stressed faces of Canadians looking forward to a week of sun and margaritas. I joined the exodus when it began, the large Canadian flag travel tags on our bags blending in with all the others that were being dragged and wheeled about me. I managed to grab a cab without too many problems, and made sure that the driver knew where I was going before we set off.

Since this was my third trip along the Jalisco/Carretera Federal Highway 200 that day, I was beginning to get the lay of the land. Unfortunately, this was by far the most rapid version of the trip, so I buckled up, tried to hang on, and hoped the cabbie would at least slow down a bit. He didn't. The reddish-brown hills covered in scrubby green, and the fields of blue-green agave planted in rows, streaked past in a blur beneath the clear blue sky. The air rushing into the cab smelled of dust and exhaust fumes. I missed Bud's smell. I missed Bud. And I was terrified by my imaginings of what might be happening to him.

Start All Over Again

By the time we arrived at the *Hacienda Soleado*, I was glad to get out of the cab; Bud always says I'm a hopeless passenger because I'm a control freak…and I have to agree that, maybe, he has a point. I balanced the two suitcases and my carry-on tote as close as possible to the entrance to the delightfully rustic adobe structure that Jack had told me to look out for.

The sign on the building announced AMIGOS DEL TEQUILA, which was promising. I pushed open one of the massive wooden double-doors, and felt the welcome tingle of air conditioning on my damp skin as I entered the dim interior.

Lovely.

The place was deserted. In front of me was a long, high bar, behind which were rows of glittering bottles, a great number of which were of a similar design – stumpy, with fat stoppers. Dotted around the rusty, Saltillo tiled floor were high marble-topped tables and leather-upholstered bar stools; the white plastered walls were adorned with atmospheric photographs of rows of giant blue agave set in a luminous landscape. I took a moment to decompress.

"Hello?" I called. My voice echoed.

Somewhere beyond the bar a door swung open and smacked against a wall.

"Coming!" A young man appeared around a corner: a tousled mop of unruly blond hair, a lopsided grin, chef whites, and a pair of large hands being wiped on a red cloth. "Can I help?"

I smiled. "Yes, I hope so."

"I'm Tony, Tony Booth," said the charmer, waving a still-damp hand. "I won't shake." He grinned. "Prepping the meat for tonight. Not quite finished." His accent was American. He didn't look Mexican at all.

Odd for a chef at a Mexican restaurant…in Mexico.

I felt suddenly nervous; I'm really not used to living a lie, but knew I had to stick to the plan. I beamed. "I'm Cait. Cait Morgan. I'm here to collect the keys for Henry Douglas's place. Do you know about that?"

I couldn't be certain that Jack had managed to get through to his friend, or, indeed, that word would have reached the hacienda, but the all-American Tony Booth grinned at me – with an all-American gleaming white smile. "Yep. Henry called about half an hour ago. Nice for you to be able to get away at such short notice. He said you're a prof. Is that right?"

I forced a less-toothy smile. "Yes, that's right. At the University of Vancouver."

Stick to the truth whenever possible, Cait.

"Gimme a sec." Tony disappeared in the direction from which he'd arrived. He was about thirty, slim and muscular, with a breezy manner, and a surprisingly good tan for a chef…they're usually so pasty. I reckoned he'd be more at home on a longboard, riding waves off the Californian coast, than in a Mexican restaurant's kitchen.

"I wrote down the security code, for the alarm," said Tony jauntily, as he handed me a single key on a leather lariat and a scrap of paper with four digits written in what I trusted was red ink.

"Thanks," I said, as cheerily as I imagined a person would if they were arriving for a week's vacation.

"Henry's place is Casa LaLa. Because he's, you know, from LA? He thinks it's funny. But I guess you know all about his so-called 'sense of humor'?"

"Henry's a friend of a friend, really," I replied. Rather sheepishly as it turned out.

Embrace the lie, Cait.

I added, more confidently, "But the friend that he's a friend of is quite a…unique character."

Tony looked puzzled and a bit concerned; I wondered what my face was doing as I tried to be convincing in my role.

He shrugged. "I guess you could say that about Henry too. In fact, you could say it about all the FOGTTs."

"FOGTTs?" I was puzzled: Tony had pronounced it as though it were a word, but I suspected an acronym…though not one with which I was familiar.

Tony nodded as he confirmed my suspicions. "The Friends of Good Tequila Trust. The FOGTTs. That's what the owners here are all called. They each own a share of the place, and each have a house on the hacienda; they've each paid their money, and – when we finally make a profit here at the restaurant – they'll each get their cut. The way this place is set up, and with some good public relations work in Puerto Vallarta, I reckon the next season could see us break through. But they're all doing okay even now…the *Tequila Soleado* they make here is selling pretty well back home in the States."

I tried to look as though I was interested in what the young man was saying, which a casual visitor – one without a partner who'd been locked up for a murder he didn't commit – probably would have been.

I struggled for small talk. "So what do you do here, exactly?"

Tony looked down at his chef whites, and resisted the temptation to make a smart crack. "I'm the chef." He smiled and waved his arms as if to signify "Ta-da."

I mirrored his smile and felt my eyebrow arch at the inanity of my own question. "Sorry – it's been a long day already. Traveling, you know?"

"Hey, don't worry, everyone gets here feeling that way. And – although I don't get to travel much – I understand long days;

I also design the menu, and do all the shopping at the local markets…so I know how very long they can be. If I'm not down in PV – that's what we all call Puerto Vallarta around here – by six in the morning…sharp…I'm not gonna get the best stuff, so I'm up and at 'em every day, and have to clean up after this place closes."

I went with, "And what sort of dishes appear on your menu, Tony?"

"Depends on what's good, and what's freshest, on the day, of course," he replied. "Today we'll be having…hang on a minute." He scrabbled in the deep pocket on the front of his apron. "Here you go, today's menu. All small plates, you understand. We're open from five until eleven-ish."

The young chef handed me a grubby piece of paper where I managed to decipher a scrawl of handwriting: "Roasted ancho, or green tomatillo, salsa with blue corn chips; red snapper ceviche; smoked mussel ceviche tostadas; barbequed pork quesadilla; mushroom empanadas; chicken mole tamales; hahas."

I was familiar with most of the items that were listed, and mentally ate my way through the list. "I didn't realize I was so hungry." I smiled, as my tummy rumbled aloud. "What's a 'haha'? I don't think I've heard of them."

Tony smiled. "The FOGTTs love them. Sort of a coconut, pecan, and chocolate macaroon; they're rich, small, and popular for dessert. I won't be making them for a couple of hours yet. Will you come to eat, or at least nibble, this evening?"

With my mouth watering, and the wonderful smells coming from the kitchen making things even worse, I realized that I didn't have a plan. Not a clue about what I was doing…nor where, when, or what I was going to eat. It also occurred to me that I was going to be hunkering down in the house of someone who'd left their place for the summer and hadn't expected any guests, so there might not be so much as a bottle of water in Henry's place. I cursed inwardly that I hadn't thought ahead, and brought supplies.

As I stood there, silently accusing myself of rank stupidity – and imagining the pathetic little cardboard-flavored chicken wrap I'd stuffed into my pocket – both of the massive doors behind me flew open and a voice bellowed, "Where's Juan? Tony, have you seen Juan?"

I turned and was confronted by a huge figure, silhouetted against the brilliant sunlight outside.

The shape continued with: "They should bring back the death penalty. It's disgusting that they can get away with this sort of thing. Where's Juan?"

Bossy female voice, booming…someone used to getting her own way.

As my eyes adjusted, and the figure stepped forward, I recognized the large woman dressed in orange I'd seen outside the florist's store earlier in the day.

"I'm sorry, Dorothea," said Tony, fluttering to the woman's side, "I haven't seen him all day. But it is Sunday, so he'd probably be in church, or at home…"

Dorothea towered over me, at about six feet to my five-three – *five-four on a tall day* – and was proportionately large in every way: a wide-brimmed orange hat was stuffed onto a headful of red curls; a voluminous, full-length orange cheesecloth dress was gathered beneath her prominent bust; her flabby, heavily freckled arms were bare, and – below puffy ankles – her feet were encased in, of all things, gold ballet flats. She appeared to be alarmingly top-heavy, and seemed to teeter on her tiny feet; I hoped she didn't topple over.

As I was sizing up Dorothea, it seemed she was doing the same to me.

"Who are you?" she asked imperiously, peering at me over her sunglasses.

"Cait. Cait Morgan." The peering was working; I felt intimidated.

"Well, Cait, that's nice for you. Why are you here? Those your bags outside? Staying somewhere here? Friends with one of the FOGTTs? Have you seen Juan? Do you even know who he is?"

I felt I was being fired at by a machine gun; I decided to give as good as I'd got.

"Vacation. Yes. Casa LaLa. Henry Douglas is a friend of a friend. No, and no."

I smiled as sweetly as I could when the woman looked quite taken aback. She gave me a look that informed me she was going to ignore me.

"So, Tony, no sign of Juan? We have to get hold of him. Can't you phone him? It's…important."

"You know he never answers the cellphone he has, and you also know his house doesn't have a phone at all," replied Tony, as patiently as a saint. "Why do you need him…on his one day off?"

Dorothea gave me a sideways glance. "There's news he must be told. Not good news. Haven't you heard?" She seemed incredulous. Tony shifted uncomfortably.

The young chef's patience seemed to be wearing thin. "No, Dorothea, I haven't heard anything. You know Sundays are busy for me; I was out early, buying fish, then in the kitchen all morning. What's happened?"

I judged Dorothea to be someone who'd enjoy whispering some tasty tidbit of gossip to a confidante…loud enough so that everyone in a room could hear. As she planned her next words, she brushed imaginary motes from her arm and adjusted her hat.

She's preening.

"It's awful. Juan's daughter, Margarita. Dead." She uttered her final word with all the dramatic import you'd expect from a Wagnerian diva, shaking her head tragically, her arms falling limply to her sides.

Tony appeared nonplused. "What? Margarita's dead? What…what happened?"

Dorothea looked me straight in the eye. "I'm not sure I should talk about it in front of a stranger." Her expression made me think of a frowning pug.

I sensed a critical moment. "Oh, don't worry, I'm just leaving," I said, as pleasantly as I could. "I'm going to be here for the next week, Dorothea, so if this tragedy is a local one, I'm sure I'll hear all about it from someone else."

You won't be able to resist…will you?

She gave it a split second's thought and took the bait. "You're right, so you both might as well hear it from me."

Dorothea drew conspiratorially close to us. I noticed that she wasn't just completely outfitted in orange, but she actually smelled of the fruit too.

Weird.

She began, "It's terrible. Godawful. Poor Margarita had her throat slit." She looked down at me, and even dared to pat me on the shoulder. "Don't panic…they've got the guy who did it. He just walked into her store, bold as you like, in broad daylight, and slit her throat. Serena saw him do it. And Al and Miguel – they're our local cops – caught him red-handed. Literally. He was covered in poor Margarita's blood."

I couldn't help myself. "You say someone actually saw a man slit this Margarita's throat?"

"Well, as good as," replied Dorothea grudgingly. "Serena – she's the woman who runs our local spa, just so you know –

opened the door to Margarita's place and there he was, strangling her on the floor."

"I thought you said he cut her throat?" Tony sounded confused.

Dorothea snapped, "He did. And he strangled her."

"Who is he? And why would anyone want to kill Margarita…let alone cut her throat *and* strangle her?" Tony was asking all the questions I wanted answered myself.

Excellent.

"I don't know who he is." Dorothea sounded terribly disappointed. "No one's seen him around here before, and Miguel told us he didn't say anything when they hauled him off. Nothing at all. He'd been in Bob's Bodega just before he did it. When he was there, he asked – in Spanish – for roses. Which Bob didn't have, of course. The man picked up some beers, some chocolate bars and some chips, he paid in cash, and left. Seems he went right into Margarita's store next door and killed her, just like that. Oh, by the way, dear," Dorothea addressed me directly, "just so you know, Margarita is the daughter of the guy who looks after all the agave plants here, our *jimador.*" She emphasized the H sound at the beginning of the word, and I noticed that even her breath smelled of oranges.

Even weirder.

She continued, looking at me, "Margarita's a florist…well, I guess you'd call her a plantswoman, really. Lovely girl. Real green thumb. You know the type? Can grow anything. And she did arrangements…did that one over there, in fact." As she made her comments, Dorothea waved her arm toward a tall, slim vase holding one perfect Bird of Paradise flower, a palm frond, and some stones…which didn't appear to have required an enormous artistic talent, but I reasoned that maybe simplicity was a virtue.

Tony shook his head. "I can't believe it. She was just here – yesterday. She brought over her accounts for Callie to work on last night. Stayed for ages…they nattered on, as they always do. I left them to get on with it, because I had to be here, of course…but Callie didn't come to give me a hand in the kitchen until too late for her to be of any real use. I have no idea what the two of them talk about, especially given how much time they spend together anyway, and…oh God…what am I saying? Margarita's dead. *Dead.*"

Tony had sounded…*irritated?*…when he'd been talking about the time his wife and the victim had spent together.

Interesting.

He continued, "I know that Margarita and Juan didn't get along, but this'll hit him hard; she's still his daughter, after all. I'd…I'd better call Callie; she's got a meeting with another of her accountancy clients down in PV this afternoon, so she won't have heard. It'd be best if she gets the news from me. Callie and Margarita get…*got*…along…real well. Oh, this is awful. My poor wife'll be beside herself. So, what's the full story, Dorothea? Callie's bound to ask. When did all this happen?"

"Eleven. Almost on the dot. Terrible," replied Dorothea. She prodded an escaping curl of suspiciously red hair under her hat.

Luckily, given that I wasn't supposed to know what had happened, I managed to stop myself from telling her that everything had kicked off just after noon – I'd heard the clock strike twelve myself.

Why would you lie about Margarita's time of death, Dorothea?

My thoughts were interrupted by the arrival of the tall, thin man in the Tilley hat and the short, slim woman who'd greeted him so warmly outside the florist's store. They entered the restaurant together, and rather less dramatically than the flamboyant Dorothea had done.

"Ah, you're here, Dorothea. Of course," said the woman.

"Yes, Ada. I thought Juan might be here. He should be told what's happened."

"I see." Ada looked at me and offered her hand. "Hello, I'm Ada Taylor, and this is my husband, Frank. Are you, umm…?" Her non-question hung in the air.

I shook her hand – cool skin, well moisturized, firm grip; she smelled of a light, floral scent.

I smiled benignly. "I'm Cait Morgan. I'm going to be staying at Casa LaLa, Henry's place."

I'm getting quite used to using my unknown host's name.

Ada returned my smile. "Nice to meet you…though what a day you've chosen to arrive." She gave Dorothea a sideways glance and added, "I expect you've heard the bad news, Cait?" Her expression told me she was in no doubt about my answer, and her accent had already informed me that she was Canadian.

I nodded. "Yes. It sounds awful. Though Dorothea here was just telling us that the police have got their man. Do you know where they've taken him?"

I have to take every chance to find out all I can about Bud's situation.

Ada opened her mouth to reply, but Dorothea jumped in before she had a chance to utter a word. "Off to the local cells, Miguel said. Came into Bob's Bodega all flustered, saying they'd have to keep him there for a couple of days. He didn't like the idea of working extra hours to keep an eye on the murdering…" She paused and shook her head, as if to rid herself of the expletive she'd mentally managed to delete. "Apparently, some major drug thing went down this morning, and all the prisons from here to Guadalajara are full of gun runners, drug dealers, and the like. Hang the lot of 'em, I say…though hanging's too good for some. They've completely spoiled the country for people like us."

I'd already judged Ada to be the submissive one in this pairing with the bombastic Dorothea, and her quiet reply backed up my suspicions, "You have a point, of course, Dorothea…but maybe they've spoiled it even more for the Mexicans themselves? They're the ones who really suffer. We can all come and go as we please, after all. This is their home, dear."

Okay then, maybe not totally submissive, after all.

Dorothea rolled her significant shoulders as if to suggest that the undeniable problem that Mexico faces when it comes to drug-running, and the terrible violence that accompanies it, was designed to specifically inconvenience her, and her alone.

By the time he joined the conversation, Frank Taylor had removed his Tilley hat. "Hey, we don't talk about all that stuff, right, Ada?" He bobbed his head, which sported a crescent of well-trimmed gray hair, then wiped his large bald spot with his free hand, before holding it toward me. I hesitated for a moment before shaking it warmly.

He had a firm handshake, kind brown eyes, a rather officious, outdoorsy air, and gave off a distinct, if incongruous whiff of…cigars.

"Hello, Frank. Nice to meet you." I smiled. "So why isn't the local jail here also full of all these drug-runners that have just been picked up?" I wasn't going to be sidetracked, so I looked directly at Dorothea as I spoke.

Dorothea's reply was intriguing. "It's too old. Cute, but old."

"What Dorothea means to say," said Frank, "is that we have some municipal jail cells in our very own police station, which, unusually, is housed within our very own picturesque, and old, town hall. I don't know how much Henry's told you about our little haven, but it's got quite the unique history you know…"

Ada Taylor spoke firmly. "Oh, come on now, Frank, Cait's obviously come here on vacation. Let the poor woman get on with it. I'm sure she doesn't want one of your lectures on the history of *Punta de las Rocas*. Want a hand to Henry's place with those bags you've got outside, Cait? How long are you staying, by the way?"

I decided to go with the flow of the conversation, for the moment. "Just a week," I replied.

"All that baggage outside for a week?" Frank sounded truly taken aback. His wife gave him a sideways glance, and Frank had the good manners to look sheepish.

Luckily for me, I didn't have to respond, because our group was joined by yet another arrival…and this was someone I was relieved and terrified, in equal measure, to see: the policeman I'd come to think of as Big Al entered the restaurant.

No longer in his fancy uniform, his light gray pants and short-sleeved, crisp white shirt seemed much more practical, though his heavy gun belt and the glittering gold epaulets on his shirt definitely marked him out as law enforcement. He was hatless, and pulled off his sunglasses as he walked in.

He stopped just inside the doors, allowing them to close behind him. He squinted for a moment, then nodded to each of us. As his gaze rested upon me, I noticed a puzzled expression pass over his face like a shadow.

He said, "I can't find Juan. Any of you seen him?" His voice was a light tenor, not unpleasant. What was most surprising was his accent; there wasn't a hint of Spanish about it.

As I took in his appearance, I noted other unusual features: his hair was fine and light, his eyes were a definite green, and he had even, white teeth. He was really not a bad looking guy. I put him in his mid-thirties…which seemed very young for his role. And that accent? Those eyes? How could a municipal cop in Mexico look and sound so American? I was beginning to realize how entirely un-Mexican the whole place felt…then reminded myself that this was a hacienda owned by a group of ex-pat investors.

But, surely, the cops would be locals?

"None of us have seen Juan," replied Dorothea on behalf of the group.

Tony piped up with, "I thought he might be at home, or in church?"

Big Al shook his head sadly. "I tried both places. No sign. Thought he might be here."

"Unlikely, on his day off," responded Frank Taylor, his wife nodding her agreement.

Big Al shrugged, put his hands on his hips and looked directly at me. "I guess you know what all this is about?"

I studied the cop's micro-expressions: he might be facing the grim task of informing a father that his daughter was dead…but he was distracted.

He's staring at me with real curiosity. Does he know who I am?

I replied, truthfully, "Dorothea told us."

I felt a blush well up from somewhere deep inside me; I'm not really cut out for lying to police officers.

With some glee, Dorothea announced, "Al, you don't know our guest, Cait. She's going to be staying at Henry's place for the next week. She and Henry…"

As I felt, once again, Dorothea's determination to be She Who Knows Everything, I felt some sympathy for the woman creep over me: she really did seem to be compelled to make herself the center of attention. My psychologist's mind wondered if she'd been ignored as a child…or whether she'd always been the center of attention – for all the wrong reasons.

Bud often accuses me of being too quick to judge; I told myself that I could at least honor his opinion by realigning my initial snap assessment of Dorothea.

As my mind raced, I noted that Big Al had held up his hand, indicating that Dorothea should be quiet. She stopped talking, but looked crestfallen. Tapping his teeth with an arm of his sunglasses, Big Al looked sternly at Dorothea. "Don't tell me who she is, Ms. Simmonds, please don't tell me..." He stared at me with great intent.

This is...unnerving.

He pondered aloud, "I've seen this woman's face somewhere before, but I can't quite remember where it was. Just give me a moment..."

My heart thumped in my chest.

Did you look up from the crime scene and spot me lurking at the window in the condo?

"Got it!" he exclaimed.

The expression on every face around me conveyed eager anticipation; I suspected mine portrayed something closer to fear, however much I tried to make it look as though I were merely...interested.

He grinned, "I know exactly who she is."

Oh no...

He looked me up and down. "This is Doctor Cait Morgan, a professor at the school of criminology at the University of Vancouver. She's done some fascinating work in the field of victim profiling. I must say that her arrival here, today of all days, is...most interesting."

His words hung in the air as all eyes turned toward me.

Brilliant. Not.

Getting Into It

I'm rarely speechless…indeed, I think the general opinion among my students would be that I'm never lost for words. But as the group took in the announcement about who I was, and what I did, I felt my mouth dry up. I swallowed, hard, and mustered a weak smile.

Even if you did see me in the window at the condo, how do you know who I am? was what I thought; "How on earth do you know all that about me?" was what I said.

As Big Al peered at me, he nodded. "I know a great deal more about you than that."

"Really?" I squeaked.

"But I am being rude." He smiled. Shark teeth. Shark eyes. "I know who you are, but you don't know who I am. Allow me to introduce myself." He saluted. "Alberto Jesus Beselleu Torres, captain of law enforcement for the municipality of *Punta de las Rocas*. If folks around here are feeling especially formal, they call me Captain Al. Of course, if someone's feeling intimidated by my presence, they tend to call me Captain Torres. At your service, Doctor Morgan." He stood to attention.

"Oh, please, I'm Cait. Call me Cait. I'm not that keen on being Doctor Morgan inside the university, let alone when I'm away from the place. So please, everyone," I tried to catch each member of our group with what I hoped was a winning smile, "it's just Cait. Cait Morgan. Thanks."

General nodding ensued.

I tried to maintain my fake smile as I added, "So how do you come to know who I am?" There was no point beating about the bush.

Al relaxed his formal stance and smiled broadly…and more genuinely, I hoped. "I wish I could say I possess cop-telepathy,

Doctor…Cait…but I recognized your face from a photograph on your university's website. I'm taking some criminology classes at the university in Guadalajara, and yours is a very good school, with a reputation to which our little department aspires. Your work on victimology is fascinating…as are theories that came out of your school some years ago on geographic profiling,"

Again, I could feel a blush rise on my cheeks; I'm not very good at accepting compliments…I'm really not used to them, I suppose.

Thank heavens that's the only place you've seen me, was what I thought; "Thanks," was what I said.

Al asked the obvious, if undesirable, question: "So what brings such a well-known criminologist to our little out-of-the-way bit of paradise?"

"She's a friend of a friend of Henry's," butted in Dorothea, aiming to re-establish her position as the local know-it-all as rapidly as possible. "Isn't that right, Cait?" She beamed at me, glowing with proprietorial pride.

"Yes," I replied. Monosyllabic responses seemed safest.

"Well, it's auspicious," observed Al. "We've all suffered a great loss this morning, as you've heard. A valued and much-loved member of our community, Margarita Rosa García Martinez, a wonderful and irreplaceable woman, was found murdered. I have the perpetrator in custody, a circumstance I would like to boast was due to excellence in police work, but, truthfully, I just happened to be on the scene at the time."

I had to take my chance, so said, "How fortunate…under such unfortunate circumstances. Dorothea mentioned that the man in question…umm…do you know his name, by the way?" I tried to make it sound like a throwaway question that had just occurred to me.

Al shook his head, and looked grim. "No. Not yet."

I tried to make sure I didn't reveal the relief I felt when I continued, "According to Dorothea," I acknowledged the woman, who beamed with pride, "the perpetrator cut the throat of your…friend, then also strangled her. Is that true?"

Al shook his head and shrugged. "I know it seems unlikely, but Margarita's throat was certainly…slashed, and the man was found with his hands around her neck. One could surmise that he was finishing off the job…making sure she was dead…or maybe he thought better of his actions and was trying to save her."

"Oh, come off it, Al," said Dorothea loudly. "Serena said he was throttling the life out of her."

"He might have been trying to save her," said Tony quietly, still wiping his hands on his apron.

Dorothea exploded, "Rubbish! If he'd wanted to save her, then why did he cut her throat in the first place?"

"Maybe he didn't." It was out before I could stop myself.

Shut up, Cait.

"What do you mean, Cait?" asked Al.

Everyone gave me their – unwanted – attention.

Yes, what do you mean, you stupid blabbermouth?

I composed myself as far as possible, and decided upon a course of action in that split second…then threw myself into it.

"Forgive me," I said, as calmly as I could, "I know I'm a new arrival here, and – of course – I'm absolutely mindful of the fact that you all knew Margarita, and must have feelings about her…grief being the uppermost at this terrible time. But, as Captain Al has just told you all, I'm a person who focuses – professionally – upon victims of crime…usually murder. What that means is that I consider a victim's life and lifestyle, their habits, and their entire life story to build a better picture of why and how they might have ended up becoming a victim. When I do this, I usually work with their families and friends to help me gain those insights, which I then interpret for those working in law enforcement, to help them with their investigative duties. I try to be a voice speaking on behalf of the victim, in a way. Of course, none of what I do is to imply that they chose to become a victim…I merely seek to illuminate how they might have come into contact with someone who meant to do them harm."

I turned to Al, and didn't have any problem in delivering an earnest look when I added, "That's one of the criticisms of my discipline that I hear most often, but there's absolutely no intention to victim-blame."

Al nodded sagely.

Encouraged, I carried on. "I have colleagues whose life's work is to look into the backgrounds of criminals, but I've chosen – academically – to focus on the victims themselves. Now, in this instance, you might not know anything about the man you have in custody, Al, but you all know a great deal about the victim. And that knowledge could help Al to discover who the murderer really is…and why Margarita, apparently, both had her throat slashed *and* was being strangled."

"But we know who the killer is," shouted Dorothea. I wondered if she had any idea how to use a normal speaking voice. "It's that horrible man. The one Serena saw."

I didn't like to hear Bud spoken of that way: I worked hard to prevent my expression from betraying my feelings toward Dorothea.

Frank Taylor leaped to my defense. "I think what Cait means is that we can find out who the *killer really is*, rather than who the *real killer is*. Isn't that right, Cait?"

Nope, you're completely wrong, was what I thought; "You're exactly right," was what I said.

"Ah, if only we could afford to retain the services of the famous Professor Morgan," said Al enigmatically. "But I can see that Cait Morgan, the private individual, is here for a vacation, not to…work on a case." He pouted a little.

Go for it, Cait.

I judged that Captain Al was ambitious…otherwise, why would a local cop in one of Mexico's smallest municipalities be a part-time criminology student? He must want to better himself. I could see how I could insert myself into the case, then try to find out who had really killed Margarita, and clear Bud into the bargain…but knew I had to go about things the right way. I didn't want to appear to be too keen to get involved…but I also didn't want to put Al off to the point where he'd feel guilty about accepting my insights.

I opened with, "You know what…it sounds like a fascinating case. With all due respect to the late Margarita and you – her friends – I think I'd find looking into it an interesting challenge…as long as you don't mind me asking you all lots of questions about Margarita, her life, and – possibly – even your own lives."

There were general shrugs around the room.

Al had the look of a hungry man eyeing up a meal. "I wouldn't want to impose," he said quietly.

Frank Taylor spoke hesitantly. "So you think you can work out who this murderer is, just by asking us all a bunch of questions?"

Al managed a weak smile – and a slight eye-roll – in my direction.

I stepped up. "Not exactly. What I do is try to understand the life of a victim, because that often opens up possible reasons for them having been killed. You see – without giving you the full lecture on the subject – truly random acts of violence are incredibly rare: more often than not, there's an existing link between a victim and the person who killed them. This is especially the case when it comes to premeditated murders. Most of those are carried out by someone close to the victim – a spouse, family member, or very close friend. That's where most investigations start, and where I'd start too: with the victim's closest family and friends."

Dorothea declaimed, "But Margarita couldn't possibly have known the man that Al has in custody; he can't be local, or someone would have recognized him already. Everyone knows everyone else around here. Oh, wait…" She dramatically clapped her hand to her forehead. "Of course – he's a hit man! That'll be it." She looked triumphant for an instant, then crestfallen. "But why? Why would a hit man come here to kill Margarita?"

"We don't know everything about Margarita," said Ada Taylor quite timidly. She seemed surprised to discover she'd spoken aloud.

Frank backed up his wife's observation. "That's true. We all knew Margarita, to some degree or other…but only professionally speaking. You know, with regards to her flowers, her plants, or her photography."

Photography? Interesting.

Ada seemed to be spurred on by her husband's support. "Exactly, dear. I've never even met her at a social engagement when she wasn't involved in the event in some way – doing the flowers or taking the photos. In fact, I've no real idea about the woman, or her interests, outside of her jobs."

Dorothea looked ready to shout something at us all when Tony spoke up; he had a way of disappearing into the background that I suspected came from having been in the food service industry for years.

Clearing his throat first – as if he didn't want to interrupt – the chef offered, "Callie knows…knew…Margarita quite well. She liked her a great deal. It's funny, though…we were saying only the other day how very private Margarita always was; she was never chatty when she was doing her floral arrangements, or her photography…or even on occasions like last night, when she brought all her accounts for Callie to work through. In the past year of them being what most folks would call 'close', Callie's only ever been inside Margarita's home once, and that was because she'd offered to help carry some equipment from her house to her van."

Let them talk, Cait. Observe. Listen. Learn.

It was fascinating to see this group gradually realize that they'd hardly known the woman who – just a few moments earlier – they'd all been sure they'd completely understood.

I noticed that Al's eyes were darting around the group as people spoke; he was nodding his head as he listened.

"You're all quite right," he said. "Even as I was driving Margarita's killer to the police station, I thought about how little I knew of the real woman."

An interesting choice of words.

He looked at me through narrowed eyes. Again. "Cait, it's clear that in just a few moments you've made people think about this in a way that we might never have done. If you could bear to give up some of your free time, I'd value your input. It won't be for long: I'll be handing the guy over to the *Federales* the day after tomorrow. They reckon that, by then, they'll have cleared out enough of the people they rounded up in the dawn raids this morning for there to be room in the system for him. Since I'm stuck with him until then, it would be a great comfort to our community if I could use that time to maybe work out who he is…and why he killed Margarita."

And it wouldn't be too bad for your career, would it Captain Torres? was what I thought; "But of course," was what I said.

Al nodded his gratitude.

I added, "I'd be grateful for the chance to get to Casa LaLa, maybe wash and brush up a bit, and unpack a few things first, but – then – I don't see why we can't just dive straight in."

Al beamed. "I'll give you a hand with your bags, then I'll find Juan and…break the news. This is my responsibility…my grave responsibility. I could collect you from here at…maybe five?"

I checked my watch. "Okay, that would be great. Thanks. Do I walk to Casa LaLa from here, or…?" I wasn't really sure how to finish my question, as I didn't know what my alternatives were.

Tony jumped in with, "No need to drive, it's the nearest building to this one. Just a five-minute walk. You have the key I gave you?" I nodded. "And the code is for the alarm, which has a pad inside the front door. The water service people will be there tomorrow, but would you like some bottles for tonight?"

"The water service people?" I was puzzled.

Tony smiled. "Yeah, every Monday, Thursday, and Saturday morning they bring water for the water coolers in all the houses, and take away the used containers. Since Henry wasn't expecting you, he didn't hold on to any containers, so they'll bring you two fresh ones tomorrow – I'll sort that out for you. Then you'll have a spare. If you can be at home around eight, the guy can show you how to put the bottle onto the unit; it's not complicated, but there's a knack to it. Then just put the empty where he tells you, and they'll replace it next time they call. If you need extra water, just let me know. But, like I say, I'm guessing there won't be anything at Henry's place at all, so why not take a few bottles now, to pop into the fridge? I'm sure you'll find your way around his place okay. The pool service people come on Friday and

Monday, so they'll show up tomorrow morning, but you don't need to be there for them. They have a key and their own code."

Oh, my very own pool!

The thought gave me pleasure: even though I can't swim, I enjoy the way a pool catches and plays with the light, and – if it's shallow enough – I can always have a little dunk.

Nope…rescue Bud, no dunking.

I replied, "Thanks, Tony. Maybe I'll see you later for a bite to eat. We'll see how my time goes with Al, okay?" My smile was genuine, because I was remembering the menu I'd read.

Tony winked at me. "Sure thing. If no one else needs me right now, I'd really like to call Callie. I think I've got the full picture. She'll be devastated by the news, of course, but it'll be worse if she hears it from someone else."

Tony clearly hoped that Dorothea, Frank, and Ada would leave.

Frank ushered his wife toward the door. "Absolutely, Tony. You've got a busy, and difficult, time ahead of you, I'm sure. Come along, Dorothea, we'll let this young man get on with his work. We retired folk have nothing better to do with our time than sit about all day, but he's got to get ready to feed us all tonight. It would be great if you could join us, Cait. We all eat here most evenings, even if it's just to see each other and catch up on the gossip."

His expression shifted from jovial to embarrassed when he'd uttered his final words.

"Oh, Frank," remonstrated his wife.

"Everyone knows what I mean," replied a red-faced Frank. Looking at me he added, "It's always fun to have the chance to catch up with a fellow Canadian. Did you know our place is called Casa Canuck?" He grinned. "You a hockey fan, Cait? Get to many of those Vancouver Canucks games?"

"Not on my money, and with the prices of the tickets," I replied, maybe a little too quickly.

"Quite right," said Ada. "We watch most of the games here, on satellite. Sometimes it feels like we live in a very sunny Prince George…almost like we never left home."

"You're from Prince George?" I attempted to sound politely interested.

Frank replied, "I had a brewery there…that was our family business, and Ada was the local butcher's daughter. A match made in heaven, right? Beer and…well, every meat you can imagine, eh? But…the kids wanted nothing to do with it, so we sold up, and now we're spending their inheritance. They didn't want to put in the work, so they won't get the profits." He raised an eyebrow toward his wife. "Besides, if our son wants to be an eternal kid, and our daughter wants to double the world population with that tofu-eating husband of hers, good luck to 'em, but they can do it on their own. I worked my way up from the bottom – my father made sure I did every job there was before he let me have any management responsibility. But kids these days…"

Ada tutted. "Oh come on now, Frank, Cait wants to get settled, and she doesn't need to hear all about how our son and daughter have, apparently, let you down. Not now, and probably not ever."

She patted her husband's arm, then gave me her attention. "Our children wanted their own lives, Cait, and that's that. If you start talking to him about hockey, or anything else remotely Canadian, then you'll only have yourself to blame if you're trapped for several hours." She smiled at me, then at her husband. "Don't say you weren't warned. Come on now, Frank, let's get home and get a few laps in at the pool before we change for appies." She led her husband out into the blinding daylight.

As Dorothea trailed behind them – a performer without an audience – Al looked at me with a kind smile and said, "Okay, let's get you installed, then I can go and do my very unpleasant duty."

We walked outside, the wooden doors closing heavily behind us, and we both shoved sunglasses onto our noses.

Al wheeled my suitcase, I wheeled Bud's.

"You don't travel light, do you?" Al observed, smiling.

No…I have a lot of baggage.

Two Days

Casa LaLa was bedecked with vivid pink bougainvillea which clambered up the adobe walls, almost reaching the terracotta tiles of the roof; geckos scuttled as we approached, and Al stayed just long enough to see that I was able to gain entry, and deal with the alarm.

Once I got inside, and had the chance to take stock for a moment, it was clear that Henry Douglas had a preference for the minimalist approach to décor…which disappointed me a little, because – to me – clutter is joy. White walls floated – starkly unadorned – between a dark wood ceiling, and floor. The paltry furnishings were also white – either disappearing against the walls, or popping against the bare planks of the flooring.

I found the bedroom, used the *en suite* facilities, dumped Bud's suitcase into the closet, then riffled through my own…trying to find something to change into that didn't need an iron.

Fifteen minutes later I was fresh from the shower, my clean hair pulled back into a ponytail, sporting cream capris, a cream and lemon over-shirt, and cream sandals. I transferred everything I thought I might need from my carry-on tote to my cream knitted purse – a Christmas gift from my sister in Australia, who knows that all my fingers become thumbs when knitting needles are involved. Then I allowed myself a few more moments to explore the outdoor areas of my temporary home.

I noted that almost every flat surface inside the house, as well as the stark metal table on the stone patio outside, had a heavy glass ashtray on it. Clearly Henry was a smoker, which was a huge relief. However, it still didn't seem right to me to smoke inside his home, so I plopped myself onto an angular steel chair next to the patio table and lit a cigarette.

The outdoor space was even more minimalist than inside: stuccoed walls painted in vivid, clashing colors, and one giant blue agave in a terracotta pot were all that surrounded the small, perfectly square pool. It all seemed somehow…familiar.

Got it!

It reminded me of the work of Luis Barragán, a famous architect from Guadalajara whose garden designs were almost a legend. Given that Barragán had died in the 1980s, and this place hadn't been built until a few years ago…based on all the technology that was wired into every minimalist corner…it must have been meant as the owner's homage to the man. Or maybe Henry Douglas, himself, had never heard of Barragán, but the designer of his home had.

I might never know.

I found the ambience pleasant; a vivid nothingness, with the shadows cast by one wall onto another providing ever-moving angles of shade. I was seeing the design in the light that Barragán had grown up with…had designed for. I hadn't understood it before.

Context is always critical, Cait.

The thought resonated: the woman in the capris who'd screamed – Serena – had seen Bud in a situation where she believed he was killing her friend, so she *saw* a killer. I, on the other hand, knew that if the florist, Margarita, had suffered a slashed throat, then Bud had been on his knees with his hands around her throat trying to save the poor woman.

Context.

And context always exists because of knowledge that you do, or do not, possess. Sitting at that table I understood, as never before, that Barragán's designs worked for gardens within the context for which they'd been conceived; as the light played against the shade, the striking palette of the walls allowed my brain to conjure up floral displays, without there being any. I had gained a unique insight from a new experience.

I might not be able to go around telling everyone I know that Bud is innocent…but maybe I can change the context of his discovery.

I unscrewed the top of a bottle of chilled water, pulled a notebook and pen from my bag, put my reading specs on, lit another cigarette, and got to work. Before I called Jack White, I needed to get a few things straight, so I wrote down a list of key points from my recollections at the airport, and what I'd learned since. Lists usually help me to arrange my thinking, and I hoped they would now, maybe more than ever before…because this was a critical situation.

I now knew that Margarita's throat had been slashed: the severing of a carotid artery means that the heart pumps blood out of the body fast…very fast…so, with a rapidly reducing supply of blood returning to the heart, the body shuts down quickly. Depending on whether she'd received a nick to one carotid, or had both completely severed, the woman would have been dead in anything between one and five minutes. Thus, the killer must have been very close by when Bud discovered Margarita because – if she'd been already dead – Bud wouldn't have been trying to stop her from bleeding out.

I'd been looking out of the window when Bud entered the bodega, and I hadn't noticed any activity inside Margarita's store at that time. At least…nothing that had caught my eye.

Then I'd seen Bud go inside her store. I had to assume that Margarita was already fatally injured by that time, and that Bud had immediately tried to help her. So…the killer had struck sometime during the period when Bud was inside the bodega.

That meant that the killer had either been hiding somewhere inside Margarita's shop when Bud was hauled off, or…they'd exited by another door.

Good start, Cait.

Once again, I pictured the street where it had all happened: I hadn't been looking at the scene every moment, but I could make up a timeline of activity. I listed everyone I'd seen in sufficiently close proximity to the flower shop that they could be a legitimate suspect. And knew I could immediately eliminate some people from that list.

Serena – of the capri pants and spa – couldn't have been the killer, nor could Frank Taylor: they'd either been together – in my sight – in the street, or inside the bodega, at the critical time.

Right…that's a start. Two down…

I checked my watch: I had fifty minutes before I was due to meet Captain Al at Tony's *Amigos del Tequila* restaurant, so – rather than making more notes – I decided to call Jack; I was anxious to find out what was happening at his end of things…though I felt a lot less stressed knowing that I had a plan in place to help Bud.

However, I allowed myself a moment or two to give some thought to what I should, and shouldn't, say before I dialed. Given that Jack had initially been all in favor of me fleeing the country, I couldn't imagine he'd be enamored of the idea that I was now going to work on the case with the local police. I decided to make up my mind when I got a sense of his mood…so I glugged my water, then punched his number into my own phone.

Sheila answered, sounding breathless. In the background I could hear barking, and was pretty sure I could pick out Marty's operatic woofs within the din.

"Hello Sheila, it's Cait. You sound busy. The dogs sound as though they're having a great time, too," I observed.

"Oh, Cait…" was all Sheila managed to say before she burst into tears.

The pit of my stomach knew – even before my brain did – that this wasn't good. "Sheila, what's wrong? What's happened?"

It's amazing how many disastrous scenarios you can run through in the time it takes for someone to blow their nose.

Sheila blubbed, "The ambulance just left. I couldn't go with Jack because of the dogs. Sandra's on her way over to look after them, then I'm going to meet Jack at the hospital. They're driving him to the ER in Abbotsford. Oh, Cait, I'm so frightened."

So am I…

I took a deep breath. I owed it to Sheila to give her what she needed, instead of looking for help for Bud. "Sheila, if Sandra's coming, could she bring her daughter with her – you know, the eldest one? She could look after the dogs, and maybe Sandra could drive you to the hospital? I'm not sure you should be behind the wheel right now."

Sheila's wonderful, and capable, though a bit prone to fuss; I could imagine how much of a state she must have been in at that moment.

I tried again. "Even if Sandra's daughter can't come, I do think someone should drive you. Can't you leave the dogs alone for a while…let Sandra get you there, then come back to see to them? I'm sure they'll be fine if you just put them out in their compound like usual." I knew the dogs would cope; Marty loves to run and play with Jack and Sheila's three animals.

Sheila sobbed, "That's just it, I can't. Daisy – you know, our biggest girl – went and got herself caught on the compound fence somehow, and Jack was cutting her out when the whole thing collapsed…and he fell down the bank into the creek. It wasn't until the dogs came rushing into the house that I realized anything was wrong. If it hadn't been for them, I wouldn't have looked for Jack until his dinner was ready, and by then he might have been…oh dear. Anyway, the dogs are all completely freaked out. When I found Jack, it was clear that he'd done more than broken his arm."

"Jack's broken his arm?"

Oh no.

"Yes, I could see the bone."

My toes curled at the thought: put me in a room with buckets of blood and I'm fine, but there's something about bones poking through flesh, or even the thought of it, that turns my stomach and makes my feet go all tense and tingly.

Maybe it's got something to do with the fact that I'm only just out of plaster myself, having managed to break the same wrist twice within the past year?

Shela kept going. "I didn't even notice his ankle. They think it's broken too. It was his face that frightened me, Cait, not his limbs. He was gray. And yellowish. Terrible. I thought he was…oh dear. So I called 911. I stayed with him. The dogs were all over us…I couldn't keep them off him, and they were clambering all over me, too. By the time the paramedics got to us, I thought for sure they were too late…but they said he's stable. They reckon he had a 'coronary event' down there beside the creek, they said, and he might have lost consciousness due to a concussion. But the dogs? They're going nuts. I can't leave them, because the fence is down. I swear they wanted to get into the ambulance with Jack."

Our Marty had lost part of an ear when he was grazed by a bullet – when he'd attacked the man who'd shot Bud's late wife – so I could well understand how four dogs could become more than a little fractious if their beloved human was injured, and then taken from them. My heart went out to Sheila…she was putting the terrified dogs' needs ahead of her own; she must have yearned to be in that ambulance beside the man she loved.

I faced a significant dilemma: Jack White had cheated death after a nasty accident, it seemed, while the man I loved was still locked up for a crime he hadn't committed…and Jack had been a lifeline for Bud that I'd been counting on.

Did I dare ask Sheila if Jack had managed to do anything on Bud's behalf before he'd been injured?

I was torn.

Poor Jack. Poor Sheila. My poor Bud.

I made my decision. "Sheila, I'm so sorry to hear what's happened. And I'm sorry I'm not there to help. I know your friends will rally around to support you – and I know you have a lot of friends. You deserve them: you guys are so giving and selfless. But – I'm sorry, but I have to ask – do you happen know if Jack managed to speak to anyone about Bud? Is there anything he told you? I'm really sorry to ask, Sheila, at a time like this, but…I have to. For Bud's sake."

I felt guilty, yet driven.

Sheila blew her nose again. "Don't be silly, Cait, of course you have to ask. All I can tell you is that Jack sent you an email. He said that it was best to get everything in writing, so he did all that before he realized that Daisy was tangled up in the fence. She's fine, by the way. No damage. Lord knows how she managed it. So check your email, and there'll be something from him there. I also know he booked himself onto flight to Puerto Vallarta tomorrow morning, but, of course, he won't be coming now. And…oh, there's Sandra coming up the drive now. I have to go, okay?"

"Go, Sheila. Give Jack my love – give him *our* love. And don't give us another thought. Tell him I'm on it. I'm more than capable of sorting this out. He's not to worry about Bud, or me, and he's to concentrate on getting better. And Sheila…all that goes for you too, right?"

"You're a good girl, Cait. I'll let you know how Jack is when I can. Bye for now."

Being referred to as a "girl" made me smile…but that was all I had to smile about. Of course I felt sorry for Jack, and hoped he was going to be alright, but…this additional disaster couldn't have happened at a worse time.

I hadn't even considered checking my emails since I'd arrived, so turned my attention to that…only to hear the doorbell chime. I got to the front door and opened it, wishing I was reading whatever it was that Jack had sent me instead.

There stood Frank and Ada Taylor, their hands full of brightly colored raffia bags. Frank's Tilley hat was perched on his head at a jaunty angle, and Ada was looking almost manically cheerful.

"We brought supplies," announced Frank jovially.

All I could do was invite them in, take the bags, and thank them profusely…while telling them that they "shouldn't have" – and meaning it. As I packed everything into the fridge and cupboards, I reminded myself that they were kind to help me, and couldn't help but realize that Ada was the epitome of the sort of woman you rarely notice, until you spot the fact that order reigns supreme thanks to her efforts. She made me think of Sheila – but without the element of "fusspot".

"We know you're meeting Al later, but we thought you could do with a proper welcome," said Ada, shutting a cupboard door one last time, and presenting me with a dish of nuts, and some sliced fruit.

My polite gene kicked in. "Would you like a drink?" I asked. I slapped my best smile on my face as I added, "Some very kind Canadians I know have supplied me with juice, wine, soda, and beer – so you have a choice."

Frank and Ada grinned at my attempt at humor.

Ada responded, "Juice for me, thank you, dear, though I usually prefer tea. Unfortunately, we didn't have an unopened box I could bring you, I'm so sorry. I find tea very soothing and even cooling, don't I, Frank? But I'll have juice for now. Shall I help myself?"

I nodded. "Please do. And you, Frank? Can I tempt you into having a beer with me?"

What are you thinking, Cait Morgan? You need a clear head.

Frank glanced at his wife. "No thanks, Cait. Juice will be fine for me too," he half nodded toward Ada, "at least, I'm sure that's what the wife thinks."

"True," replied Ada as she poured a second glass. "And for you, Cait? Do I take it you fancy a beer?"

I looked at the bottles in the fridge and gave it some serious consideration. "Thanks, but I'll stick with juice too. I'll want a clear head for my conversations with Al about Margarita."

I wanted to get to the subject of the murder as quickly as possible; Bud didn't have time for me to be engaging in chit-chat…but how to begin?

"Are you sure you don't mind giving up your spare time to do this for Margarita?" Ada's opening gambit gave me a good opportunity to dig in.

Frank corrected his wife, "Cait's not really investigating to help Margarita, dear. We all know who killed her."

"Yes, but we don't know why," was Ada's sensible reply.

"That's what I think you might be able to help me with," I said, maybe a little too quickly. "Were either of you 'on the spot', so to speak?" I knew the answer, of course, but they weren't aware of that.

"Oh yes, both of us were right there," Frank said, smiling. Ada tapped him on the arm. Frank's face rearranged itself into a more serious expression.

I suggested, "How about we sit on the patio and you can tell me all about it?" I waved in the general direction of the glazed wall that I'd folded back on itself to offer almost entirely open access to the garden.

"Can I smoke?" asked Frank hopefully.

"Only if I can too," I replied.

Frank brightened. Ada tutted.

"He doesn't need any encouragement, Cait," she admonished. "Him and his cigars. They're all the same around here. In fact, I think it's why he wanted to come here to live: when Greg told us about the place, he kept going on about how wonderful it was to be able to sit outside and puff on a cigar anytime."

"Greg?"

I haven't met a Greg.

Ada smiled. "Greg's in PV today; you won't have a chance to meet him until this evening. Greg is Greg Hollins. He's the one who told us about this place…as an investment, you know? Lovely man. So tell me, are you single, Cait? Greg is. A bit older than you, of course, but he's single."

Ada's surprising change of topic – and her knowing look when she mentioned that Greg was unmarried – threw me for a moment. I saw Bud's face flash upon what Wordsworth would call "my inward eye".

"Yes, I'm single. Totally single." I replied with as much conviction as possible.

Forgive me, Bud.

"What, you've never been married?" The look on Ada's face told me I might as well have grown a second head.

I decided to laugh it off. "Yes, I've just turned forty-eight and I've never been married, and have no children…and no significant other, either." I waited for the inevitable look of pity that creeps across the faces of those who are married, or are parents, after I make such a statement.

"No children?" asked Ada brightly.

It was Frank's turn to tut. "Just because she doesn't have kids, it doesn't mean she's weird. From what Al said earlier on, she's made a very successful career for herself. Besides, kids – who'd have 'em? Ungrateful so-and-sos."

"That's enough, Frank," said Ada quickly. "I hope I haven't insulted you?" she asked me. The genuine concern on her face deserved a thoughtful response.

"Not at all, Ada. Frank's right: my career has most certainly been the biggest part of my life, and…well, not everything's for everybody." I didn't add that the only person before Bud with whom I'd ever been in a long-term relationship had turned out to be a sociopathic alcoholic who'd beaten me, made me feel less than worthless, and had ended up dead on my bathroom floor.

Not the time, nor the place, Cait.

"And now you live in Vancouver?" asked Ada, still bright.

I felt as though she was the one pumping me for information, when it should have been the other way around. I resolved to try to move ahead on a more of a *quid pro quo* basis.

"Do you know the Lower Mainland?" They both nodded. "I live in a little house on Burnaby Mountain, about halfway up, on the way to the University of Vancouver's Burnaby campus. That's where I teach. I like it very much."

"But your accent's from Britain, isn't it?" asked Ada.

I smiled. "Yes, it's a Welsh accent. I'm from Wales, originally."

Ada looked delighted. "Frank's granddad was Welsh, isn't that right, Frank?" Frank nodded patiently. "But he wasn't a Taylor. Where exactly are you from, dear? Might we have heard of it?"

"I'm from Swansea…"

"That's where that Zeta-Jones girl is from, isn't that right, Frank? And Tom Jones was from near there too, I know. Fabulous voice. Jones was Frank's grandfather's name, and he was from…I think it was Aber-somewhere. Was that it, Frank, dear?"

Frank didn't seem to be very engaged. "Yes, dear, that's right," he replied. I had no doubt that he'd hardly heard what his wife had said, and that, mentally, he was somewhere else entirely. He rolled the end of his fat cigar in his mouth, then rested it in the large ashtray on the patio table.

"That murderer was in there killing Margarita when I was right next door, you know." Frank made the statement with grim determination. "Imagine. I was that close to him that I could have stopped him…if only I'd known."

Ada shook her head. "Don't start that again, Frank."

I took my chance. "How close were you, exactly, Frank? Were you literally next door to the flower store?"

Ada opened her mouth as if to answer on her husband's behalf, but Frank gave his wife a firm look, picked up his cigar again, and manipulated it in his fingers as he replied. "I'd gone down to the *Rocas Hermosas* Resort on the seafront, right opposite Margarita's flower shop. I wanted to see a guy who works in the bar there. He's great at getting these things for me at a reasonable price." He looked lovingly at his cigar. "Anyway, I'd just left him, and was wandering through the gardens, waiting for this one to finish at the spa. What was it today, dear? Mani-, or pedi-, or both? I lose track."

"Both." Ada wriggled her neat French manicure at him.

Frank continued, "We'd agreed I'd pick her up when she called me. You never know how long Serena's going to be, do you, dear?"

Ada shrugged, with resignation. "No, not really. She's very much a *mañana* person, Cait, so you're never quite sure when she'll start on you…or finish. Once you've got your feet in that basin, well, there's not a lot you can do about it really, eh?"

For two retired people, I couldn't imagine that a small delay when you were getting a pedicure would be a big issue, but Frank struck me as the sort of man who liked a schedule for his days.

He tutted. "So there I am, hanging around waiting for Ada, when Serena comes out of her spa and calls over to me."

So far, Frank's account agreed with my own observations, and augmented them.

He continued, "She had this big cake box with her. Told me it was Bob and Maria's wedding anniversary, and invited me to join the celebration."

Ada added, "Bob and Maria are the couple who own the bodega next door to Margarita's flower shop, Cait. Bob's Bodega. Lovely couple. Married forty years. Isn't that just wonderful?"

"I was getting to that," responded Frank a little impatiently. "They own Bob's Bodega, as Ada said, and they are, indeed, very nice people. Of course I said I'd join Serena, though I have to admit that I was a bit puzzled about Ada's situation…I mean, if Serena was out in the street, what was Ada doing?"

Ada said, "I told you I couldn't leave, Frank. Serena had finished me, but I had to wait where I was for my toes to dry properly. There's no point getting them done if you're going to ruin them, right, Cait?"

I nodded and smiled, though my personal experience of pedicures is non-existent: just the thought of anyone touching my feet makes me squirm. In fact, I suspect I'd knock out someone's teeth if they tried to grind down my hard skin, or paint my toenails.

Again, Frank tutted. "Anyway, while Ada was sitting around waiting for her toes to be ready for the world to enjoy, I went into the bodega with Serena. That man – the murderer – he even held the door open for us. Can you imagine? I was that close to him. There he was, all smiles, and he was just about to go and kill poor Margarita."

Frank and Ada both shook their heads, disbelief and anger etched on their faces.

Frank pressed on. "Al and Miguel were already in the bodega because they'd known about Serena's plans for a while; they'd agreed to get all kitted up in their dress uniforms to make the anniversary celebration something special. Of course, Bob and Maria were delighted by all the fuss, and they wanted to cut the cake there and then…but Serena said she knew that Margarita wanted to be there for the cake-cutting and had agreed to take photos, so she said she'd go next door to get her, since Margarita was late. A minute after she left, we all heard her screaming. In fact, I'm pretty sure anyone within a mile could have heard her…she's got one heck of a pair of lungs on her that Serena. Luckily, Al and Miguel were right on the spot, though they were a bit hamstrung by their silly outfits. And that's when all hell broke loose."

"I heard the screams too, from inside the spa," chipped in Ada. "It frightened the life out of me. I popped my sandals on, as carefully as I could, and rushed out into the street."

"Were you all alone in the spa?" I asked…as innocently as possible.

"No. Dorothea was in the back getting a massage," replied Ada. "Well, I guess by then she'd have been getting dressed after her massage. Serena runs the place alone, and she'd just given me the final coat on my fingers, then she'd gone outside with the cake that she'd brought through from out back."

"Is there more than one way in and out of the spa?" I asked.

Ada looked puzzled by my question. "There's a door that goes to the lane behind, and the front door, that's it. Why?"

"No reason," I lied.

So...Ada and Dorothea had been in the same building, but not together, during the critical few minutes between Serena leaving the spa and Bud going into the flower shop. And there was a back door to the spa.

Interesting.

Could I picture Ada slashing a florist's throat? It seemed unlikely. There again, my years of studying criminal psychology have taught me that you really cannot judge a book by its cover: some of the most warped minds have been possessed by perfectly average-looking people. I wondered how large a woman Margarita had been; if she was a plantswoman, and used to working the land, the chances were that she'd have been physically capable...and there was Ada, a seemingly happy wife, mother, and grandmother, about five feet five tall, weighing around a hundred and ten pounds. Not an obvious suspect.

Of course, there was still Dorothea to consider...she was a much more substantial person.

I asked, "What brought you two to *Hacienda Soleado*?" I decided I'd take my chance to gather a bit of background...now that I'd established that at least one of my guests had, indeed, had the opportunity to murder Margarita.

"That was Frank," replied Ada. "And not just because he could sit about and smoke his cigars all day. In fact, we came here because he was bored, didn't we, dear?"

"Bored?" I asked.

"I'd sold my brewery in Prince George, and we'd been on a few cruises, taken a couple of trips to be with the grandkids, redone the bathroom...and the kitchen. You know the sort of thing. But I missed the work." He smiled wryly. "Before I sold up, I couldn't wait to pack it in. The business had changed so much in the last few years I was running it, with all the big players squeezing out our type of small operation, you see. The day I walked out of there, I thought I'd be happy to never work another day in my life. But then the wind changed, and everyone started looking for the small and micro-brewery products, so if I'd only hung on…"

"Come on, Frank. You know the time was right," said Ada.

Frank nodded. "Yeah, it seemed right at the time, and I got a good price. We met Greg on one of our cruises. We palled up over the dinner table, and kept in touch afterwards. He mentioned this place he was investing in, and it seemed like a good fit. I get to dabble in the tequila business and use all those years of knowledge about bottling, distribution, and all that…and we get to live in a home we were able to design exactly as we wanted, right here, at the hacienda. We moved in four years ago, and – I have to be honest – it's worked out great. Greg's quite a driving force for the business. He and Juan – poor Margarita's father – organized all of the distillation and bottling construction before we got here. Dorothea was an investor before us…she met Greg on a safari in Africa. Then we came along. I get involved in just enough of the business stuff to keep my mind sharp, and we get wonderful weather pretty much all year. We don't miss the weather in Prince George, do we? And Ada's never bored, are you? As long as she's got her books, she's happy. She's addicted to all those blessed murder mysteries."

Time to Talk

I stood to collect the glasses we'd used. I didn't want to hear what either of them was going to say next, because I was pretty sure I knew what it would be.

"Ada always solves all the crimes in her books before they tell you whodunit, you know," said Frank.

There you go.

"I bet she could help you work out who this guy really is," he added eagerly.

Oh dear.

I smiled. "Why thank you, Frank; I'm sure Ada could be very helpful, but, if Al is going to be giving me any sort of confidential information – you know, autopsy results and that sort of thing – then I…probably shouldn't share it." I hoped that would stall them.

Ada gushed, "But we don't need to know all of that to work out who that awful man is, right? We know he did it, and we know how, and where, and when, so an autopsy wouldn't help at all. I'm pretty sure everyone here wants to help Al crack the case before the *Federales* get involved. We don't see much of them around here, but when they do anything at all, it's all flash and bang, and sticking their noses into things that don't concern them. We should all pitch in."

Nip this in the bud, Cait.

I sat down again and gave both Ada and Frank a meaningful look. "I know you want to help, but in a case like this – which hinges on gathering and interpreting information – the more people who get involved, the more opportunities there are for miscommunication, or misunderstanding. We psychologists learn about many theories relating to the human psyche: for example, the way the individual operates within groups and society, and the ways in which that might have some bearing upon their behavior. If Al and I are trying to work out who this man is, and why he killed Margarita, I need to understand what it was in Margarita's life – whether that be an incident from many years ago, or a trigger word she might have innocently used that day – that might have set an 'unconnected' killer in motion. Or…did they actually know each other? And, if so, then why would the killer choose that specific time to take action? Or – if he's a hit man, as Dorothea suggested – then who might have hired him, and why? I suspect that the best way you can help is to start by telling me what you knew about Margarita. As a person. That would be good. But I really would prefer it if you would let me help Al alone. Is that okay?"

Ada looked crestfallen. "I suppose," she said quietly.

"Margarita never got over the deaths of her mother and her siblings," said Frank, diving right in. "They died when she was about ten, I think. That's what her father, Juan, said, anyways. Their house burned down. The mother and two brothers died, and Margarita was left with that terrible scar on her face."

"Scar?" I was curious.

Ada jumped in. "Of course, you never met her. Poor Margarita had a very bad burn scar up her neck and onto her face. There was no way she could hide it, so she didn't bother trying. Some people reacted to it quite badly. I know a couple of brides who were happy for her to do their flowers, but didn't want her taking the photographs at their weddings. Sad really; I mean, Margarita couldn't help it."

I took my cue. "About her being a photographer – how did that play a role in her life?" I couldn't imagine how being a florist could put Margarita in danger, but photography offered a whole host of possible scenarios.

Promising…

Frank answered. "She'd always taken photos of her arrangements, and her gardens…to show them in albums, to help sell her services. I think I'm right in saying she had a keen interest in nature photography in general, right, Ada?" Frank's wife nodded. "Then, when they built the *Rocas Hermosas* Resort about six years ago, she took the store opposite it. The one where she was killed. They have weddings at the resort, and they also need their own floral decorations and garden maintenance; she had all those contracts. She kept the gardens looking good, brought in flowers for the public areas, looked after the plants inside, and – when brides were planning their weddings there – she was right on the spot to provide any special floral requirements. I think it was then that she saw the chance to do a bit more business, and she started offering her services as a wedding photographer. I'm pretty sure she was doing well at it. We've never heard any complaints, have we, dear?"

"Oh no," replied Ada. "She was very good at the photography thing. She had this way about her: you never felt as though she were fussing…or that you were tripping over her. Afterwards, when you saw the photos – which were always very flattering, as well as crisp and clear – you wondered why you hadn't really noticed her. But it wasn't just a way for Margarita to make money: she took her cameras – big, lumpy things – with her wherever she went. I know she took some wonderful shots of the flower market in PV, for example. You should check out her website."

I pulled out my phone, and pounced. "Do you know what it's called? I'd like to see what she did."

Frank replied, "Same as the name of her store, Margarita Flores. She said she wanted to keep things simple."

I suddenly realized my phone wasn't connecting with the Wi-Fi at the house, so we all hunted about for something that looked like a password – which Ada found on a sticky note on the fridge, in the kitchen. Once I'd connected, I managed to find the late florist's website quite quickly.

"Thanks, that's a great help. I'll check it through when you've gone," I said, putting my phone to one side.

Please take the hint.

Ada noted, "She wants us to leave now, Frank. Put that cigar out, and she can get on with her investigating."

I felt bad: I didn't really mean to kick them out so unceremoniously, but I was desperate to read the email that Jack White had sent to me. I looked at my watch; I only had ten minutes before I was due to meet Al.

Ada must have spotted the panic that flashed across my face. "Don't worry, you've got plenty of time, dear." Her voice was pitched to soothe, but I heard annoyance in there too…as an undertone. "When people around here say that something will happen at a certain time, it's just a vague suggestion. You'll get used to it. Most things happen eventually, just not when you thought they would. Like I say, you'll get used to it. Eventually it might even stop annoying you…though you've only just arrived, so you're still thinking like a Canadian rather than a Mexican."

"There aren't really a lot of Mexicans here, are there?" I ventured. "Considering we're in Mexico, that is." I wondered how Ada would react.

Frank replied, "You mean that the *Hacienda Soleado* is a bit like a theme-park version of the country, right?"

I nodded.

Ada smiled indulgently. "We're all imports here, dear; we've decided how we want it to be, and we've made it that way. When we bought into the place, and then everyone started building their houses, we all made an agreement that this would be our own vision of the world as it should be. All the best bits of Mexico, without any of the horrible things, you know? That's how we like it. We're a bit of a mixed bag, I suppose. We're Canadian; Greg is from Australia originally, though he hasn't lived there for a very long time; Dorothea, Henry, and Dean and Jean are American – oh, you haven't met Dean and Jean, have you? Nice couple. African American. Three grown sons, all in the…well, the armed services, of some sort. Dean had some type of job with the US government…something to do with supplies, I think. He's always vague about exactly what he did; says it was a very boring job. They moved about a lot over the years, I know; funny life, I should think. He says he enjoys being away from a desk. He helps Greg with the logistics for the FOGTT – you know, the Friends of Good Tequila Trust. He's very…" she searched for the right word, "…effusive. Always telling jokes. Big man. Big character. Big laugh."

Ada finally paused, and I thought she'd finished, but it seemed she was just catching her breath.

She ploughed on again. "Jean's not so talkative, but very nice. Keeps herself to herself a lot. They only moved here last Christmas. They bought out a nice couple from Seattle who said they wanted to move back there to be closer to their grandchildren, but, I don't know…there was something fishy about all that. They must have needed their money out of the Trust for some reason or other, because they sold up so fast. Anyway, when Dean and Jean arrived, he just threw himself into the tequila business, didn't he, Frank?" Frank nodded dutifully. "Dean seems to love it; he's taken to it like a duck to water. And Jean? She goes into PV to do that *tae kwon do* boxing thing. Volunteers at the American hospital in PV too. Like I say, they're very nice. Their house is called Casa Nova. Dean jokes about that a lot…thinks it's hilarious because…well, it means

New House, of course, but there was that man who was a right one for the ladies, too, you know?" She raised her eyebrows as she spoke.

I jumped in while I had the chance. "So everyone here's an outsider. Even Tony – which is a bit unusual, isn't it? An American chef at a Mexican hacienda?"

Frank replied, which surprised me. "Tony's a good chef, and he's really into all that stuff about local ingredients, and new flavor mixtures. He can be a bit…too experimental, on occasion. But, usually, he makes dishes all the FOGGTs enjoy. Not too spicy, if you know what I mean…not like some places. But he reckons it won't be long now before more visitors to the area make our hacienda a dining destination, which would be good. As long as we all get priority for the seating, of course."

I wonder if you all pay to eat there, was what I thought; "Of course," was what I said.

Ada chipped in. "I suppose you could say that *Hacienda Soleado* is a bit…fake, if you like. If you go down to the seafront, you'll find that the village there is a little more authentic. It's small, of course, and dwarfed by the new resort. I suppose these days you really have to go way up into the hills to find the old way of life. Along the coast here it's newer developments, tourism, and a mish-mash of the sort of Mexican-ness the tourists expect, and then…well, poverty. When it comes to the proper locals there are the ones who play up to the tourists to attract the *pesos*, and the ones who want nothing to do with them, and choose to live a subsistence lifestyle that we outsiders always look at and pity. But it's their choice, right?"

For a woman who liked a mani-pedi, and a good murder mystery, Ada Taylor seemed to have quite a lot to say for herself. I imagined that her desire to chat, and impart what she probably regarded as 'information', was often stifled by the domineering presence of Dorothea, and that her down-to-earth approach to life had been honed by decades of child rearing and husband wrangling.

She stood, and said, "Come on, Frank; let's go now, dear."

Frank harrumphed his way toward the front door. "How about we meet you at *Amigos del Tequila* later on for a bite? You could bring us up to date after your meeting with Al." Frank looked hopeful.

"I'd enjoy that," I said, half-truthfully, "but I don't quite know what Al has planned for me, so I can't commit to a time."

"How about you take our cellphone number, and we can keep in touch?" suggested Ada. "Texts are good."

"Good idea." We exchanged numbers. I was glad I'd bought a decent roaming plan for the week that Bud and I had planned to be in Mexico…together…on a proper vacation.

Oh…Bud.

As soon as the Taylors had set off toward their Casa Canuck, I nipped inside, shut the door, and checked through my emails until I found Jack's message. I opened it and read as fast as I could, which, given that I'm a speed-reader, was pretty quick.

Hi Cait – I won't beat about the bush, this thing with Bud is bad. I've spoken to an old CSIS colleague of mine in Ottawa, and he's promised to get in touch with an associated operative in the area, with whom I can liaise when I arrive. Funny thing…I know the person in question, but never knew they were "in the business". Good cover.

Ottawa's not happy about the situation.

I'm on a flight at 11:05 AM tomorrow. I should be at my condo by about 6:15 PM. I'll phone you when I get in. Meanwhile, here's some advice: don't get involved, keep your head down, stick to your cover story, and don't let anyone know what you do for a living, especially not about your one-time role as a consultant with the Integrated Homicide Team here in the Lower Mainland. Henry thinks you're a friend of ours (me and Sheila) so stick to that. Act like you're on vacation.

If you mix with the folks at the hacienda, be careful not to give yourself away. Steer clear of the cops and the crime scene, and, above all, make absolutely no effort to contact Bud. I'm guessing this murder will become a hot topic there: stay out of the conversations. Just hunker down next to Henry's pool and read a book or something.

I trust you to do this. I know it's what Bud would want. He's following protocol, and you need to follow it too. Bud will hope that you've left. He'll probably think you have. So be as good as not there.

Bud's likely pretty safe if he's at the local cop shop. Once he's in the general population, if anyone finds out who he is...given his most recent role in the international gang and drug-running task force...he could be in grave danger.

NO ONE can know his name, and NO ONE can know about his background. I'm sure you understand why.

If you go anywhere near him, the chances of someone making a connection increase. So don't.

I know it'll feel like a long time until I get there. Call, text, or email me if you want. See you soon. Jack.

There was no information about Bud, his "colleagues", or what the heck was going on with regard to possible CSIS involvement…nor was there a single useful suggestion from

Jack that might save Bud. Nothing. There were no contact details, no names. Not a number or an email address. Nothing that would allow me to follow up on Jack's plans…which were now not going to be put into action. Just a series of warnings to steer clear of Bud…and that one ominous comment about how Bud would be in danger if he was dumped into the general prison system. That suspicion had been gnawing at me since Al had handcuffed Bud, so it didn't help at all to see that Jack felt it necessary to spell it out.

Oh Bud.

I reminded myself that I hadn't actually told anyone who I was or what I did for a living – Al had done that on my behalf. So the cat that Jack was telling me I had to keep hidden at all costs wasn't just out of the bag…it was running about the place, yowling as it went.

I couldn't stay out of it now. No matter what Bud might have expected, and no matter what Jack had hoped…I was on the case. In fact, I wasn't so much on it, as up to my neck in it…because I was about to meet the cop leading the inquiry into discovering Bud's identity, and I'd promised to help him do just that, while I was being implored – okay, instructed – by Jack to do the exact opposite.

What could possibly go wrong?

Power Hour

I closed up Casa LaLa and headed down the slight incline of the rocky track that led to *Amigos del Tequila.* It was well past five o'clock, but the sun was still high in the sky, and the humidity was almost unbearable. As I walked, I kicked up dust, which stuck to my sweaty legs. I hate humidity, but had agreed to come to a place where I suspected I'd have to learn to live with it for a week because it was my only real chance to get to spend some alone time with Bud.

If only I'd said no…then Bud wouldn't be in this predicament.

I was at the adobe restaurant and bar in a matter of moments; the walk had seemed a lot longer when I was dragging the bags up to the house, even with Al's help. Once again, I pushed open the doors to the building where I'd made my fateful decision to help out the cops, and – once again – the place was deserted.

I shouted, "Hello?" Nothing.

I was at a bit of a loss as to what to do next. Wait outside for Al? Settle myself on a stool and wait for someone to show up? Peer into the back of the building from where Tony had emerged that afternoon?

I'll peer.

Beyond the bar was a short corridor, which led to the washrooms, then the kitchen. I pushed open a pair of swinging doors, stepped into a small but gleaming kitchen, and shouted, "Hello?" Still nothing.

Odd.

Surely Tony wouldn't just leave the whole place completely unattended? I walked farther into the kitchen. No one in sight. The humming of refrigeration units buzzed in the air, and a wonderful aroma of herbs, spices, and cooked meat filled my nostrils. My tummy rumbled; nuts and fruit weren't able to hold me for long, it seemed. Covered containers of ingredients stood ready to be used, *mise en place*, and a couple of pots were bubbling on a gas range.

Definitely odd.

There was a door in the far wall of the kitchen that I assumed led outside, so I opened it and stuck out my head. I immediately spotted the blue pickup truck that had roared past the crime scene just as Bud had been discovered. I wondered who it belonged to.

Could it be Tony's? He'd been quite keen to tell everyone that he'd been out buying fish, then in his kitchen, all morning. If his wife and Margarita were friends who spent a great deal of time with each other – which was something he'd mentioned with some…emotion – then might he have a reason to want the plantswoman dead? His "alibi" might be difficult to prove, and I hadn't seen who'd been driving the truck.

"Hello?" A voice carried through from the bar, interrupting my thoughts.

"Back here," I called in response, as I allowed the back door to close again.

Al's head appeared through the swinging doors. "Where is everyone?"

"I don't know," I replied. "Is this normal, for there to be pots boiling and food prepped, but no one here?"

Al shrugged. "I don't know. It seems odd to me. Haven't you seen Tony? Callie? Anyone at all?"

"Not a soul," I replied.

Al drew his gun.

Good grief – that's an alarming reaction.

He gestured for me to walk toward him, while he approached me and whispered, "Have you looked out back?" I nodded. "Anyone there?"

"Not that I could see, but there's a blue truck there. Does that belong to Tony?" I tried to make my question about the truck sound innocent.

Al moved across the kitchen a lot more stealthily than I had done – *I'm not really built for stealth* – and pushed open the back door, peering outside.

He whispered over his shoulder, "It's Juan's truck, that blue one. I'm surprised he's still here at the hacienda; I thought he'd be pretty keen to get away after I gave him the news about his daughter. Tony's truck isn't out there, nor is Callie's car. If it wasn't for the fact that the place is wide open, and there's food cooking on the stovetop, I'd say they'd left the property altogether. I'm going to check their apartment upstairs. You stay here."

He came inside, allowing the back door to close, and disappeared up a narrow staircase that led from the kitchen. I've watched enough movies in my time to know that if someone carrying a gun tells you to stay somewhere, you do exactly that, so I didn't follow him.

I registered the information that a truck belonging to Margarita's father had been at the scene of her murder that morning, within the critical time frame…but reasoned that the truck could have been driven by either Juan or Tony…or even Tony's wife, Callie, I supposed.

Then I ran through some possible reasons for why the *Amigos del Tequila* currently resembled a restaurant-y version of the *Marie Celeste*.

Had Juan killed his own daughter…and had now caused some sort of harm to the couple who ran the place? Or was he just wandering his fields, bereft, and grieving? Of course, if either Tony or Callie Booth was responsible for Margarita's murder, then it did make perfect sense that they'd have done a runner…but there was food actually cooking on the stove, which made that idea seem unlikely; if Tony, or Callie, or both of them had planned an escape from justice, why would they bother putting anything into a pot, let alone turn on the heat?

Standing there on my own, with steam and spices in the air, I realized I was literally dripping with sweat. It was running down my back in a most unpleasant manner. I decided to be "helpful", so turned off the gas flame under the pots, then my curiosity kicked in and I lifted their covers. Water. Boiling water. That was all.

Curiouser and curiouser.

I replaced the lids, but immediately felt as though my nasal passages were on fire. My eyes were stinging, and I started sneezing uncontrollably.

Gas? Poison?

I grabbed a roll of kitchen paper: what it lacked in absorption and softness, it more than made up for in proximity. I thought my head was going to explode. I had to get out, away from…what on earth was it? I knew that I recognized something about whatever I'd inhaled, but I couldn't get a fix on what it was exactly. I pushed open the back door and stood on the step to catch what little fresh air and breeze there might be outside, fanning myself with my hand. I did the best I could with the kitchen roll, and gradually the sneezing subsided. But my eyes? They were a right mess. I must have looked as though I'd been crying for hours.

"Their stuff's all over the place upstairs, but there's no sign of them," announced Al, who was suddenly about three inches away from me. I nearly jumped out my skin.

When I turned, he looked alarmed. "What's wrong?"

"There's boiling water in the pots over there," I replied, my voice thick with mucus. "And…some sort of pepper, or jalapeno…umm…oil, I suppose, because there's nothing to see in the pots but water."

"What? Pans full of jalapenos and water? I don't like this. It's weird. It doesn't feel right."

You're not kidding.

I nodded my agreement. "What do you suggest we do?"

I watched, with relief, as Al holstered his weapon. "I'm going to get hold of the FOGTTs. They can decide what they want to do for themselves; Tony and Callie run this place on their behalf. Come into the bar with me and give me a few minutes to make some calls. Maybe you can grab a drink? You look like you could do with it. Let me check that the washroom is safe, then maybe you can wash your face with some cool water. Let's both stay out of the kitchen as much as we can; all sorts of capsicum-based things can be nasty stuff…like a steam version of pepper spray."

"Yes, cool water's a good idea," I replied, sniffling.

I followed Al into the restaurant. He drew his gun again as he pushed open a heavy door labelled *baño* with a silhouette of a figure wearing a full-length dress. He declared it "clear", then ambled off.

In the washroom I stood and looked in the mirror at the mess that was me. I wanted to cry…though my eyes were already watering heavily. Instead, I had some choice words with myself, washed and wiped my face – *mascara's overrated anyway* – and then headed to the bar to grab a cool drink and catch up with Al's news.

I was surprised to find no Al, but instead a man I guessed was Dean, of the Dean and Jean pairing described to me by Ada. Seeing him now, I realized he was, indeed, the Black guy I'd seen arrive on the crime scene. I guessed that his wife, Jean, would turn out to be the Black woman in the tennis outfit I'd seen join him there…they'd definitely been a couple.

Dean and Jean. Casa Nova. Oh dear.

If I'd had any doubt about the man's identity, it didn't have a chance to linger. He came toward me, offering a massive hand and an equally large smile. I put him at about six feet five, around two hundred and fifty pounds, and somewhere between sixty and sixty-five. His head was shaved, or, at least, completely bald, and he was wearing the most lurid Hawaiian shirt you'd ever want to see. If my eyes hadn't been sore already, that shirt would have done the trick all on its own. His voice was a deep bass, and it resonated in the empty bar.

"You must be Cait Morgan. I'm Dean George. Dean is my name, not my occupation, you understand." He grinned.

I wonder how many times you've said that.

He continued, "Al's outside talking to the rest of the FOGTTs, or at least those he can reach on the phone; I just happened to be arriving. Gonna meet my child-bride here. You'll like her. Everyone does."

He was still holding my hand, but now in both of his, and I was beginning to get a crick in my neck from looking up at him. It occurred to me that *Punta de las Rocas* seemed to be inhabited by very tall people: Ada was the only person I'd met so far who was of what I thought of as normal height.

"Oh my goodness me, honey-pie, what on earth is going on here today? Our little piece of paradise is quite out of sorts. First poor Margarita, dead, and now Tony and Callie have disappeared. What is the world coming to?"

Has Scarlett O'Hara just arrived?

I turned to see that the woman who was walking toward us was quite a vision, but there were no crinolines involved. Her hair was snowy white and cropped very close to her head. She was about five-two, weighed around ninety pounds, and – despite probably being close to sixty – didn't have a wrinkle on her face. There was almost nothing to her, except a waft of jasmine, a hint of coconut, and an aura of gracefulness and quietude that seemed to surround her. Dressed completely in white, she carried herself with casual elegance. Her eyes, and her voice made a huge impact; the rest of her was almost insubstantial.

She reached up to her husband's neck, which was just about as far as she could manage, and he bent his whole body right down, so she could kiss him on his bald pate.

"Now don't you worry, honey-pie," she said, doing her best to look her husband in the eye, "Captain Al will get all this sorted out." She looked at me. Her expression changed. "Are you the woman who's supposed to be able to help him?"

Jean George's ethereal charm had evaporated. Her tone was dismissive, to say the least, and I was being treated to an expression that her husband couldn't see, which I suspected was the point. She had decided to be hateful toward me, that much was clear.

I wonder why.

"Oh, come on now, honey," boomed Dean, "Al speaks very highly of Cait. He said she's known all around the world for her work. We're lucky to have her here. You know we all want Al to crack the case before the *Federales* get here, don't we?"

Jean nodded and smiled coquettishly at her husband.

As she did so, it struck me that Dean had used almost the exact same words as Ada had done when speaking about the case. I reckoned that was maybe because they were friends, and co-investors, and they'd all been at the crime scene – so the topic must have come up at some point.

Al strode back into the restaurant. "Dorothea, Ada, and Frank are on their way, and you guys are here already. Greg's not back from PV yet, and, of course, Henry's not around at all. I'm taking Cait with me to the station, where we're going to get to work. Between all the FOGTTs, I'm asking you to call anyone you can think of who knows either Tony or Callie to try to find out what's going on here, and you can all decide what to do with that food on the counters in the kitchen before it goes bad. Avoid the pans of water in there, though – Cait reckons they have capsicum in them. You might want to wait until they cool a little, then dump the water. I'll call you later to find out how you're doing, or you'll call me if you can locate Tony or Callie, okay? I'm not going to hide the fact that I'm concerned. If we can't get wind of them, I'll set the wheels in motion for state-wide law enforcement to be on the lookout. But we need to find out where they are, locally, if we can; them not being here might be...quite innocent."

Dean and Jean nodded. "I always think it's best if folks do their own housekeeping, before they involve outside elements." Dean grinned. Directly at me.

Odd.

Al addressed me. "Come on, Cait. This has been a terrible day, and it doesn't look like it's going to get easier as it gets older. I'll show you our 'facilities'. I'm not bragging when I say we have the best-looking police station in all of Mexico. So let's go. Your eyes okay now?"

I nodded, and we got to the door as Frank and Ada arrived.

"I've explained everything to Dean and Jean," said Al, as he propped the door open with his body. "I haven't the time to go through it all again. They can explain." With that he all but pulled me outside.

"Here you go, Cait," he said politely, as he held open the passenger door of the dusty white police car for me to get in.

A bit different than when you shoved Bud in here, was what I thought; "Thank you," was what I said.

We sped off down the hill in the gathering gloom as I wondered if it would ever be possible to get used to the way the sun just drops out of the sky at southern latitudes; for some reason, I've always found it deeply unsettling.

I checked my watch. It hadn't long turned six, but I was already feeling tired – the stresses of an incredibly long, and emotional, day were taking their toll – and I was aware that I was hungry. But at least the wind that buffeted me through the open car window was refreshing. Al drove us back to the tarmac road, and we turned left, as though heading toward the *Rocas Hermosas* Resort, but before we arrived at the road that Bud and I had headed down so joyfully that morning, he turned left again, onto another track that led up the other side of the hill we'd just descended.

By the time we parked, it was dark, however, that didn't really matter, because the building at which we'd arrived was floodlit…and it was quite a sight. I even heard myself say "Wow!" when I first saw it; I noted that Al smiled proudly at my exclamation.

"What style of architecture is this? Does it have a name?" I asked, puzzled.

The whitewashed adobe building had a traditionally Mexican tiled roof, but there was a square gray stone clock tower in its middle, just like something you'd see on a Welsh church of the Norman period. That particular stone wasn't local, that much was clear, because all the local hills had reddish-gold soil. Mirrored wings of a two-storied structure jutted out at angles, like an arrow pointing away from us, and – beyond that – I could see the long body of the building extending straight behind the tower had three stories, rather than the two-level structure of the wings. Every single window in the entire building was encased in a decorative metal cage. All in all, the building appeared to have been created in a blend of French and Spanish colonial styles, with a bit of local Mexican flavor thrown in for good measure.

Al shrugged. "How about we call it a *Punta de las Rocas* special?" He smiled. "It was designed for a French family with pots of money and a wild imagination," he said enigmatically. "And it's my home." His voice conveyed a surprising amount of warmth.

I was puzzled. Again. "You live here? I thought we were going to the police station."

"This is the police station, at this end," Al indicated the wing to the left. "My home – I live in the mayoral apartments – is in the other wing. The municipal hall is the main body of the building, the tallest part of the building. It's everything, all rolled up into one. The current mayor – the *intendente* – didn't want to live in his official apartment, so they offered it as a perk for the top cop in the area. That would be me. Captain Al." He grinned. "Juan Martinez is the *intendente* at the moment…I don't know if you knew that. Margarita's father."

"How did he take the news, by the way?" I asked, as solicitously as possible.

Juan might be a suspect…his truck was on the scene.

Al surprised me with a loud "Ha!" He turned in his seat to face me. "On a day when everything is off…everything is wrong…that was one of the most wrong parts of it. I finally managed to track down Juan; I found him wandering his fields of agaves. I broke the terrible news about his daughter as gently as I could. But…all he said was, 'I see'."

Al paused; I chose to say nothing.

He continued, "I'd just told him that his only daughter had been brutally murdered – but that at least we had the guy who'd done it – and that's all he said. No questions about who the guy was, or why he might have done it. He just walked away from me, and that was that. What do you make of that, Cait? What does his reaction suggest to you?"

I took a deep breath, and played with my chin a bit to cover the fact that I was carefully considering my reply: I'd seen Al emerge from Bob's Bodega when Serena had screamed, and Frank had told me the two cops had been in there when he and Serena had first arrived…but I still wasn't one hundred percent sure about exactly when Al and Miguel had actually gone into the bodega, or even if they'd done so together, so – until I knew more – I had to act knowing that Al himself could still be Margarita's killer.

I puffed out my cheeks, then replied, "The father's response could mean any one of a number of things. I heard it mentioned, earlier today, that Juan and his daughter didn't get along well, so it might be that there was such great enmity between them that he was…glad to hear that she was dead. Such a response would be unusual – but not unheard of. Or…it could be that you witnessed how this particular man deals with any shocking or tragic news: I know that his wife and sons died in a house fire that also physically scarred Margarita for life, so maybe – in dealing with that loss – he's built a wall around himself that keeps him safe from the worst blasts of tragedy and loss."

Or it could be that Juan killed his daughter, and misjudged his response when you told him about her death.

When Al eventually responded, he surprised me. "You've learned a lot in a few hours. Is that one of your skills? Getting people to tell you secrets about others, or themselves."

I pounced. "Well, if it is…you could start by telling me a bit about your background, and how you came to be 'Captain Al'." I wanted to find out as much as I could about the man, because he seemed such an unlikely person to be holding his position.

Al asked, "What…sitting here, in this car, in the darkness?"

I forced a chuckle. "Why not? No time like the present. Then it's done. After all, you do seem to know a lot about me, so it's…only fair."

Al nodded. "Okay then. Short version. You comfortable?"

I dared, "Am I allowed a cigarette?" I could tell by the smell of the car, and of Al himself, that he was a smoker.

He shrugged. "Let's both smoke, but let's go to the little table and chairs over there." He signaled toward the side of the building. "It'll be more comfortable than this – my mobile office – where I spend too much of my time as it is."

As I hauled myself out of the police car, I was brutally aware of how my entire body was aching. Tiredness will do that to you.

We settled ourselves on two plastic chairs, lit up our cigarettes…and Al began. "My mother was quite the woman. Still is. An artist. Loves pottery. She moved to Jalisco State to follow her muse, and got pregnant by my dad in Guadalajara. He was a player in a mariachi band. Ma said he was a fabulous musician, but I was too young when he died to ever be a good judge of his skills. She gave birth to me on her way back to her family's home in South Carolina. Her name's Beselleu. Belle Beselleu. Old family. Money. Her parents threw her out when she showed up at their front door carrying a *mestizo*. So she went back to Guadalajara, and set up home with my father. She told me she married him, but…who knows? From what I can remember, it was a pretty good childhood, but my dad died when I was fourteen, and – although Ma managed to keep us going for a while – eventually we went back to her parents."

Al's eyes betrayed complex emotions.

"I'm sorry you lost your father when you were so young. That must have been difficult for you. Did your mother's family accept her…and you…when you returned?"

Al's eyes narrowed, then he replied acidly, "By then, they said, I 'looked quite white'...which the Beselleu family was pleased about."

I dared, "Your hair and eyes are remarkably light, for a local."

Al nodded. "Funnily enough...not really. Historical factors come into play, you see."

I conceded, "I only found out that I was able to use Henry's place at relatively short notice, so have to admit I did what so many do...I packed my bags and jumped on a plane, heading for a bit of R & R in the sun. Didn't have a chance to read much about the history of the area. It's...unlike me. I try to find out about places I'm visiting, ahead of time."

Al shrugged. "Good for you. Not a lot of people do. But this area, like so many these days, needs tourists to survive. Not all of them care about anything more than what's available at the breakfast buffet. The part of our history that's relevant to my personal tale is that when the forces from the French Intervention reached Jalisco in 1865, they mixed up their blood with the locals as fast as they could. They might not have been in the state for long, but they sure left an impression. My dad had the light-colored hair, greenish eyes, and taller stature that you often see hereabouts. As did I. Still do, of course, and, with my ma's blood too, I could 'pass for white'. That was what my Gram Beselleu – my mother's mother – used to say. I...I didn't like my mother's family, but my ma needed to be there, so I did as I was told. As a teen in South Carolina, I was known as Al Beselleu. I stopped speaking Spanish, picked up the local accent and manners, and got myself a good education. Eventually, I attended university in South Carolina, where I was 'allowed' to take Latin American studies. By then, Gram's health was failing, so Ma got her way with her father...she sure could wrap that man around her pinkie finger."

I caught the twang of Al's once adopted, but now absent, accent, and half expected him to add a quick "y'all". But he didn't.

Al pressed on, lighting another cigarette. I followed suit. "I graduated and decided to take some credits toward a master's degree at the University of Guadalajara. When I got there, everything felt so natural to me that I stayed. I felt as though I'd come home, which, of course, I had. But by then I'd become so 'American' I wasn't accepted by the locals, so I started using my full name, Alfredo Jesus Beselleu Torres."

"So did you study Latin American politics? Law?" I was interested in what had brought him to *Punta de las Rocas* as a cop.

"No. I prefer to understand the fascinating and bloody history of my country, the *Estados Unidos Mexicanos*, through the eyes of its writers and artists. I was an arts grad: art, literature, cultural aspects of the Latin American civilizations from pre-Columbian times to the present day. Whatever the name of the country, and whomever might think they're in charge, I truly believe that it's those with artistic talent who have reflected – and even shaped – the way that the people of this region of the world see and define themselves. That's what I wanted my post-graduate work to be about: how art can give a people its identity, even as the warring politicos argue about titles, names, ownership…and loot."

Al's voice became more passionate as he spoke. I was surprised by this increasing warmth of tone…nothing else he'd spoken of since my arrival had seemed to spark such fervor in him.

I commented, "That's an interesting point of view."

Al leaned forward in his seat. "Non-Mexicans seem to know nothing about our culture. They think it's all about painted pots and sombreros…but it's so much more than folk art – and even that's been dumbed down for the tourists. Sure, many people will have heard of Frida Kahlo and Diego Rivera, but who knows about José Joaquín Fernández de Lizardi, who wrote the first Latin American novel? Or about the poetry of Manuel Gutiérrez Nájera? There are so many artists who have helped us become who we are. Have given us the fire in our blood."

As he spoke, I could hear Al's enthusiasm and frustration, and made a mental note to do some internet surfing when I had a chance. It's true that psychological theory is supposed to be "universal", but I don't believe for one minute that we psychologists understand everything about the human condition: I've always suspected that artists and creative types know more than we do, in their own ways.

I said, "I came here hoping to have some time to dive into gaining a better understanding of Mexican culture – not having had a chance to do so before I arrived – but, with this case to consider, maybe we could put all that on the back burner for now?" I knew I had to get him back on track, or I'd never get ahead.

Al nodded. "I guess," he replied. "So, where was I?"

Before I could respond, or try to steer him, he'd picked up his life story. "Oh yes, I was at the university in Guadalajara. Even though Ma had a trust fund in the US, I didn't have much money at that time, so I lived in a pretty sketchy part of the city. It's a great city, but every place has areas where you don't go out after dark unless you're making trouble, or at least expecting it, right?"

I agreed. "Oh yes, every city has those areas; the Downtown Eastside in Vancouver, for all its creeping gentrification, is still a pretty wild place, especially between dusk and dawn."

"Then you might understand what I mean," he continued. "All around me I saw the results of poor, or no, education and low – or even no – incomes…and the pervasive evil, and stranglehold, of the drug-running economy. Instead of sitting in an ivory tower talking about art and society, I decided to get involved, and help. I volunteered with youth groups, mentored kids who wanted to get out but didn't know how, and, after a few years of getting to know the beat cops there – the ones who try to keep kids out of trouble instead of throwing them into the system so they come out ten times worse than they went in – I realized that I could do more good by becoming a professional rather than remaining a volunteer. I did my police training, and this post came up. I did some research into this place – you know, its history, how it came to be what it is today and so on – and applied for the post. They offered it, and I took it. And now, when I get my criminology degree as well, I think it's a career where I can progress and do even more good work as I move ahead."

A good man? Definitely ambitious.

I asked, "Are there many young people walking the tightrope between success and failure in *Punta de las Rocas*?" Given the little I'd seen of the area so far, I found it hard to imagine.

"You'd be surprised," he said. "Serena? The one who found Margarita's body?"

I nodded.

"Serena has two younger sisters who were on their way down the wrong road. Now they're both back at school, and they help out at a local restaurant in the evenings and at weekends. They wanted to run off to Guadalajara…thought it was glamorous…and that's when Serena asked me to get involved. Her sisters hadn't broken the law, as such, but they found the young men with the flash cars in PV exciting, and used to get themselves all dressed up to hit the tourist bars along the coast. Serena saw the way they were heading. Maybe now they'll stay here and settle down…and not become a part of the flood of young people leaving our villages."

Now I can drag this back to Margarita.

I asked, "Was Margarita ever a wild girl? Or was she someone who followed the 'good path' to womanhood?"

Al smiled and looked up at the black, starry sky. "You can see whatever you want in that, up there…allow it to be a backdrop for your dreams. For Margarita, the soil was like that: she saw it as her blank canvas, allowing her to dream. She worked it, planted things in it, cared for what grew there, then cut and arranged what she'd helped create. She made her dreams a reality…from the dirt. She knew that both the right and wrong roads existed, but what she traveled was her very own road."

"She sounds…interesting."

Al nodded. "She was, but she wasn't outgoing or showy. She always did…her own thing. Her scar – the one she got in the fire that robbed her of so very much – molded who she was. She once told me she was so badly bullied at school that she left earlier than she'd really wanted to. It was then that she threw herself into learning about the land, plants – and nature in general – on her own terms. It meant she didn't have to mix with people too much. When she turned eighteen, she inherited her mother's holdings just up the hill here, so she had her own home, and her own land to do with as she wanted."

I was beginning to get a picture of Margarita, though I still couldn't see how her role as a plantswoman – however wonderful or knowledgeable she might have been – could have led to her murder.

"I'm sorry to ask, Al, but are you quite sure that everything Margarita grew was…legal?"

Al gave me a sad look. "You too? It's not all about drugs here, you know, Cait." He sounded disappointed.

"Hey, I had to ask, Al. Believe me, I understand what you're saying – after all, I'm from British Columbia, where cannabis is grown in legal, government licensed facilities…but the trafficking of illegally grown marijuana, and so many other drugs, is still massive. There are still illegal grow ops hidden within perfectly respectable suburban subdivisions, not to mention out in remote areas where the conditions are perfect for fast growth and turnover."

Al stood. "You're right, of course. We have flybys around here. Well, not this area so much, because it's not such a big deal here, but across the state in general. They use heat-seeking equipment to detect the growth of a 'certain type of vegetation', shall we say? However, I happen to be one hundred percent certain that Margarita was only growing what she said she was growing."

"And what did she grow?" I asked. I was imagining all sorts of exotic specimens.

Al beamed a warm smile. "Roses were her thing. I'll drive you to her place in the morning. You'll get a kick out of it. Anyone would. For now, how about I pour us a drink?"

"Well, I was rather hoping you could tell me some more about Margarita and the crime scene; I'd like to get a better understanding of where it all happened."

What I really wanted to know was if there was another way to get into or out of Margarita's store, that could have been used by the killer without anyone – me included – having seen them from the street, but I couldn't ask that of Al, because he "knew" that Bud had killed Margarita, so the logistics of the crime scene were of no interest to him…and weren't supposed to be of any interest to me.

He shrugged. "Okay, but let's go inside. I'm starting to get cold."

I was relishing the still-warm air and the chance to be comfortably un-sweaty…then reminded myself that the evening might feel delightful to me, but for someone who was used to much higher temperatures, it might feel a bit chilly.

"Okay," I agreed. I gathered my bits and pieces together, then walked through the heavy wooden door at the police station end of the building that Al pushed open for me.

As I peered into the gloom, I could only make out vague shapes, then Al threw some switches and the whole building lit up. To my right, someone gasped, and I turned, startled.

There, inside a cage fashioned out of heavy iron bars, was Bud. He was lying on the floor on a dirty mattress that looked as though it were made of straw.

Like an animal.

"Oh, Bud…" was out before I could stop myself. I hastily added, "But…is that him?"

Will Al work out that I blurted out a name?

"Yes, that's him alright," replied Al. His tone assured me that he hadn't noticed my blunder.

You've got to be more careful, Cait.

I looked at the man I loved and hoped I was controlling my micro-expressions well enough that Al wouldn't be able to work out the storm of emotions surging through my entire body.

Bud was wearing long gray pants and a white, short-sleeved shirt; I reckoned he must have been stripped of his own, blood-soaked clothes to preserve them for forensic investigation. A metal plate and mug were on the floor of his cell, so I guessed he'd at least been fed, and given something to drink. I couldn't spot any bruises, so trusted he hadn't been beaten.

No…Al's not that sort of cop.

Finally, I noticed that Bud had been cleaned of blood, and was grateful for that; what with the heat, and the flies, it was certainly for the best. I suspected that Al and Miguel would have taken photographs of the blood spatter that Bud had been covered in when he'd been carted away from the flower shop. Also, I knew Bud well enough to work out that he'd actually dropped off – he has a certain look about him when he first wakes.

That's a good sign.

The man I loved blinked, screwed up his face, and rubbed his eyes in the brightness of the lights.

Good, that's giving him a chance to hide his surprise at seeing me. Oh, poor Bud, I love you, and I'm here to do all I can to rescue you.

Al said, "Nasty looking beggar, isn't he? Could be from anywhere...though the blue eyes suggest he's not local. What do you think?"

"What do I think?" I replied loudly.

Too loudly?

I moderated my tone a little, but made sure Bud would hear every word. "I think you've got yourself a killer in a cage, Al, and we'd better work out exactly who he is before you hand him over to the *Federales* the day after tomorrow. Of course, as we've agreed, us working together to figure out why Margarita was killed will give us the best chance of establishing who this fellow is. You didn't say whether you'd circulated a photo of him – have you?" Al shook his head.

Thank heavens!

I took my chance, "Good, and I suggest you keep it that way. It would be better for your career plans if you're able to tell the *Federales* that you've established his identity for yourself by the time they come to pick him, rather than letting them work out who he is – from a photograph."

That's you brought up to date with what's happening, Bud...and that's how I'm playing it from here on.

Al nodded. "Yes…you make a good point. But come on…I don't know if he speaks English or not, but I don't want us to talk in front of him. Let's go to my office. Follow me." He spoke surprisingly sharply.

I cheerily replied, "Lead on."

Once Al had turned away from me, I dared a glance directly toward Bud, within which I did my best to convey all the love, pity, hope, and determination that I felt. I had no idea whether Bud would pick up on such a complex message in the flicker of an eye, but I'd done all I could; I didn't dare mouth anything to him. Then I followed the jailer of my beloved to his office…and wondered how best to move my investigation forward.

I might be in for a long evening; I have to make sure it's productive…for your sake, Bud.

Margarita Time

It felt completely disorienting to be so near to Bud, and yet for him to be so utterly beyond my reach. I didn't close the door to Al's office after I followed him in on the off chance that Bud might be able to hear something…comforting.

The office itself was neat and tidy, with tall, old-fashioned wooden filing cabinets lining three whitewashed walls, surrounding a tired-looking desk. It was a small room, with the same worn hardwood floors that ran through the entire building, as well as a similar heavily plastered ceiling. It was oppressive; Al had turned on three fans, one in each of three corners, and the cross-draft they created pulled in some cool air through the open barred windows which filled the fourth wall.

I sat in a worn leather-covered swivel seat. I tried to stop it spinning, but it seemed to have a mind of its own.

"It does that," said Al, pulling a folder from a drawer. "Miguel says it's a haunted chair."

"And why would 'Miguel' say that?" I asked.

Al picked up on my double query. "Miguel is my right-hand man. Well, he's my only man, actually. Just the two of us. And he works the short hours."

"Does he live here, with you, too?"

Al chuckled wryly. "No, he doesn't, thank heavens. I don't say that because I dislike him; Miguel's a good man, but he lives with his wife, four daughters, his mother, and his brother." Al sighed. "Poor guy…he lost his eldest last year. It's been…devastating for him."

"What happened?"

'Lost" can mean…so much.

Al looked at the file in his hand and laid it on his desk. He sighed and rubbed his hands over his face. "It was *el Día de los*

Muertos, the first day of November, last year. It's a big deal around here, The Day of the Dead. Of course, it's nothing like most foreigners think…nothing like 'Halloween'. It's a family day; a day for remembering our ancestors. Miguel's eldest, Angélica Rosa, was supposed to be with her family that night, but she never arrived."

This doesn't sound good…

Al shifted in his seat. "I mentioned a local restaurant earlier on…where Serena's potentially wayward sisters help out?" I nodded. "Well, Rutilio is Miguel's brother, and his restaurant is directly behind what was today's crime scene: it faces the sea, with its back to Bob's Bodega, Margarita Flores, and Serena Spa."

Okay…so the chef I saw in the lane between the buildings might have been the cop Miguel's brother, Rutilio, was what I thought; "Sounds like a good location for a restaurant," was what I said.

Al shrugged. "Back then, Miguel's daughter was helping at her uncle Rutilio's restaurant, and it wasn't unusual for her to walk home alone after they closed up. I should explain that – at that time – Rutilio wasn't living with his brother…he had his own place…didn't move in with Miguel until after…it happened."

Al paused for a moment, then sighed and shook his head sadly. He pressed on. "Anyway, Angélica Rosa was eighteen, after all, and that night in particular was a busy one, with people traveling to and from family gatherings, so everyone assumed she'd be safe. But she never made it from the restaurant to her father's house. Miguel was annoyed at first…he thought she'd gone off to have some fun with her friends, instead of spending time with her family. So I didn't get involved – officially, if you see what I mean – for a while. Not until he got nervous, in the early hours of the morning. Then he started checking, and realized she wasn't with any of her friends…so he called me, and I did everything I could locally, but I also called it in to the *Federales*. Miguel was…well, he wasn't able to act in his professional role at the time. Couldn't think straight…so I took the lead on it."

I ventured, "And the *Federales* found her?"

I could see the pain in Al's eyes as he spoke. "Eventually, yes. She was laid out, wrapped in white sheeting, hands folded in prayer, on a bank near the edge of a side road about fifty miles from here. No…sexual interference. A mercy. Miguel was overwhelmed by the news, of course, but then – as if losing his daughter wasn't bad enough – when he went to Guadalajara to identify her body, they kept him there. Locked him up. The questions went on for days. It…it nearly broke him. By the time the medics worked out when his daughter had been killed, and it was established beyond any doubt that Miguel couldn't have done it himself – because he'd been with his family at the time – he was…a mess."

At least they only questioned me for twenty-four hours when they thought I'd killed my abusive ex-boyfriend, Angus, was what I thought; "That must have been dreadful for him," was what I said.

Al didn't make eye contact with me, instead he continued to study the embossed leather panel set into the top of his desk. "They allowed Miguel to come home to his family, but he needed to take weeks off work, to recover. Not that I believe he ever has – not fully. And even then the *Federales* kept buzzing around *Punta de las Rocas*, asking questions about him. Then – unfortunately – there was another killing, with exactly the same *modus operandus*. Luckily for Miguel, there was early, and strong, evidence about when the body had been deposited on the roadside where it was found, and it was quickly established that it would have been impossible for Miguel to have been involved.

Which was good…for him. Though not for the second victim, of course."

"I understand what you mean. Though Miguel was, indeed, fortunate to have an alibi…did the Federals make a big song and dance about checking it out?"

Al finally looked up. "They didn't really need to: Miguel was on his knees in front of the altar at Our Lady of Guadalupe, in Puerto Vallarta, saying a Requiem Mass for his dead daughter at the critical time…where a good number of people saw him. It was a big deal around here: he and his family carried out a simultaneous crucifix of Requiem Masses. Miguel's mother went to her old hometown in the south, his wife to hers in the north, Miguel was east of us, in PV, and his brother, Rutilio, was here in *Punta de las Rocas*, to the west. That sort of thing doesn't happen too often. It's one of the old ways of this area. Everyone who lives here went to one of the services; most stayed in *Punta de las Rocas* with Rutilio, but I know that Margarita went with Miguel to PV, as did several other locals. They all told the *Federales*, in no uncertain terms, that there wouldn't have been time for Miguel to get from the place where the body was found to the church, where he was, obviously, very much front and center at the Mass. And, after that, there were any number of friends and extended family members dropping in on him at his home through the evening, and his brother stayed with him all night, even though the rest of his family members were away. So the heat was off him, at last, and he eventually returned to work."

"I'm so sorry that it took a second life being lost to allow Miguel the chance to grieve properly – and to be cleared."

A wry smile crossed Al's face. "What you say is sad, but true. Most unfortunately, there's been another murder – by the same killer – every month since. Well, not exactly every month…it's been just over the four-week mark each time. In fact, if the 'Rose

Killer' keeps to his schedule, there'll be another dead teenager within the next few days."

I felt chilled. "'The Rose Killer'?"

Al rolled his eyes. "The media's name for him. As I told you, Miguel's daughter's name was Angélica Rosa, and the serial killer – because that's what we now know him to be – always puts two red roses in his victims' hands, between their praying palms. There have been seven victims to date. Seven young lives…state-wide…gone." He snapped his fingers. "Just like that. But…it's not a case I can do anything about: the *Federales* are the ones charged with finding this monster who somehow convinces girls not known to be off the rails in any way to drink themselves to death, before he lays them out on the side of the road, far from their homes, and their distraught families."

"They die from alcohol poisoning?" I was puzzled. "That's very unusual; you have to drink a great deal to die that way. It's hardly what you'd call a dependable way of killing someone."

"You're not wrong," said Al, finally sitting back in his seat. "It's unusual, and horrible, and utterly depressing. The theory is that – although there's no evidence of sexual interference – the killer takes pleasure from watching the girls get drunk, then…die."

"Really? There's evidence that the killer watches until death? Or is that being assumed because of the way the bodies are arranged?"

Al smiled. "Good questions. They found some evidence in the case of the second girl that the killer had force-fed her the alcohol, bringing her out of unconsciousness several times, making her drink more…and that he drugged her, too. And, yes, there's evidence that the killer was with the girls until they were deceased: they were positioned where they were found after death. There are…evil people in the world, Cait. But I guess I don't have to tell a prominent criminal psychologist that. However, I only know such details about the first two cases because, after that...well, there was never any reason for me to be informed of the *Federales'* findings, to be honest, and any meaningful details dried up in the media. It is a big case. It needs a lot of manpower. But...well, of course it struck close to home, because of Miguel's loss, and then how he was treated."

Get this back to Margarita...and Bud, Cait.

"Just as close to home as Margarita's death has been," I said.

"Indeed." Al pushed the folder he'd been fiddling with across the desk. He sighed, heavily. "Anyway, here's the file – such as it is, so far – on Margarita's case. I can't see any reason why you can't have a look at it, Cait. After all, we're on the same side, right?"

"Absolutely," I said and reached for the folder.

"How about I get us a cold beer from my apartment, while you take a look at that? Do I need to warn you that some of the photographs are disturbing? No – I dare say they're exactly what a professional like yourself would expect."

I flashed him a reassuring smile, and he was gone.

I flicked through the file: it contained some notes, and crime scene photographs, that was it. I studied the photographs; the ones showing Bud, covered with blood, standing in the cell within which he was now confined were the hardest to take. The ones showing Margarita with her throat clearly cut from ear to ear didn't make for pleasant viewing either, of course, but they were more...informative, and I was able to study them more dispassionately. The notes were in Spanish, and I could only just about read them – not because my translation abilities were lacking, but because Al's handwriting was appalling.

"How are you doing?" Al arrived and put a well-chilled bottle of *Pacifico* on the table in front of me. I grabbed it by the neck and took several big gulps; by the time I relinquished my grip on the bottle, there was only about a quarter of the beer left.

"Thirsty?" Al was smiling, and still holding his full bottle.

I smiled back. "Just a bit. These notes – are they written by you? It's…it's a bit difficult for me to read them."

"Spanish not up to it?"

"I could do with some help," I replied. I didn't go so far as to actually lie by saying I that couldn't understand Spanish: he inferred it.

Not my fault.

He took the folder from me. "Most of my notes are about the crime scene, Margarita, and the suspect, as you'd expect; I'll read them to you."

I sat back in my rickety chair and sipped my remaining beer as he spoke.

"Margarita Rosa García Martinez, age thirty-three, height five feet three inches, weight approximately one hundred and ten pounds. Address: *Hacienda García*, *Punta de las Rocas*, Nayarit. Found deceased at her flower shop, Margarita Flores, *Rocas Hermosas* Resort, *Punta de las Rocas*. Throat slashed, displaying a deep, ear-to-ear wound. Suspect found on site, with hands around the victim's throat. Suspect's name, not known; country of origin, not known. Body and suspect found in situ by Serena Marquez García, of Spa Serena. The suspect had been encountered by Roberto and Maria Gutiérrez, owners of Bob's Bodega, when he went into their store to purchase supplies. He spoke Spanish to them and paid in cash. They directed him to Margarita Flores as a place where he could purchase roses." Al paused and looked up at me. "I wondered why he wanted to buy roses. Maybe it was just a ruse, to have an excuse to enter the flower shop? What do you think?"

It was a romantic gesture…

I gave some careful thought to my reply. "An interesting question. But…why didn't he just buy flowers at the bodega?"

Al smiled. "That's easy. I know that Margarita had often told Roberto that she promised to not sell beer if he promised to not sell flowers. It was their little joke." The smile faded on his face. "She didn't like it that Rutilio literally gives them away at his place of course…"

I interrupted, puzzled. "I thought you said that Rutilio had a restaurant?"

"Yes, but he always has cheap roses in plastic collars that he gives to the ladies at their table when the check is being paid. You know the sort of thing? It gives him a chance to speak to all the women."

"Rutilio's a bit of a ladies' man?" I asked.

Could be interesting…

"You might say that," replied Al enigmatically. "He thinks highly of himself, and, to be fair, he's a pretty handsome guy. But a 'ladies' man'? I believe that's what he'd like to think – but he's not known for having lots of girlfriends, locally. What he and the tourists get up to, I don't know…though I've received no complaints on that front. The only reason he's ever been on my radar is because of problems with the sign for his restaurant: it's a giant fluorescent portrait of his face, and it shines out in the night. The local fishermen say it frightens their catch away from the shore, and the folks who live close to the restaurant have complained ever since he erected it about a year ago. I think I've managed to calm things down, and now he's promised to turn it off no later than midnight."

A sign with his face on it? Even more interesting…

Al sat forward in his seat. "The killer asking about where he could buy flowers? I thought that might suggest that he wasn't alone…that he might have had a woman with him."

Al's words made my heart race. I tried to sip some more beer, but my bottle was empty. I held it up, and pouted.

Al asked, "Another?"

Thank heavens you're the perfect host.

I smiled. "Thanks. I'm thirstier than I thought."

He left the room, giving me time to gather my thoughts.

When Al returned with my second beer, he looked grim. "Even just talking this through with you is helping, because I've just been thinking that if…the perpetrator…did have a woman with him, then maybe they were staying somewhere local." He sat at his desk and picked up a pad and pen. "I'll check it out in the morning."

Oh, no…

I jumped in with, "As you see best, but I think it's more likely that the killer sought out the flower shop with a purpose. He was simply giving himself a cover story – as you suggested – and not expecting to be found on the scene. By the way, am I correct in understanding that Serena went into Margarita's store because she'd offered to take photographs of the bodega owners' wedding anniversary celebration? And that's also why you and Miguel were on the spot, wearing full dress uniforms?"

Al smiled, and he leaned back in his chair. "Like I said, you're good at finding things out, Cait. Yes, that's all true. Serena had made the arrangements: we were all to meet at the bodega; she'd baked and decorated a surprise cake, and Margarita was to record the event for posterity."

"So you and Miguel were inside the bodega when the suspect was in the flower shop?"

Al nodded. "We were a little late for the appointed time, but the best shade for parking a car down there is near the spa, at the opposite end of the building to the bodega. We thought we might catch Serena at the spa before she left, but she was already out in the street when we arrived. She'd bumped into Frank Taylor and was trying to get him to join in, so we ended up beating her into the bodega. Miguel and I went in just before the killer left. He held the door open for Serena and Frank to enter. Yes…I was that close to a good friend when she was murdered – and to the man who did it – but I…could do nothing to save her. I couldn't stop him." He drank deeply from his bottle. His frustration was palpable.

My mind was racing, as I took stock: Roberto and his wife Maria, as well as Miguel and Al, were all in the bodega, while Serena and Frank were in the street. None of them could have killed Margarita, because they'd all been in the company of others when the poor woman's throat had been slashed…I knew this because, allowing for the time it would have taken her to bleed out, she must have been attacked about two or three minutes before Bud entered her store. And yet another problem slapped me in the face…at that critical time, not only had Serena been in the street with Frank, but two cops had also been there…so no one could have left the flower shop through its front door without being seen.

Not good.

"If Margarita was simply a wonderful plantswoman, with a spotless reputation and a quiet personality – who lived the sort of life that didn't bring her into contact with anyone who might wish to do her harm – then this is an unsolvable puzzle," I said. Aloud as it turned out.

"As you say," said Al thoughtfully.

I dared, "But I understand that Margarita wasn't just a woman with a fabulously green thumb; she was also a photographer. She…might have photographed something she shouldn't have." It was an avenue worth exploring. "So…what else can you tell me about the victim?"

You're a victim profiler, Cait. Get on it!

Al thought for a moment, then said quietly, "Margarita and I knew each other…quite well, I believe. I think it might be because we both felt we didn't fit in too well with other people: her scar…my mixed-race background. I can't say we were close, but I did know her better than most. Maybe not as well as Callie Booth knew her, but I knew her in a different way. As you have already been told, she was a good photographer. Birds, landscapes, and plants were Margarita's favorite things to photograph. Yes, she took photographs at weddings and social functions for the money, but her cameras were almost a part of her. She was always ready to shoot, so…hmm…yes, you make an interesting point. Maybe she did, inadvertently, photograph something she shouldn't have done." He sucked on the end of a pen.

Yuk!

I pressed on. "Where did Margarita go, Al? How did she live her life? Where might she have been, on a regular basis, to spot – or photograph – something out of the ordinary?"

Al sat back. "Right – that's not in my notes, but it will be, soon. I know all this, and it might be relevant. Margarita's life was simple, but her business needs dictated what she'd do on any particular day. She might gather flowers at her own hacienda early in the morning, before their blooms opened in the sun, then she'd jump onto her bicycle and take them directly to her store. If she'd ordered flowers that she didn't grow herself – special blooms for a function or a wedding, for example – she'd cycle to her store, collect her little van, and get to the big flower market in PV very early, then do all the arrangements back at her store. On days when she didn't have a special occasion, she'd fulfill her contractual agreements with the *Rocas Hermosas* Resort, tending to their gardens and plants, or delivering displays she'd made to other locations. Her store was open to the public from ten until noon, then from three until six each day. She never took a siesta, she always worked…out in the heat of the sun, or in the torrential downpours we have here in the summer months. If she didn't have contract work, she'd cycle back to her place when her store was shut to work on her plants there. When she closed up, she might drive to some locations with arrangements. I know she did that for the *Amigos del Tequila* deliveries, because it meant she was less likely to run into her father; he works at the *Hacienda Soleado* all day, tending the agave there, but he's finished by four-ish, so she'd only go there when he'd left. Then she'd drop the van back at the store, and cycle home."

She really did get around…a lot, was what I thought; "She sounds…well, organized, and fit, with all that cycling," was what I said.

Al chuckled. "She cycled most places because she loved it, and because it was cheaper than putting gas in her van. People around here have to be careful with money because there's not much of it about, and their income can be highly seasonal. However, in Margarita's case…I swear she loved her bicycle more than any person. Especially her father."

I jumped in. "So what's the story there? Do you know the cause of the rift between Juan and his daughter?"

Al drew closer, becoming more conspiratorial. "Honestly, I don't think either of them came to terms with the loss of Margarita's mother and brothers: I understand that she and her father were distant from that point on. He hardly visited her when she was in hospital recovering from her burns. At least, that's what she told me. He's never spoken of it."

Juan's truck was on the scene…a possibility there.

I said, "It's such a shame when a tragedy like that can…well, cause such a deep fracture within a family. One might have hoped that both Margarita and her father would have sought solace for their loss from each other."

Al sipped his beer thoughtfully. "You're right…but there it is. And, with Juan being both the mayor of the municipality and the one responsible for the agave crop at the hacienda belonging to the Friends of Good Tequila Trust, he and Margarita have been at loggerheads over the past year or so."

"How so?"

"As mayor, Juan has a responsibility to the whole community for certain aspects of municipal life, one of those being the water supply. Our water comes from a collection of public springs up on the hillside…springs that were designated by one of our far-sighted forefathers, Juan Carlos García García, as being essential to the public good. However, as the man also responsible for ensuring a good crop of agave at the *Hacienda Soleado*, Juan is employed by one of the biggest water users in the municipality."

I was puzzled. "I thought agave didn't need much water to thrive – they're desert plants, aren't they?"

Al smiled. "You're right, agave plants don't need much water to survive…but making tequila uses a lot of water. As such Margarita accused him of putting the interests of his employers – the FOGTTs – ahead of the interests of the local community. She was also very angry that Juan had sold off a large portion of his land to the developers who built the *Rocas Hermosas* – the resort down on the seafront near today's crime scene – and then went and sold off even more to the FOGTTs."

I was pretty sure I was missing something. "Hang on a minute, Al…are you telling me that Juan – Margarita's father – owned the land where the *Rocas Hermosas* Resort is built?" Al nodded. "And he owned the land where the *Hacienda Soleado* is now?" More nodding. "And he's the mayor…the *intendente*? And the *jimador* at the FOGTT property?" He nodded again.

Good grief…

I continued, "How come? I know this is a small place, but one man seems to own a lot, or at least once owned a lot, and has a lot of power. How does that happen?" Scenarios featuring rampant corruption were racing through my mind, so I thought it best to ask.

"Ha!" cried Al. It seemed it was quite his thing. "Of course. You don't know. A quick history lesson will explain…"

Really? Please let it be quick.

I wondered if I'd given away my frustration when Al almost giggled, then made a serious face.

He sat up straight, and said, "Okay, here are the facts – I'll trust you to keep up. As I mentioned earlier, the French arrived, they married, and they bred. General Phillipe Dubois was a well-connected French general, and he married the daughter of the most powerful family in this area. It was a good political match. When the French were defeated, Dubois was allowed to stay, with all of his lands intact, because of the influence of his wife's family. He dropped his 'Dubois' name and adopted her family's 'García'. There are a lot of people in *Punta de las Rocas* with García somewhere in their name because Dubois, aka the husband García, and his wife, García, had six sons and five daughters, all of whom stayed and were granted land of their own from within the family's huge holdings. Then they married and had children, many of whom also stayed…so the land was sliced into smaller and smaller pieces as the overall size of the extended family grew."

I'm not really sure where this is going…or how it can help Bud, was what I thought; "That sounds…complicated," was what I said.

"Indeed – and it led to some terrible feuds, over the years. But there's something else you need to understand: we Spanish adopt both the name of our father's and of our mother's families, which means that – around here – it's possible to run into a lot of people whose name contains García twice. It can become confusing. The eldest son of the original couple, Juan Carlos García García, never married and never had children of his own. He traveled a great deal, especially in the southern states of America, and he was recognized as a talented negotiator and diplomat, involved in both local and international politics; his talents allowed him to keep at least his – sizeable – part of the family's fortune in one piece through revolutions and wars, and – by the mid-twentieth century – he was in a position to grant that the lands held at that time by the children of the García family would become their own property, which they could then dispose of as they wished, without it having to be constantly divided. In other words, Juan García Martinez, our mayor – and Margarita's father – has inherited land from at least five deceased family members. People used to have more children than they do these days, so, as there have been fewer offspring to inherit, and as siblings die, the land is now becoming consolidated again into fewer hands. Margarita inherited her land from her mother's side of the family when she reached the age of eighteen. It was, at one time, three parcels of land, which all happened to abut each other…which isn't always the case. Her father's lands, for example, weren't joined together at all."

I was beginning to see a glimmer of a new motive for Margarita's murder. "Do some people inherit a parcel of land they can't access…because they have to cross another person's land to get to theirs?"

Was Margarita – literally – getting in someone's way?

"Very perceptive," replied Al. "When it was all between brothers and sisters, I guess things could get a bit heated, but now we have people who haven't been closely related for a couple of generations – who might have moved away, even –

who need to work together to make the land viable. Access is just one issue. The other is water."

"Water?" I was surprised. "But you mentioned a 'public' water supply."

Al nodded. "It's all well and good attracting the tourists, but they use so much water it's alarming. I swear they just sit in those condos on the seafront and leave the taps running all day. Within the last few months, it became a real hot-button issue hereabouts. You see, it's been dryer than usual for the last couple of years, so anyone who has a 'private' spring on their property is doing much better than those who rely on the rains or the communal – 'public' – springs. It's been tough for a lot of people, and Juan hasn't helped at all…some say…because he hasn't tackled the subject of a sustainable water supply for all."

Interesting.

I offered, "His daughter thought he should put the needs of the community ahead of his personal finances? That selling his land to developers for a seaside resort, and for the FOGGT investors, just put greater pressure on the local water supply?"

Al shrugged. "I'm in law enforcement, so I'm not supposed to have an opinion. But, if I were pressed…I'd say that our mayor, the estimable Señor Juan Martinez, doesn't care about anyone but himself. He'll sell every square inch of land he owns one day very soon, then disappear into the sunset with a well-padded bank account."

I had to ask, "Will he now inherit Margarita's property?"

Al nodded. "As far as folks hereabouts know, he's Margarita's only living relative. Certainly her closest, so I believe he'll get her entire *hacienda*…and, with it, one of the most productive and reliable springs on the hill. Margarita also owned two large waterfront parcels, handed down from her mother's side of the family, and I happen to know that she wanted them to remain wild and accessible to all. She'd go there often, hiding in the sand dunes, or behind huge rocks, photographing birds, plants, and, sometimes, the fish that come close to the shore. She loved that land. Back in the old days, everyone wanted hillsides where they could raise agave and animals – only the ones who wanted to fish were interested in the beaches. Now, of course, it's a different story: look along the coastline…it's not just the beaches that are golden, it's the land itself. It's the new gold rush."

I gave everything that Al had told me some thought. First – Juan would clearly benefit greatly from the death of his daughter: he'd inherit land, and a lot of it…so, he had a decent motive to kill her. Second – his pickup truck had been on the scene…even though I couldn't be certain he'd been driving it. Third – he hadn't seemed overly upset when Al told him his daughter was dead. Was it that dreadful…and that simple? A man had killed his child for the money he could make? Where exactly had Juan Martinez been when his daughter was killed? Had he been the person driving his truck past the crime scene that morning?

I need to find out the answer to that one…

When Al thumped his desk, I jumped. "I don't think Juan would have hired a killer to get Margarita out of the way."

Why would you even think he might? was what I thought; "Why not?" was what I said.

"If Juan had wanted Margarita dead, he'd have probably just slit her throat himself. I think he's got it in him." Al made the statement wearing such a grim expression that I was quite taken aback. "But he didn't. That guy in there did it." He sucked his pen again. He'd sounded almost disappointed.

Of course…you "know" Bud did it…but, from my point of view, that's a telling thing for you to have said.

My tummy gave an almighty growl, and I blushed.

Al grinned. "I've got an idea. Why don't I take you for something to eat at Rutilio's? It's Sunday, which is Grill Night, when all he does is salsas and salads, and then meat and vegetables on the grill. He reckons the smell of the meat attracts the tourists staying at the *Rocas Hermosas* Resort, and that when they see how wonderful his place is they'll keep going back all the time they're staying there. I don't know about that…but it's a good night to go. Meat's not cheap, but he makes it go a long way. We could keep talking about Margarita, if you like. Or you could even have one to drink." He smiled wistfully. "She couldn't stand them. Margaritas. Margarita didn't like margaritas."

"Yes, I get it," I said softly. "Okay, I'm game, and I am pretty famished. Let's go." I tried to sound cheery. It meant I could meet Rutilio, and maybe get a proper look into the alley behind the flower shop, to check out if the store had a back entrance…which was the only way I could imagine that this otherwise impossible murder had taken place.

I pulled my purse onto my shoulder. "Do you need to do anything with…the prisoner, before we leave?"

Oh Bud…

"No. I gave him some more food, and water when I fetched us these beers. I thought…I should."

Good. Thank you.

"Will we have to pass him on the way out?"

"Let's not," replied Al. "We can go through the back and around to the car that way. The trip won't take long; it's only about ten minutes away."

Yes, I know…but you don't know that.

Al flicked light switches, and I imagined Bud being plunged into darkness again. My heart ached for him, but I knew that the only way I could help him was to press on with my investigation.

We set off in Al's car once more and made our way toward the blackness of the sea. In the distance I could see the lights along the *Malecón* in Puerto Vallarta, glittering like a diamond necklace set in a jet velvet case, and all I wanted to do was take Bud by the hand and enjoy the night air.

Time to Dine

Upon our arrival at Rutilio's Restaurant, we were greeted by the chef himself with a booming, "Alfredo!"

As the two men exchanged friendly banter, the first thing I noticed about our host was his wide, white smile; the folds in his tall chef's hat looked like an elongated version of his teeth. Having only seen Rutilio from a distance, that morning, this was my first chance to get a close look at him: what I'd believed to be a red shirt was, in fact, a red chef jacket; his black pants appeared to be almost uncomfortably – and certainly unsettlingly – snug; a heavy gold neck-chain flashed within a thatch of dark chest-hair.

I understood what Al had meant about Rutilio being good-looking, but he seemed to be trying just a bit too hard to be dashing, for my taste. I hadn't noticed his facial hair from my perch in the condo: he sported a mustache across his top lip that couldn't have been more than four hairs wide, and it looked as though someone had used a Sharpie to draw a line around his jaw- line.

You must spend an age in front of the mirror to look that way.

"Pleased to meet you. I am Rutilio," said the grinning chef, holding out a welcoming hand.

I hope none of those arm-hairs make it into the food I'm about to eat, was what I thought; "Hello. Likewise, I'm sure. I'm Cait," was what I said.

"And what are you doing, Alfredo, bringing a woman…and an older woman like this…to dinner?" Rutilio had spoken to Al in Spanish; he'd obviously decided I couldn't possibly speak his language, and I made sure that my expression didn't give away the fact that I understood every word he'd said.

I wasn't pleased about being referred to as an "older

woman", and his "like this" referred – I assumed – to the fact that I probably looked as though I had lived through a long, tough day…which I had.

Al glanced at me sideways, then replied in Spanish, "She's going to help me find out who that guy is who killed Margarita." This was the first time I'd heard Al speak Spanish, and he more than changed his language, he changed his register; it dropped at least half an octave and took on a much harder, more aggressive edge.

Interesting.

Rutilio spoke to me in English. "Ah yes. You are the Canadian. You speak strangely, I hear, but you will help make Alfredo's career take off."

It seemed that the entire population of *Punta de las Rocas* had Al's career progression in mind. And what did Rutilio mean by me speaking "strangely"?

I don't speak strangely.

"I've volunteered my time to help Al, yes…but I don't know what you mean about how I speak."

Shut up, Cait.

Al and Rutilio had the good grace to exchange embarrassed glances. The chef flung his hands in the air and beamed even more widely; I hadn't thought that possible.

I judged that Rutilio was trying to defuse the situation by declaiming, "Come. Sit. Eat. I will bring drinks."

Since none of the other diners paid any heed to us, I assumed he must treat all his guests the same way.

He continued, in bombastic tones, "Tonight we grill. We grill everything. Chicken, beef, pork. Everything. Even the vegetables we grill tonight. But the salad? No. We do not grill the salad." He laughed loudly at his own joke.

He was the only one who did.

Al and I sat at a small table inside the restaurant. The place surprised me: I'd expected something more...authentic. Instead, the walls were bedecked with Mexican blankets – which also served as under-cloths on the tables, on top of which were paper covers, with patterns cut into them. The walls displayed sad sombreros and even a few plastic lobsters. Tealight candles danced inside colored glass jars on each table, and the background music was elevator-style mariachi. I cast my eyes over the giant plastic-covered menu, which offered a dizzying array of burritos, tacos, fajitas, salsas, margaritas, and tequilas – among other traditional Mexican fare. I noted that, despite their presence on the walls, there were no lobster dishes on offer.

I couldn't help but longingly recall the much more appealing menu at *Amigos del Tequila.* Rutilio's prices seemed fair enough, but the small sheet that was attached for Grill Night displayed one, much higher, set price for the evening's offerings. I decided what I wanted in about thirty seconds, then raised my head and looked around. I noted that all the tables outside were occupied by pale-skinned tourists like myself, and that there was only one other table being used inside. The couple sitting at it waved to Al, and he waved back.

"Friends?" I asked, knowing full well who they were.

"It's Roberto and Maria. They own the bodega. It is their wedding anniversary. For them to come here is very unusual. It's very expensive, by local standards."

I dared to wave as well, hoping they'd come to speak to us. I was thinking they might give me more insights into Margarita – from a local perspective. I was in luck; the man spoke hurriedly to his wife and came toward our table, smiling. Upon his arrival he nodded at Al, grinned at me, and held out his hand.

"I am very pleased to meet you, Doctor Cait." I stood and shook his hand.

I guessed his English must be good, given the location of his store and the fact that pretty much all of his customers must be English-speaking. "Would you like to join us?" I asked. "Your wife too, of course. I understand it's a very important day for you both, and maybe we can send you on your way with a celebratory drink? Or maybe coffee?"

It was clear to me that they'd finished their meal and were almost ready to leave.

"We do not drink, thank you very much," replied Bob. "But my wife would like the chance to greet you, and coffee would be good." He turned to his wife, nodded, and gestured to her to join us, which she did.

"I am pleased to meet you, Doctor Cait," said Maria, smiling. She almost curtsied.

As the couple settled themselves at our table, I noted that Bob and Maria were well-matched, at least physically. Both were about my height and about my girth – so…short and plump – and they both had kind, gentle eyes. The folds in their faces had been formed by smiling, not frowning, and their hands moved automatically toward each other's, as though they were joined by an invisible force that kept them close.

Maria was a giggler, that was immediately evident; Bob whispered something to her, and she couldn't stop herself from tittering after that. I wished I could have heard what it was that he'd said, because I could have done with a smile myself. I suspected it was one of those "couple-y" comments that makes no sense to an outsider but builds bonds in a relationship, and keeps it fresh.

Oh Bud…

Rutilio arrived with coffee for our guests, as well as chips, salsa, and water for Al and me. He took our orders and set off to prepare our food on the grill, as well as the margarita that Al had insisted I needed, and deserved. It seemed as though an impromptu little party was about to break out, and – although I felt sorry for the anniversary couple – I knew I couldn't afford to let that happen.

Steer the conversation toward Margarita, Cait.

"It's a delight to meet you both," I said honestly. "I'm guessing you already know that I'm going to be working with Al to try to find out who the prisoner in his cells might be?"

They both nodded; Bob spoke. "Yes, we know this. News travels very quickly around here, as Alfredo knows." I noted that the Mexicans tended to call Al "Alfredo," whereas the imported residents seemed happier to refer to him as "Al"; as he'd said, he was a man equally – even if only partially – accepted by both groups.

I continued, "So, if it's okay with you, I'd like to take this chance to ask a few questions about Margarita. I'm trying to understand her life, you see?"

Bob nodded. "Yes, we all would like Alfredo to be able to show the *Federales* he is clever," said Bob.

What is it with this community? Why are they all so supportive of Al?

"Great," I said, "so what sort of a person would you say Margarita was?"

Bob and Maria looked at each other and spoke very rapidly in Spanish, their voices low, their heads close. I found it difficult to catch every word, but I understood enough.

Finally, in English, Bob said, "She was wicked. Very wicked."

Having already heard what they'd whispered, I feigned shock.

Al looked genuinely horrified. "You can't mean that. She was a very gentle woman. She was kind and thoughtful." He sounded…*wounded?*

Bob and Maria nodded toward each other before Bob added, "That was what she wanted people to think. Since she was a child, she has been mean. Spiteful, and keeping secrets. She does not like people. She has no husband, no children. She said she did not like children."

Maria chipped in with a caustic, "And she did not say Mass."

That seemed to really seal it for the short, portly couple with the – weirdly – still-smiling faces.

Al looked less concerned. I suspected that, like me, he was registering the dislike this couple had for the dead woman as more a reflection of their own values than of Margarita's.

I decided to probe a little further. "What do you mean, she kept secrets?"

This could be fertile territory.

Again, the couple chattered to each other in their native tongue; they spoke in half sentences, not needing to finish them.

Maria spoke, more gently than before. "It is difficult to say. But she always seemed like a woman who knew something that she was not going to share. She had a look in her eyes that said: 'I know'. But she did not say what she knew."

Interesting.

"Can you give me an example of what you mean?" I needed to know if Maria had really seen Margarita say, or do, something that might have given someone cause to be afraid of her knowledge.

This time the couple didn't confer; they said "Si" simultaneously, then laughed. Bob gestured that his wife should speak first.

"One day last week she was inside our bodega when Greg arrived." She paused, then asked, "You know Greg?"

"I haven't met him yet, but I know of him," I replied.

Maria nodded her understanding. "So…last week he arrived at our bodega in a hurry. Margarita was already with us. Greg needed some snacks for people who were coming to his house, and he came to us; he likes that we have a very good supplier of nuts. Because he was a nut farmer for most of his life, he is very fussy."

Where's this story going? was what I thought; "That's only natural," was what I said.

Luckily for me, Bob stepped in with, "He was paying me, and said he was glad he could come to us to provide supplies he could rely on for good quality…and Margarita said she knew how important good, reliable quality was to him."

Maria jumped in with, "But she said it in a way that I didn't think she meant snacks. Her eyes, her expression. She was saying something she was not saying. This is what I mean."

Very interesting.

Bob spoke up. "It was the same another day…another evening, when we were both outside the bodega, closing the doors at night. Margarita had come back to her place for something and asked if we could give her some milk, even though we were already closed. Of course we opened the door and gave her the milk. As we were locking the door again, Dorothea walked by, on the way to her car, I think, and Margarita held the milk to the sky and said, very loudly, 'Milk from the local animals, you cannot do better. The best quality, very fresh. Local milk, local cow.' Dorothea laughed a funny laugh and went on her way."

Al and I exchanged a puzzled glance.

Maria added forcefully, "Margarita had a face that was sly when she spoke this way. She was mean. She kept secrets. And she did not go to church…except when Miguel's daughter died. She attended the Requiem Mass with Miguel that day, but it was unusual for her."

Al silently chewed on the end of the straw that poked out of his glass of water.

"And you say that Margarita had been spiteful since she was a child?" I asked.

I have to keep this going…wherever that might be.

A quick conference resulted in Bob replying, "Yes, but maybe this is understandable. It was very sad when her mother and her brothers died. When she went back to school, the children were very mean to her. One of our boys was in school at the same time. He was older than Margarita, and he tried to stand up for her when some of the others made fun of her scar. But she beat our boy, who was helping her, then told him he was to leave her alone. He tried to help her again, another time, but again she turned against him. We spoke to him about it, but our boy said she did not want to be helped. So it went her whole life. Margarita never asked anyone for help. She did everything for herself, by herself. That is not good. In life you need family and friends. She needed a husband. It was sad, but she was a very lonely person because she chose plants, not people."

It appeared that Al could be silent no longer. "She had some friends, Roberto. I think that Margarita and I were friendly, and Callie and she were good friends."

I didn't dare frown at him; if it had been Bud butting in, I would have done.

Maria smiled. "Ah, Callie Booth. She is very young, very modern. She is from America, where they do not lead very religious lives. Maybe this is why she and Margarita were close. And you are right, the two of them spent much time together. I do not think that Callie's husband liked this. We could hear her say to Margarita, sometimes, that her husband had phoned her to tell her to come back home because he needed her help."

Tony could have been driving that blue truck.

I could see that the couple was getting restive, and I suspected that running the bodega meant their days began early.

"This has all been most helpful," I said, "and I don't want to keep you chattering all night, but I do have one more question, if you don't mind. If your name is Roberto, why is your store called Bob's Bodega?"

The couple giggled in unison. Maria covered her face, and slapped her husband gently on the arm.

Bob raised his hands in mock submission. "Ah, that is me." He grinned. "It costs less to have the man paint 'Bob' rather than 'Roberto' on the sign. We saved a little money," he leaned toward me and whispered, "…and it makes the foreigners feel happier to come into the store, I think. They like that I am 'Bob', which is Anglicized, not 'Roberto'."

When our food arrived, the anniversary couple took it as their cue to leave. Al insisted that their coffee was to be our treat, and they happily went on their way as I tucked into my mixed grill, which comprised a chicken breast, a pork chop, a small steak, a skewer of grilled peppers and mushrooms, and a couple of pieces of grilled sweet corn.

I've hardly eaten all day…I need protein.

It was clear that Al was as famished as me, so we both sat there, eating quickly and silently, nodding and smiling occasionally as the food on our plates disappeared…and I gradually began to feel more human. After about fifteen minutes, both our plates were empty, and a young girl wearing a full red skirt and a white, peasant-style blouse whisked them away. I realized I'd hardly touched my margarita, and I could see that the ice had almost completely melted. The guests at the outside tables were starting to drift away. It was gone ten o'clock.

"Let's take our drinks outside," suggested Al. "We can enjoy the sound of the surf as we talk."

He rose, and I followed. He offered me a chair, which I accepted, and I sipped my drink. It was still cold enough for me, because I'm not a big lover of icy drinks – my European upbringing is to blame for that – but it was strong. Too strong. And sharp. A lime margarita would not have been my choice.

"Good, right?" asked Al.

I decided to be honest. "It's a bit acidic for me, and it's very strong."

Al grinned. "I guess Rutilio was a bit heavy-handed with the tequila because you're such a special guest."

"Is yours as strong?" I asked. Al had already knocked back two drinks that looked to be the same as the one I was sipping at.

Again Al smiled his slightly lopsided grin. "I might be of mixed race, but when it comes to tequila, I am Mexican through and through. It might sound terrible, but I was drinking tequila when I was very young. I would slip off with my father to the bars where he played his guitar. Remember that I told you he was a mariachi player of some note, and that is how my mother met him?" I nodded. "Well, did you know that mariachi was invented in Jalisco State?" I nodded again – which appeared to please Al. He continued, "When I joined my father in the bars where he played, I would drink tequila with water. Just the young tequila, not the strong stuff, of course, because I was still young, too. My father and mother would argue about it. However, it stood me in good stead when I went to university." As he reminisced, he smiled warmly. "The number of drinking games I won, ah yes. And the number of times I beat someone at a game of pool because the other guy was so drunk…it made me some money, my ability to drink tequila. Maybe you think that's very bad of me?" His eyes twinkled.

"Not really," I replied. "I'm Welsh. The Scots have Scotch, the Irish have Guinness, the English have bitter, but the Welsh don't really have a national drink, which, I think, is because we'll drink anything and everything, so long as there's a lot of it. The Welsh tend to drink quite a lot, Al, we just don't make a song and dance of it. Well," I corrected myself, "maybe we do make a bit of a song of it, because hymns and rugby anthems are likely to be sung when sufficient has been drunk...but that's about it." I decided that knocking back the margarita was the only graceful way I was going to get myself a more pleasant drink.

As I did just that, Rutilio appeared at our table. "Good meal?" Al and I praised his abilities at the grill, as he drew up a chair and made himself comfortable. He waved as patrons left their tables, and two young girls cleared around us, obviously used to their tasks; I wondered if they were the previously wayward sisters of Serena, from the spa.

Other than for them, the restaurant was deserted. Rutilio said quietly, "This is my property. My home away from home. There are no customers here. Please...feel free to smoke now, Al."

Al grinned. "Thank you for observing the laws, Rutilio. Cait – you may smoke."

I didn't need to be told twice.

Rutilio called to one of the girls in Spanish, "Bring the bottles."

When she did, the tray she bore looked alarming: a dozen empty shot glasses and four stubby, dimpled bottles, similar to those I'd seen at Tony's restaurant earlier in the day.

Rutilio opened one of the bottles with clear liquid in it. "And now, as my guest, Cait Morgan, you will learn about tequila," he said. "We will begin with this, the youngest. I am guessing, like most visitors, you know nothing about tequila?"

Oh, no...I need to focus on what I'm learning about Margarita, was what I thought; "You're right, I don't," was what I said.

As Rutilio filled three glasses from the bottle, Al's cellphone rang. He answered, listened, said "Si" a few times, and finally popped it back into his pocket. He stood and said, "I must go. It is Tony and Callie. They have been found. They are at their apartment."

I asked, "Are they both okay?"

Al shrugged. "Callie had a minor accident in her car near PV, and Tony went to collect her. She is not hurt, which is good. She was upset by the news about Margarita and lost control on the highway. It sounds as though her car is in bad shape. She wants to talk to me…about something Margarita said to her. Tony says she is getting herself cleaned up. I must go. Do you want to come, Cait?"

Has the Pope got a balcony? was what I thought; "Absolutely. Maybe I can come back some other time to learn about tequila?" was what I said.

Rutilio leaped to his feet and bowed with mock gallantry. "Anytime you like. But I have poured these glasses now, so raise them with me, and here's to a safe journey and a good meeting."

He picked up one shot glass, Al picked up another, and I felt I had no choice but to pick up the remaining one. The two men didn't knock back their drinks, but, instead, took down the liquid in two savoring mouthfuls. I did likewise: my lips burned… then my tongue burned…then my throat.

Tequila's really not my thing.

I forced a smile as I thanked Rutilio for a wonderful meal. Al insisted upon settling up, and as he paid, he winked at Rutilio and asked in Spanish, "What, no flower for the lady?"

Rutilio shrugged and replied gruffly, in his mother tongue, "It is the summer. The season when the tourists are looking for a bargain, so they do not spend much money. That means I have to save every *peso* I can, so no flowers for the women until October when the rains stop, and the people with the real money come back again."

Al shrugged in response. As we left, he whistled a tune that had been playing on the loudspeakers at the restaurant; I wasn't at all convinced that he was in the best shape to drive, and I thought I'd be doing myself two favors if I could talk him into letting me see the crime scene before we headed to his car.

I decided to give it a go. "Since we're so close to Margarita's store, is there any chance I could just take a quick look inside? I was thinking that I might gain some insights by seeing her place of work. I wouldn't need long."

I dared a sweet smile, but Al hesitated. I urged, "Just five minutes. That's all I'll need. Or don't you have the authority to open up the crime scene?"

That should do it.

"Of course I have the authority," replied Al huffily, "and I have the keys with me. I don't have to hand them over to the *Federales* until they take the prisoner, so, yes, let's go. I think it would be good for you to see Margarita's store." He strode off toward the building that housed the crime scene.

Hurrah for ambition…and pride.

Time to Smell the Roses

It surprised me that there was no tape announcing a crime scene across the door to Margarita's flower shop, but I was completely shocked when Al opened the door and turned on the lights. I'd expected a pool of blood to be covering the floor – as I'd seen at the time of Bud's discovery – but there was none.

"Where's all the blood?" I asked. It seemed a reasonable question to ask…and not one that would give away my secret.

"Ah, yes," replied Al, clearing his throat. "That was Miguel. After the photographers left, and Margarita's body was gone, he collected the knife, which we found next to her, then, it seems, he decided to mop the floor. His brother brought him a bucket and brush. He thought it would prevent the flies from congregating." He cleared his throat again. "Miguel has been trained in crime scene preservation, but he found the sight of the blood…upsetting, so his brother and he…did this."

I could tell by Al's expression that he was feeling a mixture of emotions; embarrassment and anger were clearly uppermost, but I could also sense…pity.

I was pretty sure he was doing his best to excuse Miguel's actions because of his colleague's own recent tragic loss of a daughter. It's an aspect of murder with which I've become only too familiar: the way it completely changes the lives of all those left behind…and how they are treated by others. Right now, the main reaction in the local community to Margarita's murder was shock, but I knew very well that once I managed to work out who'd really killed her, there would be ramifications for Miguel's…overzealousness.

Margarita had installed low-energy directional lamps, the type that take time to reach full luminosity. When they did, they replicated daylight, without giving off too much heat, which I judged would be ideal for a floral store where color and temperature are critical elements. Obviously, Margarita had been a woman for whom detail was important.

The store was so small that I felt immediately closed in…even though the whole room had been painted white. To the right was a workbench, allowing space to build arrangements; to the left was a small counter with a cash register. The rest of the room was almost entirely full of flowers in layered rows of buckets – all of which were also painted white – which left very little floor space. My heart sank when I noted that the entire back wall housed a refrigerated unit with sliding double glass doors – of the type that holds drinks in grocery stores. However, in this case, it held more buckets, a few of which contained flowers.

Oh no…I was counting on another possible exit point.

The store was cool, but the smell was almost overpowering – a mixture of floral fragrances, which was to be expected…but there was an undertone of chemicals.

"Did Miguel use bleach when he cleaned?" I asked.

Al looked puzzled. "He didn't say he did, but who knows?" He sounded exasperated.

"If he did, he'll have compromised any blood forensics," I noted.

Al sighed. "I know, but that doesn't matter, right? I have the guy." He sounded testy.

Careful, Cait.

He asked, "What does this place tell you about Margarita?"

I suspected that Al was beginning to get impatient with me, so I decided to "do my thing" – just a little bit…to show him that I could, truly, be useful to him. "Okay, let's see…her attention to detail is everywhere: the lighting, the temperature, the layout allowing her to see and access her entire stock, the white décor to allow the colors of the flowers to stand out, as well as her cleared workspace and her super storage ideas – see how she's stacked her photographic equipment underneath her workbench?"

Al nodded as I pointed to the neatly piled black plastic cases.

I continued, "She's got schedules pasted to the wall: the planner shows she's well organized, but it also shows that she has no personal time – the hours where work tasks are allocated run from six in the morning until seven every evening, and she has 'home work' planned in for after that. This tells me that Margarita lived to work, rather than working to live. One thing, Al – I can see she had a wedding planned for the day after tomorrow at the *Rocas Hermosas* Resort. See…here? The name is Sullivan, and they ordered '24 *rosas rojas con gyp*'. Maybe you could get hold of the family and tell them they'll need to make new plans?"

Al nodded and took out his notebook. "That's thoughtful. A good point. I shall do that." He scribbled down the details, copying them from the wall planner.

I added, "There's nothing personal here: everything is related to her plants, the flowers, the business…her professions as a plantswoman and photographer. There are no photographs of her, or of her family members, and there isn't even a mirror. This place is all business. *She* is all business. Her plants are her life. In fact, I get no sense of Margarita the person in this store, just Margarita the businesswoman."

I took the five steps needed to get to the refrigerated units at the back of the shop and peered in. "Are these the type of roses that Margarita grew, or would she have bought these at the market?" I nodded toward the two buckets of red, and one bucket of yellow, long-stemmed roses that were accompanied by a huge bucket full of "Baby's Breath".

Al smiled. "She didn't grow those." He looked around and spotted a photograph on the neat cork noticeboard. He pointed. "These are Margarita's roses," he said proudly.

The photograph showed pink, shrubby roses, with full, slightly nodding heads. Some canes were trained onto arches. It was as though I could smell them – a true rose scent.

"Constance Spry," I said.

"Pardon?"

"It's the name of the rose. Constance Spry, named after the famous English flower arranger. She was quite the woman in her day and really popularized the concept of floral arrangement as an art. How wonderful. Obviously Margarita knew her field: it was Constance Spry who changed how people thought about floral arrangements. She introduced unusual materials, containers, and shapes. She herself was very involved in the cultivation of old English roses, and when David Austin introduced his first English Rose in 1961, he named it after her. This is that rose: classic, a true rose pink, with a true rose scent. Beautiful."

Al looked surprised. "You seem to know a great deal about roses, and those who arrange them," he said quietly.

Maybe it was the stress of the day, maybe it was the tequila, but I could feel myself fill up with tears.

Not now, Cait.

I whispered, "It's because of my mum. Her wedding bouquet was arranged by a woman who trained under Constance Spry herself, at her Flower School in London, England. The woman who made my mum's bouquet was known throughout South Wales, and my mum and dad had to drive into the wilds of the Welsh Valleys to collect the bouquet the day before their wedding. It was quite an undertaking, they said."

"They told you this?" Al seemed intrigued.

I sighed. "Yes. My mum spoke of it often. They didn't have much when they married – nothing, in fact, especially by today's standards. But that was one thing she spent money on. I remember she had a pressed rosebud from her wedding bouquet that she would show me when I was a child."

"Are your parents…deceased?" Al's tone was gentle.

"Yes, they are. They died quite a few years ago. A stupid, tragic accident. They were driving…oh, it doesn't matter where they were going. All that matters is that I didn't have a chance to say goodbye."

"I know how that feels," said Al with obvious emotion. It seemed that my very personal revelations were allowing him to open up to me.

Of course!

I knew the answer before I asked the question. "You and Margarita? You had feelings for her?"

Al dropped his head. "She was a very private person, as I have said. And – as you have correctly surmised – she didn't have much room in her life for personal relationships, but I enjoyed her company, when I was able to share it. I had...maybe 'hope' is too strong a word, but I hoped for hope. Do you understand?"

Al looked unusually vulnerable at that moment, and his anger upon finding Bud kneeling over Margarita's dead body made more sense to me. In fact, considering that he believed Bud to be the man who killed the woman for whom he clearly felt affection, Al had behaved in a very honorable manner toward Bud, clothing and feeding him in the jail as he had.

My respect for him increased. "I'm sorry, Al. A sudden loss…any loss…is difficult, and I know there's nothing I can say right now to help you deal with it. But I can try to help you by being proactive, and trying to solve this mystery."

"Yes," said Al gently. "It will help me if I can find out who my prisoner is…and understand why he took Margarita's life."

We were both silent for a moment.

I didn't look at Al – he deserved a little privacy. Instead, I took in all that I could about Margarita's store. Unfortunately, what I saw was that there was literally nowhere for anyone to hide, and there was no way in or out, except by the front door.

So how on earth did someone get into the store, kill her, and get out again, unseen, within a three-minute window, when there were two cops, and at least two other people, in the street outside the door?

I noted that Margarita must have had a lot of money tied up in stock: the most valuable, and delicate, blooms were in the refrigerated unit at the back of the store. I noted the still-plump heads of almost two dozen red, and dozen yellow, roses. Then I noticed something glinting between the dark green leaves.

"What's that?" I said, pointing at the shiny object and bobbing my head about to try to make it out.

Al drew himself from his reverie and stepped forward. He slid open the floor-to-ceiling door of the refrigerated unit and moved one of the buckets of roses. There was a chrome handle in the back wall. He pulled at it, and a section of the back wall of the store swung outwards.

"It's a door!" I tried to sound surprised rather than jubilant.

Al stepped into the refrigerator, then out through the narrow opening. It was a tight squeeze, but it was clearly big enough for most people to fit through.

Once he'd stepped out over the foot-high lip, he called, "It's the lane. Her van is here. I guess this is where she loaded in her chilled stock," he said. He stepped back into the refrigerator, shut the door, then joined me in the store again, sliding the glass door shut, "I've driven along the lane many times, and it's quite obvious that the spa, the bodega, and the restaurant all have rear entrances that lead out onto it, but I wasn't aware that this existed. Not that it matters…except that it means the murderer didn't know about the way out." He smiled. "That's useful to know, right?"

"I certainly think we've learned something very useful in the past few moments," I replied truthfully.

The discovery of a way to access the crime scene that avoided the street meant I now had a way forward…but I had to stop myself from getting overexcited. I took one last long look around the store: I like gardens, though I'm not a big fan of cut flowers…but the idea that Bud was coming into this store to buy flowers for me meant a great deal to the romantic woman I keep locked deep inside my psyche.

It's the *idea* of giving and receiving flowers that's lovely, rather than actually having them…because I hate watching them die, little by little, in a vase. As I looked around, I was keenly aware that I was surrounded by decay; there must have been hundreds and hundreds of dollars' worth of flowers, all about to wilt, then rot. What a shame.

Like Margarita herself…what a waste.

As though he'd picked up on my feelings, Al said, "If you're done, let's go. It feels…bad here. And I'd like to find out what it was that Margarita said to Callie. It might be nothing, but it could be something…illuminating."

I dared, "Hoping for hope?"

He nodded. "We can at least do that."

We left the store as we'd found it, full of the smell of death.

Too Late

Al parked the police car outside the back door of *Amigos del Tequila*…where I'd spotted Juan's truck earlier on. We entered the kitchen, which was deserted, and, this time, there were no aromas of food.

"Hello?" called Al.

Footsteps descended the staircase in the corner of the kitchen, and Tony appeared, shh-ing us as he did so. "Callie's finally asleep." He nodded toward the apartment upstairs. "Let's go into the bar," he added, heading off through the swinging doors. We followed. Tony flicked switches, and the lighting above the rows of bottles that stood in front of the mirrored wall of the bar came on. "Drink?" he asked us. "I'm having one, so, please, let me get one for you guys too."

"*Pacifico*, please." Al and I spoke in unison. We all smiled.

As Tony poured the beers, I could see that he seemed to have aged since I'd met him earlier in the day.

Shock can do that. But so can…other things.

"How's your wife?" I asked.

Tony smiled. "She's fine, physically. They checked her out at the roadside, but she wouldn't let them take her to the clinic. She hasn't got a scratch on her, which is a miracle, but…mentally, emotionally, she's a mess. She said she'd been crying at the thought of Margarita's murder as she was driving and just…misjudged things a bit. She came off the road and crunched the car up. She called me when it happened, and I just…went. I hardly remember driving there. I saw her on the far side of the highway, but I had to pass her, because of the median, then drive back again. It was awful. I was so close to her, and yet she was out of reach…all I could do was keep going."

I know that feeling.

"You said she wanted to speak to me?" asked Al.

"Yes. When we got back here, everyone was sitting around eating. Dean told me that, in my absence, all the FOGTTs raided the kitchen and decided to sort out their own food...which was fine by me, of course. But then Callie started crying all over again; I guess she felt relieved to be home at last...but she started blubbing that Margarita had told her something, and she needed to speak to you. Urgently. Ada Taylor managed to calm her down a bit, and she and Jean took her upstairs. Dorothea went off to her house and came back with some sleeping pills. I wasn't very keen on Callie taking them, but Dorothea insisted. She can be...overwhelming. To be fair, I think she means well, but you'd think she'd have learned her lesson by now."

I had to ask, "How do you mean?"

Tony shrugged. "I heard that she talked a lot of her friends who shared the gated community where she lived in Florida into investing with some guy she knew and...well, everybody lost everything. So she sold up, moved all the way over here, and sunk every cent she had into this place. Which I guess is what you would do, right? But...she still tries to bend everyone to her will. Like tonight. Callie finally agreed that taking something would help her relax, and she's in a very deep sleep now, which I'm sure is a good thing...though I didn't think she'd just go out like a light when I called you. Sorry, Al. Would you mind dropping by in the morning? I've got to go to the market early, and then I thought I'd go visit Callie's car and give it a good looking over; I got them to tow it into Bucerias, but think it might be a lost cause. It was old and battered anyway. I don't know what we'll do without it. The insurance won't buy us a replacement. Oh well, Callie's safe. That's all that matters."

"I'm glad she's okay," said Al, draining his bottle.

"Another?" asked Tony. Al nodded; I declined. I glanced at my watch. Almost midnight. That meant I'd already had a twenty-two hour day, and I could feel myself more than flagging.

It must have shown on my face as I drained my beer, because Al suggested, "How about I walk Cait to Casa LaLa, then come back and have that beer with you, Tony? You okay with that?"

"Sure, go ahead. I'm not going anywhere, and I need to wind down before I hit the sack." He, too, looked at his watch, then added, "I've gotta be out of here before seven in the morning, but I've got an hour left in me yet."

I didn't want to impose on Al. "I'm sure I can remember the way; I can get to Henry's place on my own. You stay here, Al. But – before I go…I have to ask – Tony, when we were in your kitchen earlier today, there were two pots full of boiling water and, I think, capsicum oil. Why was that?" I hoped to solve at least one of the day's mysteries.

Tony smiled. "Don't laugh – it's a thing I do." He looked embarrassed. "I'm not really a superstitious person, not in the way that some of the older generation can be around here. The things they get up to with their ancient sayings, habits, and beliefs…they seem to mix it in with Catholicism and it's all accepted by the church. But I do have a few little things that I like to do, and one of them is to season new pots with white pepper. A Mexican guy I worked with in a kitchen years ago said it makes the pot 'sweet'; in other words, everything it cooks will taste the best it can. You don't want to get too near the pots when they're boiling, though, 'cause the pepper in the steam can really do some damage."

That's it? Weird; was what I thought; "Yes, I learned that for myself when I peered inside them," was what I said.

Tony looked embarrassed. "Unpleasant for you. Sorry. Need a flashlight to get you back to Casa LaLa? I have a supply out back…you could save the battery on your phone that way…the flashlight app sucks juice."

I accepted his offer, which meant that Al and I were alone for a moment. I took my chance. "Could I meet you here in the morning, to find out what Margarita told Callie?" I was desperate to know.

Al gave it some thought. When Tony reappeared, and handed me a heavy flashlight, Al asked him if he thought it would be alright for me to be with him when he spoke to Callie.

Tony shrugged. "I don't see why not. I suggest you give her a call around eight, or nine, to check, and explain who Cait is. I didn't have a chance to do that with…everything that happened. She should be awake by then, so if she's okay with it, you guys can come over to talk to her."

Al and I nodded our agreement. We all said goodnight, and I made my way out into the night.

Everything looks different by flashlight, so it took me about fifteen minutes to get back to Henry's place. I got inside, turned off, then reset the alarm, and headed straight for the washroom. The bed looked very appealing as I changed, but I ignored the temptation to just slip between the sheets and sleep. I picked up the pad of paper I'd made notes on earlier in the day and curled up on the sofa. It was comfy. Too comfy. I got up, canceled the alarm again, and pulled open the doors to the patio and pool. I managed to find a dimmer switch for the lights and set them at just the right level to be able to sit and write. The metal chair wasn't as comfortable as the sofa, but I needed to be alert – as alert as I could be.

Come on, Cait – Bud needs you.

I'm good with lists. They help me organize my thoughts. So that's how I began. Having established that there was a rear entrance to Margarita's store, I decided to begin with a list of those I believed had the opportunity to gain access to the flower shop undetected, in the few minutes before Bud had entered it.

OPPORTUNITY

Unknown persons?: killer *MUST* have been on scene in the three/five minutes around time Bud entered flower shop, so *MUST* have been visible to me, or hidden from sight somewhere, or in the roaring blue truck. *Stick with the people I know were there*.

Ada and Dorothea: both were at the spa, but not in sight of each other. Spa has back door onto lane. Each had the time and opportunity to change blood-spattered clothes inside the spa before they entered the street. (Note: Door from the refrigerated unit to the lane would be a very tight squeeze for Dorothea. Possible?)

Dean and Jean: both appeared after the crime scene was discovered. Where had they been? Arrived from opposite ends of the building at different times. Had they been together, or not? Where would they have changed their clothes? *FIND OUT!*

Rutilio: was in the lane behind the crime scene around the time of the crime. (Note: Did he see anyone in the lane at the time? Wouldn't he have mentioned that? Did Al even ask this? ***CHECK THIS!***) He could have changed his clothes inside the restaurant kitchen.

"Truck driver": this is Juan's truck – but was he driving? The driver of the blue pickup truck that sped away just as Bud was discovered *could* have been Juan, Tony, Callie or Greg. (Ada said Greg was in PV, but he might not have been.) Any one of these would have had the chance to clean themselves up before they were in public view. (Also *could* have been total stranger in truck?)

Bob and Maria: in the bodega at the time of the murder.

I paused, and questioned this assumption: all I knew for sure was that Bob and Maria had both been in the bodega when Al and Miguel had entered – I didn't know for certain that they had both been there when Bud was buying our supplies. Either one of them could be providing an alibi for the other. I put a question mark beside their names.

They'd told me that Margarita was not the good person Al had thought her to be. Did their dislike of her run so deep that they might have wanted her dead? Had she "said something she was not saying" to them? Did they both, or did one of them, have something to hide that Margarita had found out about? Was there somewhere inside the bodega where they'd have had the opportunity to change out of blood-stained clothing before Al and Miguel saw them?

Serena and Frank: with each other in the street at the time.
Al and Miguel: with each other at the time.

Okay, that was opportunity sorted, and the field was narrowed a little. Now, what about motives for those with the opportunity?

MOTIVE

Bob and Maria: disliked Margarita's lack of religious devotion, lack of a family life. They might have had secrets she knew about.

Juan: probably inherits his daughter's land. He and his daughter were already estranged. At loggerheads over his roles and responsibilities. LAND. WATER.

Greg: what did Margarita mean when she said to him that he knew the value of a "reliable, good-quality supply?"

Dorothea: what did Margarita mean when she mentioned "local milk from local cows" to her? Why did Dorothea lie about the time the crime took place?

Ada, Dean, Jean, Tony, Callie, Rutilio: any one of them might have a secret that Margarita had found out about, maybe because of her photography, and she might have obliquely mentioned her knowledge to them. This applies to possible outsiders, too. (NB: Tony not keen on closeness between Callie and Margarita)

Clearly, I had more work to do in this area. Finally, I addressed the question of the way in which Margarita had been killed. She was a small woman, but probably strong. That accepted, any one of my possible suspects could have slit her throat from behind, when she wasn't expecting it.

But who would choose that method?

It was such a violent way to kill someone that it suggested the hand of a man to the psychologist in me, rather than that of a woman. But…I couldn't rule out a woman as her killer. The right woman, with the right motivation, could do it – easily – because it's a method that requires surprisingly little force, just accuracy and determination. So, no…the method didn't eliminate anyone – except, possibly, Ada Taylor…who really was quite a small, and relatively frail, person. No…I couldn't eliminate even Ada, because she really wasn't that old, and was lithe, so might well have the ability to do it.

Can the weapon help me?

The knife was found at the scene, but, because of the presumption of Bud's guilt, Al wasn't going to follow that as a line of inquiry. Besides, even if it was plastered with the killer's fingerprints, that wouldn't be discovered until long after Bud had been transferred to a jail in Guadalajara full of vengeful drug dealers. Too late to save him, in other words. Without having seen it, I had to assume there was nothing particularly unusual about the knife itself or I suspected that Al would have mentioned it. Anyone can get hold of a knife, and it's easy enough to conceal one in a pocket…or a purse.

I paused again and remembered that I had two chefs in the frame; chefs work at their knife skills, and are possibly less squeamish than others when it comes to slicing into flesh. Could the knife, and the method, therefore point to Tony, or Rutilio? Or maybe to Callie, who helped her husband in *Amigos del Tequila's* kitchen, as well as doing people's accounts. And then, of course, Ada was the daughter of a butcher. And Juan worked with blades in the fields all day, tending his agave. Did Jean's liking for *tae kwon do* suggest a violent streak? And, while Dean might have retired from a boring government job, he might be an avid hunter or fisherman in his spare time…or he might pursue any number of hobbies that would allow him to sublimate anger, while developing good knife skills.

I stood up, stretched my neck, and looked at my watch. It was one in the morning. I was exhausted and keenly aware that I wasn't thinking as clearly as I might. I pushed the glass doors closed, locked them, and headed for the bed. I could do a better job for Bud if I slept. I just hoped he was managing to get some rest himself.

Thinking of Bud made me think of Jack. I sat up with a start: who was Jack's contact? I hadn't given that any thought; who could be the "operative" with "good cover" that Jack had referred to? Someone I'd met already? Or someone completely unknown to me? Was it important that I worked that out as well?

Then another thought occurred to me: Why on earth would there be an "operative" of any sort in the area? My mind was racing – in circles, as it turned out.

Cait – rest!

As I lay on my back, seemingly staring at the inside of my eyelids, I felt hot tears trickle toward my ears. For the first time since I'd dragged myself out of my own bed, in my own little house on Burnaby Mountain back in beautiful British Columbia at three in the morning to get ready to fly to the sunshine with my beloved Bud, I felt as though I was living in the real world.

It had taken that many hours of seeming unreality for me to get here: the worst possible place imaginable.

Wake-up Call

When I woke the next morning, I was immediately aware that a bus must have run over me as I slept because my entire body was aching. This realization told me I needed to head for the painkillers; but, before I even pushed back the bedclothes, I became aware of something else…some items of mine were not where I'd left them the previous night.

Stay very still, Cait.

From where I lay, I could see that my hairbrush was now close to the taps on the basin surround in the bathroom, and not on the outside edge of the vanity, where I'd left it. My shoes were still in the corner of the bedroom, but they were sitting on their soles – which was not how I'd left them. And my clothes hadn't been that neat when I'd dropped them onto that chair.

I strained my ears: was there another person in the house?

Beyond the windows I could hear birdsong. I also identified the faint hum of the refrigerator in the open-plan kitchen, beyond the bedroom. I'd left the bedroom door a little ajar the night before…now it was half open. My heart thumped. Minutes passed. I lay there listening to every little sound…until, eventually, I had to give in to my screaming bladder. I pushed back the bedclothes and sprinted to the washroom. When I emerged, I was wrapped in my robe and carrying a can of hairspray as a potential weapon – it was the only thing with heft that wasn't attached to a wall.

I crept toward the bedroom door. If there was someone in the house, they'd already know I was up and about. I strode out into the main room, wielding my hairspray and ready for anything…but there was no one lurking, ready to attack me.

I checked the front door; it wasn't locked, and the alarm wasn't set. Recalling the previous night, I was certain I'd locked the door when I came in, but knew I'd turned off the alarm to be able to go out onto the patio. Maybe I'd been more tired than I'd thought, and maybe I'd forgotten to reset it.

How convenient for the person wanting to break in.

I opened the front door and checked the lock. There were no scratch marks, no scuff marks. It didn't look as though the lock had been picked. Maybe someone had a key? I remembered that Tony had said that the pool service people had a key for the place…and the water service people, too. Who among the FOGTTs might also have access to one?

I shut the door, turned the lock, and gave my attention to the main room of the house. Yes, someone had moved a few bits and pieces – but only things that belonged to me. When I went back into the bedroom, I could see that Bud's suitcase had been shifted, inside the closet. It was obvious that someone had searched the place while I was asleep, and it was also clear that they had done it so quietly, and professionally, that I'd slept through it all.

Unnerving…but interesting.

My watch told me it was almost half past seven, so I decided to make myself some coffee; the Taylors had kindly brought me a small jar of instant granules. As I watched the kettle boil, I gave some thought to what my "visitor" might have been looking for…and what they might have found.

Oh no…the notes I'd made about my suspicions – and my purse and its precious, and dangerous, contents.

I'd left them all on the patio table the night before. I pulled open the concertina glass doors and saw that everything was exactly where I'd left it.

Thank heavens.

I surmised that the intruder hadn't dared open the heavy, noisy patio doors, so – as luck would have it – no one had read my notes…nor had they found Bud's bits and pieces – which could identify him – in my purse.

I took my coffee to the patio, lit a cigarette, coughed a fair bit – *yes, Bud, I know you're right about me giving up* – and reread my notes. I added a comment: "Why does everyone seem so keen to help Al with his career?"

I wasn't sure of the significance of that question, but knew it needed to be answered…at some point. I decided to get myself showered and ready for the day before the water service people arrived at eight, but no one arrived. Luckily, I still had enough bottled water to make another coffee, and I decided to check my email once more, hoping against hope that there might be something there that could help Bud.

Nothing.

While I was online, I began to dig into my suspects' backgrounds.

I trawled through some lists of South Carolina families – *who knew there were so many French family and place names there?* – and found Al's. I managed to discover that his maternal grandfather had inherited a fortune from his forebears and had gone on to make a pile more for himself, while his maternal grandmother – the Gram Besselleu to whom Al had referred – had come from another French line, Dubois, and had brought her own money to the match. All of which knowledge begged the question: Why would a scion of such a wealthy family be working at all?

I checked out Frank's old brewery, which had an easily discoverable, and significant online footprint. Frank was mentioned in glowing terms in the company's "About" section and a bit more digging showed me that the freshly relaunched business was, as he'd said, doing very nicely indeed.

Tony's Facebook page was fascinating; he obviously kept in touch with folks who'd known him at various restaurants where he'd previously worked. And I found a wedding photograph of him and Callie. They made the perfect beach-wedding couple – he was casual in a white linen shirt and pants; she looked delightful in her flowing white dress, with flowers in her hair. Fit, bronzed, healthy, and muscular, they certainly looked happy, but then, who wouldn't on their wedding day?

Unfortunately, I found nothing about Dean or Jean George, nor Dorothea Simmonds or Greg Hollins.

I wandered around a few general websites that allowed me to find out more than I'd ever thought I'd need to know about making tequila, then took a few minutes to check out the place where I was staying.

It was clear from their own website that the Friends Of Good Tequila Trust – *I bet they wished they'd come up with a name that made for a more natty abbreviation that the FOGGTs* – had invested in the most modern tequila-making equipment possible, including autoclaves that shortened the cooking time for the *piñas* – the hearts of the agave plants used to make the drink. I also learned that they produced the four most popular types of tequila: *blanco*, the youngest, and therefore the quickest to produce, which is clear; *reposado*, which the Mexican government decrees must rest in the barrel for at least two months, and sometimes stays there for a year; *añejo*, or aged, which must – legally – be in a barrel for at least a year; and, finally, extra *añejo*, which must be in the barrel for at least three years. The FOGTTs' website further made it clear that they didn't make *oro* tequila – the type that's young and colored with caramel to make it smoother, nor the *cristalino* type – *añejo* that has its color filtered out with charcoal.

I sat back for a moment or two before I plunged into the sales pitch for the FOGTTs' *Tequila Soleado* brand of all four types of tequila, then gave in and read through the superlatives. They all seemed to be well reviewed by aficionados: triple-distilled and naturally fermented, their smooth, complex flavors and reliable quality – as well as the excellence of the extra *añejo*, aged in French white oak barrels – were often commented upon, especially in the US, which I was unsurprised to discover was, apparently, the fastest growing market for tequila. It seemed that the FOGTTs had invested in good agave, the right equipment, and the right people to make good tequila. Their website suggested their investments had been well-placed.

I finished my coffee, recalled what I'd been warned to expect regarding local timekeeping, and decided I'd hang on until someone appeared with my water supplies before I headed off…which gave me time to find out a little about the circumstances surrounding the death of Miguel's poor daughter.

A few clicks took me to the website for the region's newspaper, *El Informador*, where I checked on news about the "Rose Killer". It seemed that most of the information centered on the first and second victims, as Al had mentioned, and which I happen to know isn't unusual in terms of a serial killer. The police often use the media when they're hunting the killer of one, or even two, victims but – once they realize they might have a serial killer on their hands – they tend to become more circumspect with their sharing of information.

In addition to what Al had told me, I discovered that Miguel's daughter had been killed immediately after she'd gone missing: her time of death had been estimated by analyzing her stomach contents, due to the length of time that had passed between her going missing and the discovery of her remains. The second victim, however, had been found much more quickly, and there seemed to be a question of exactly when she'd died; the information the journalists had gleaned from the autopsy seemed to suggest she'd been dead before she even disappeared.

That's…odd.

I read on.

The second victim, a nineteen-year-old girl from a "good home", had no boyfriend, had been attending her local college to study as a beautician, and had disappeared one afternoon. The initial reports said she'd been last seen about ten minutes before three, when she'd set off to walk to her home from a friend's house. She was found just after dawn the next morning, about forty miles away – and the subsequent autopsy on her remains had put her estimated time of death at about two o'clock in the afternoon on the day of her disappearance.

This last point was – according to the reports – a puzzle that consumed the *Federales* for quite a while, and one that had put the friends who'd all claimed to see her alive later than that in the frame as certain liars, if not murderers. They'd all been questioned multiple times.

Further reports told me that it had then been discovered that a police car had driven along the road where the victim had been found at about six o'clock on the evening of the day she'd gone missing, thereby establishing that the body must have been placed where it was found after that time, because it hadn't been there when the police had passed the spot in question. The article went so far as to mention that it was this critical fact that had led the *Federales* to no longer believe that Miguel Juan-Carlos García Perez, the father of the first victim, Angélica Rosa, was responsible for killing his daughter – because he couldn't possibly have been involved with the placement of the body of the second victim.

So what Al had told me was correct: if Miguel hadn't been seen by dozens of people saying a Requiem Mass for his daughter in Puerto Vallarta on the evening that the second victim was found, and then had an alibi for all his time until that victim was discovered, he might not have been cleared…at all.

I wonder how Miguel felt about the discovery of that second victim? Some complex emotions there, I bet.

I moved on to the most recent article about the Rose Killer, which dealt with all the killings to date. By the time the piece had been written – just a week or so earlier – the coverage simply stated the facts, and warned young women that they should not walk alone after dark…in quite alarming language. The simple statement of facts was almost chilling: approximately every four weeks a young woman's body had been found on a remote roadside, swathed in a white sheet, her hands closed as if in prayer, with two red roses clasped between them. It had been established that each victim – except, notably, the second one – had been last seen at night. Hence the warnings, I supposed. It also stated that they were all small, young women, most no more than five feet tall, and weighing around ninety pounds.

I haven't worked on any ongoing serial killer cases, because, fortunately, they're much rarer than spree-killing cases. Sadly, I worked on too many of those during the period when Bud hired me to consult for his homicide teams. However, I've studied many of the so-called "classic" serial killer cases; the deviant psychological factors observed in true serial killers are of interest to any criminal psychologist. Thus, I know only too well how the psychopathy of a serial killer can be triggered by physical appearances or attributes, and I've also learned that they can be highly specific in their choice of killing method. I therefore read with interest that Angélica Rosa was the only victim who'd died of simple alcohol poisoning; all the other victims having ingested large amounts of diphenhydramine. The report helpfully explained that the strong antihistamine is widely available in sleeping pills, and found in about sixty percent of all homes.

Maybe the killer wasn't pleased that his first victim took so long to die, and revised his method with his later victims?

There were photographs of families dazed with grief, and snaps of the victims, all of whom smiled from the newspaper's webpage on my phone in wide-eyed innocence.

All dead. Terrible.

I clicked away from the tragic images and once again settled in my little corner of the garden. It seemed so odd that this place already felt so familiar…indeed, I felt strangely peaceful, given my circumstances, and those of poor Bud. I was acutely aware that all I could do while waiting for Al to call, or for someone to show up with water bottles, was…think.

I lit yet another cigarette as I mused on the fact that I've spent decades studying people, and, although it might be generally accepted that I've accumulated a great deal of knowledge about why humans do what they do – and how they signal their true thoughts rather than their intended ones – I'm more than ready to acknowledge the fact that I really know only a fraction of what I wish I did.

But Bud having a secret background? With CSIS? How had I not noticed him lying? Until yesterday morning – *was it only yesterday morning?* – I'd thought I knew him well. I puffed angrily as I reminded myself that I'd made a decision to not dwell on the things he had chosen to keep secret from me…but I could feel the hurt…my vulnerability…creeping up on me again.

Stop it, Cait.

"You're looking thoughtful." It was Al, standing just a few feet away from me. I jumped. He added, "I knocked, but you didn't answer. I hope it was okay for me to come in?"

I locked that front door, I know I did.

Didn't I?

I'd already decided not to mention the break-in to him; what was the point? Nothing had been taken, and what "evidence" did I have? My photographic memory's ability to show me that items had been moved? Also, although we were working together, I didn't want him to focus on me.

I blurted out, "You just startled me. I didn't sleep too well. Nor nearly long enough. Yesterday was quite a day." I waved toward a chair as an invitation for him to sit, but Al declined.

"If you'd rather not pursue this any further, Cait, we'd all understand. After all, you're supposed to be on vacation." His words hung on the morning air.

I sensed something different in his attitude; he seemed to be on edge.

Is he angry? With me? What have I done?

I stood. "We're on a mission, Al. You and me – we're going to find out who this guy is, and why he killed Margarita. Right?" Al nodded. "Tell me, has he said anything this morning?" I was desperate for an update on Bud's condition.

"He ate his breakfast, drank his water, but not a word. When I got back there last night, he was fast asleep. Like a baby. Not a care in the world. How can that be? How can a man kill and not feel remorse?"

I believed I'd identified the source of Al's anger, and was pleased that it wasn't me. However, my greater relief came from the knowledge that Bud seemed fine.

For the time being…and time's getting shorter.

I wanted to get going. "Well, we're not achieving anything by hanging around here. I'm not going to wait for the water service to deliver after all…might we go to see Callie now?"

"That's why I came. I thought we could walk over together. I haven't been able to get an answer on the phone at their apartment, so she might still be asleep…and maybe Tony's still out, buying supplies for the restaurant. But…well…I don't like the idea that she took pills prescribed for Dorothea; she's a much…bigger woman than Callie."

I agreed. "Right, let's go then, but just give me a moment and I'll just pop to the…you know…before we leave." I did just that.

A glance in the bathroom mirror told me that – since I'd packed clothes I thought I'd be wearing to wander Mexican beaches, holding hands with the man I love – I looked as though I were jolly, and relaxed…which was not at all how I felt. At least the coral hue of my lightweight tunic gave me the illusion of having some color, and the bit of sunburn I'd managed to get on my nose while sitting at the airport the previous day had, thankfully, turned from pink to brown. My white capris were roomy, and stretchy, and summery, and the long white scarf I'd tied in a bow around my ponytail topped off the look – literally.

You'd be proud to be seen with me, Bud.

Finally ready to leave, I shoved my notepad, phone, and ciggies, into my purse and shut up the house, then Al and I walked down the little hill to *Amigos del Tequila*. When we arrived at the back of the building, I wasn't at all surprised to find that the door to the kitchen was wide open, and there was no one about.

It seems to be the normal state of affairs for the place.

Al sighed. "I'm supposed to get it through to people that crime often happens because of an opportunity presenting itself. Why do people not lock their doors?" He shook his head with resignation as we entered. "Hello?" he called. There was no answer. He turned to me. "Let's check upstairs."

I nodded, and was grateful that he didn't feel the need to unholster his gun, on this occasion. We climbed the steep, narrow staircase, and emerged into what was obviously the scene of a disturbance: clothes and decorative items were scattered about the furniture and the floor. The room was in total disarray.

I gasped aloud.

Did the same person do this who was in my place last night?

Al turned and said sharply, "What's the matter?"

"It looks like the place has been ransacked," I said.

Al beamed – a glint in his eye. "I've been here before. This is how they live."

As we stood there – surrounded by discarded clothes, books, papers, files, soda cans, drink bottles, dirty mugs, and plates – I wondered how anyone could live surrounded by such a mess.

I know my home's not pristine, but even I'm tidier than these two.

I spotted a laptop and a tablet, so accepted Al's assertion that this was normal for the Booths…because any thief would have made off with such items. However, that knowledge didn't make the mess any prettier to look at.

In front of the tiny kitchen was a breakfast bar, which was completely covered by piles of paperwork. I noticed that at least this seemed to be in something of an orderly arrangement, and – as I approached, and peered – I spotted accounts, receipts, and records for *Amigos del Tequila*, Serena Spa, and the FOGTT. Tony had told me that Callie did accountancy work for people – at least it looked as though her work had some order about it.

"Would you check in the bedroom?" asked Al. "The bathroom is silent. Callie might still be asleep."

I nodded and knocked on what was obviously the bedroom door. There was no response, so I opened it a crack and peered in. There were two mounds in the bed.

"I think they're both still in bed," I whispered to Al over my shoulder. "What do you want me to do?"

Al shrugged.

I knocked again and said, "Hello." Nothing. I stepped into the room and announced loudly, "Rise and shine. Time to get going." But neither lump stirred. My instincts kicked in and I reached for the pulse point on Callie's neck. I couldn't feel anything, but she wasn't cold.

Good sign.

"Al, come here and check for Tony's pulse," I called.

There were no obvious signs of a struggle in the surprisingly tidy bedroom, and there were no signs of blood. I pulled Callie's arm free of the bedclothes and held her wrist. Finding a pulse is a lot harder than you might think; it's especially difficult when your own heart is pounding. Luckily, I noticed Callie's eyelids flutter.

"She's alive," I said announced triumphantly. "However, I'm concerned that she's so deeply asleep. How's Tony?"

"The same," said a grim Al from the other side of the bed. "I know Callie took Dorothea's pills, so she might still be under their influence. But as for Tony being like this? He and I had a few more drinks last night…but this is not…normal."

I scanned the bedroom, but saw no sign of pills, or a pill bottle. "We don't know if Dorothea brought Callie one or two pills, or a whole bottle, do we?"

Al pulled out his cellphone. "I'm calling an ambulance. These guys need to be checked out. Then I'll call Dorothea and find out exactly what she gave Callie."

Al left the room to make his calls. Once again, I turned my attention to the Booths' bedroom. There was a glass on Callie's nightstand; I peered at it, then scrabbled in my purse for my reading-cheats, shoved them onto my nose, and took another look.

White crystals.

Tony's side of the bed didn't have a nightstand, so – without touching anything – I bent down to look under the bed. A beer glass lay on its side on the floor. I pulled a pen out of my purse, stuck it into the glass, and rolled it along the floor until I could see it properly.

More white crystals.

I toyed with the idea that maybe neither Tony nor Callie liked to swallow pills, and that both of them had chosen to grind sleeping tablets into a drink…but thought it unlikely.

Al stuck his head through the doorway, and I told him about what I'd seen in the two glasses. As he walked into the bedroom, and took a good look at both glasses himself, he said, "An ambulance is on its way, and Dorothea says she gave Callie a whole container of her sleeping pills, and she thinks there were about forty pills in the bottle. She can't remember what they're called, though she told me they have a Z in their name. It seems she buys them at a pharmacy in PV, where they know what she takes. She's checking with them."

I stood back, allowing Al to kneel to examine the beer glass on the floor.

I offered, "Sleeping pills are BZRAs – benzodiazepine receptor agonists – often referred to as Z-drugs, so we can't even guess what she gave Callie, because the 'Z' isn't that useful. We'll have to wait."

Al looked puzzled. "You seem to know a lot about sleeping pills. Why's that?"

"You'd be surprised how many medicine cabinets I've been through when I've been working for the local cops as a victim profiler. Checking out a person's medications can tell you a great deal about them…and not only about how they're doing physiologically. It can give useful insights into their lifestyle, and sometimes even their psychological makeup. Different sleeping pills are prescribed for different types of sleeping disorders, so I've researched which are which so that I can assess the contents of medicine cabinets more accurately. For example: the Z-drugs are used to treat people who can't get off to sleep easily, rather than those who wake up during the night. They're available under a variety of brand names that differ from country to country, or, sometimes, as a generic; they've been around for a while, so the patents on some of the earlier formulations have expired. If Dorothea was getting her pills here, in Mexico, she might have been getting a generic. Whichever case it is, they're certainly not the sort of pills that should ever be mixed with alcohol, and – worryingly – it's possible to overdose on them quite easily. That said, we can't even be sure that it was Dorothea's pills that Callie and Tony were dosed with…if that's what those white crystals mean. So it really would be best if these guys were shipped off to a place where their vital signs can be monitored."

Al was pacing around the small room. "The ambulance shouldn't be long. I guess it helps that it was me who called it in. Sometimes my position here helps in practical ways."

Al looked just a little proud, but I was feeling totally useless.

"Let's go back into the main room, and leave this door open," I suggested. "We can still see and hear the Booths from there, but I won't feel as though I'm…intruding so much."

Al agreed. I was tempted to tidy up their living room – *odd, for me* – but I resisted. Instead, I stood in the middle of the mess and looked around, carefully noting what I saw. There was a tiny desk against one wall, and upon it sat a jotter beside the base unit for the handset telephone, but no handset. I picked my way across the room and peered through my glasses at the last notes made on the jotter – by whom, I didn't know.

M mileage?

S wax?

FOGTTs barrels vs bottles? Not enough or too many?

The "M" and "S" notes had been crossed through; the "FOGTT" note hadn't been. Not terribly helpful, as notes went, but they must have meant something – or at least enough to be useful – to whomever had made them.

I returned to study the only area of order in the room: the piles of accounts arranged relatively neatly on the breakfast bar. I spotted a yellow sticky note poking out of the pile that related to Serena Spa. The word "WAX" had been written in a green highlighting pen with a question mark next to it. I looked at the sheet it was stuck to: lists of expenditures, all for consumable supplies. Someone – presumably Callie Booth – had highlighted the line for wax in green pen, and I could see why. The amount spent on wax supplies at the spa had been pretty steady for five months, then had dipped down to about half the usual cost. Clearly Callie had needed to ask Serena about this fact. That explained one cryptic note on the telephone pad.

I turned my attention to the other piles. Nothing jumped out at me. There were no yellow notes on the FOGTT papers, but there were a couple of sheets with scribbled calculations – not so unusual for financial paperwork. One was largely covered in multiplications and divisions; it looked as though Callie Booth preferred to use her brain rather than a calculator. I looked at the figures for a few moments but couldn't fathom their significance. All I could see was that both the multiplication and division seemed to be using the same base figures.

Odd – checking her own work?

As I replaced the FOGTT pile, I spotted another relatively neat pile of papers beneath a plate that still bore signs of a partially consumed fried egg. I found that this mound related to Margarita Flores. Again, I couldn't see any sticky notes, yellow or otherwise. Undaunted I picked up the papers and started to flick through them, hoping to spot something that Callie had highlighted; if "S" had referred to Serena Spa, then the "M" could mean Margarita Flores.

Sure enough, Callie had run a green highlighter pen through a list of gas costs. She'd also scribbled a big question mark across the whole page. I read through the figures but couldn't understand why Callie had highlighted that particular page. It looked as though Margarita had made fairly regular trips to one specific gas station with a Bucerias address, with an occasional visit to another place in Puerto Vallarta. Her overall mileage figures were at the top of the page, and a quick calculation told me that she was getting great gas mileage. I wondered what she drove, because Margarita's van was getting her better mileage than I got. I wondered if, maybe, her van was a hybrid vehicle.

Al's cell phone rang, and I watched him as he listened, scribbled something in his notebook, thanked the person on the other end, and tucked his phone away. "That was Dorothea, who's spoken to her pharmacist. She says Zaleplon is the name of her pills, and she's certain there were forty-seven capsules in the bottle. Now at least we can tell the paramedics what Tony and Callie have taken." He sounded relieved.

I shook my head. "But…Zaleplon is traditionally blue. The residue I saw in the glasses was white."

Al looked crestfallen. "Really?"

I heard a siren in the distance.

Al brightened. "Here they come. I'll go show them the way." He bounded down the stairs.

After he'd gone, I took photos of the notes on the jotter and the sheet of gas expenses from the pile of accounts for Margarita Flores, as well as the sheet with all the scribbled calculations from the FOGGT file. I wasn't sure what it all meant, but I felt it was important.

If Margarita had been speaking to Callie about her gas expenses and mileage figures before she'd been killed, might Margarita have mentioned something that had put Callie in danger?

How can information about gas costs and mileage be life threatening?

The next thirty minutes was manic: when the ambulance arrived, Al and I were told to make ourselves scarce in no uncertain terms, despite Al's position. At least that meant we were able to meet all the FOGTTs as they came running to *Amigos del Tequila*. Initially, they all assumed that Callie had been taken ill as a result of her car accident the previous evening, and were then aghast when Al and I told them of the state in which we'd found both Tony and Callie.

Unsurprisingly, Dorothea had been the first to arrive, and – when she found out what had happened – I suspected that if she'd had something to physically flagellate herself with, she'd have done it. She loudly informed everyone who arrived that she'd told Callie to take just one pill, and that she shouldn't drink. She wailed that she'd never forgive herself if the couple died because she'd given them her pills.

Ada managed to calm her a little, with the suggestion of a stiff brandy, and everyone agreed that was a good idea, so we all made our way into the bar.

The poor paramedics had a terrible time getting the stretchers down the apartment's steep, narrow staircase; the angry shouting and wild gesticulations that accompanied their progress verged on the farcical…and stood in stark contrast to the seriousness of the situation. They'd just left when the final FOGGT arrived; it was my first chance to meet Greg Hollins.

He was about Bud's height, but slimmer, and had an air about him that reminded me of Peter O'Toole at his most lugubrious. He had a deep tan, wore leather flip-flops, and a rumpled white linen shirt with matching pants. He held a Panama hat in one hand, and there was the stub of a fat cigar clenched between the fingers of his other. He must have been seventy years old if he was a day…or else he was in his sixties and had lived a hard life.

"Ah yes, the illustrious Cait Morgan. G'day," he said.

His strong Australian accent surprised me: Ada had told me that Greg hadn't lived in his native country for many years, so I'd expected his accent to have toned down a little. However, I reasoned that I'm always being told that my Welsh accent is still strong, despite more than a decade of living in Canada, so maybe he, like me, had managed to keep his native twang.

The twinkle in his eye was unmistakable as he greeted me, and his grip on my hand didn't waver as he said, "I find it hard to believe that a woman as beautiful and, if I may say, curvaceous as yourself is still single." His eyes wandered to my bust and dwelt there.

You're investigating, Cait – don't put him in his place…as he deserves.

My reply was stunningly polite, given his leering. "You're single too, I hear," I said.

Play along, Cait.

He released my hand, stood to attention, and saluted. "At present, ma'am, but…possibly not for long." He winked.

My internal slime-o-meter hit new heights; Greg Hollins was a disgusting, aging lothario, with skin like dried tobacco leaves, and an aroma to match.

I reminded myself – forcefully – that he was a possible suspect, so I had to take my chance to find out all about him…however unpleasant that might be.

"Let me pour you a drink," he offered. I noticed that Dorothea, Ada, and Jean were on their second brandies. I heard Dorothea utter the words "for the shock", which seemed like a good enough excuse for everyone else to continue helping themselves to Tony's bar supplies.

"Thanks, I'll have a bottle of water," I replied.

"Your wish is my command," said Greg greasily, as he slunk off to the bar and returned a moment later with a bottle and a glass. As he poured, he said, "You were the talk of the place last night, my dear. Dorothea Googled you before she arrived for the evening, so she was able – as usual – to be the fount of all wisdom for our little group." I took the glass from him, barely managing to avoid his hand touching mine as I did so.

Yuk!

He pressed on, "You're quite the woman, I hear. Bright – a Mensan, no less – and famous for changing the way the criminology community thinks about victims. No mean feat, I'm sure. Though I've never been a victim of anything in my life – except wounds to my heart, suffered at the hands of many, many beautiful women."

Double yuk!

I braced myself and set off on my journey of discovery. "I'm sure you're just as fascinating," I said, as coquettishly as I could.

He grinned. "I'm nuts!" He waited for me to bite.

I won't.

He carried on, undaunted. "Well, I used to be nuts…but I've retired, now. Nuts. Macadamia nuts, to be exact. Started on my own land in Australia, ended up with holdings in Guatemala, South Africa, Kenya, and Hawaii. Got fed up with nuts, so I sold up, and here I am. Now I get to smoke my cigars wherever I want and drink my own tequila. What could be better?"

Greg's strong accent was matched by a full-on Australian attitude; I was just waiting for him to say "Strewth".

He moved even closer to me. "You're Welsh, I hear. Loads of Welsh in my family, way back. Quite a number of your lot got shipped over to 'serve at Her Majesty's pleasure', right? Stealing sheep, I wouldn't be surprised." He laughed and nudged me. Hard. "No need to go chasing sheep when the women look like you, though, right?" He winked again.

I gritted my teeth and smiled, as graciously as possible. I asked, "You were in PV yesterday, when Margarita was killed?"

Go for it, Cait.

His face fell, and he nodded. "Terrible. Very sad. Not that I knew the woman myself, you know. But it's always sad."

"Where were you exactly?" I asked.

Bluntness might be the only thing that works with this guy.

He stared into his own glass. "Here and there, you know? Dropping in on friends, checking out the beaches, taking in the views."

Bikinis and binoculars, I bet.

He finally looked up. "But Al's got the guy who did it. I don't need an alibi, right?" He grinned and held up his hands in mock surrender, but his micro-expressions told a different story.

He's worried about something and trying to hide it.

"Breakfast, Cait?" Once again Al had managed to get within feet of me without my noticing him.

How does he manage that?

"Yes, please. I'm absolutely starving," I said – possibly with too much enthusiasm. Unbelievably, it was still only just gone ten. "Where shall we go?" It was clear to me that no food would be served at *Amigos del Tequila* that day.

Dorothea piped up. "You should go into Bucerias. Don't go down to Rutilio's, he'll rip you off. They shouldn't be allowed to get away with it. And he's the worst of the lot."

I stood, pulled my purse onto my shoulder, and was ready to leave with Al, when a short, elderly man entered the bar from the kitchen. His clothes were tattered, and filthy, and he held a large, battered straw hat rolled up in his hands, which looked as though they themselves were made from coarse leather. His face was a mask of dark, folded, weathered skin, his sunken jet eyes glittered, and his head was covered with a slick of black hair. As he spoke, I noticed he had almost no teeth at all.

"Margarita," he said gravely.

No one moved. I noticed that the general emotion displayed was…*embarrassment?*

"Oh, Juan, you poor thing. Let me hug you." Dorothea threw her arms into the air and rushed toward the tiny man.

Juan? Juan the *intendente*; Juan the *jimador*; Juan the murdered Margarita's father.

Not what I'd expected.

Seconds In

As I stared at Juan, I considered the possibility that the man had killed his own daughter; even Al had said Juan was capable of such a deed. His clothes hung off his tiny frame; I reckoned they'd seen many hours in the fields that day already, unless…he never washed them.

My online research had told me what a *jimador* did – his job was to cut the leaves from the agave plant at exactly the right time, so that the sugars in the remaining heart of the agave, the *piña*, were at their best for making tequila. It seemed to be extremely skilled, yet physically exhausting, work: the *piñas* often weighed up to seventy pounds each and they needed to be cut from their roots and pulled out of the narrow rows of plants by hand; a *jimador* might cut and move eighty to one hundred *piñas* each day.

I'd seen acres and acres of the spiky blue-gray plants growing in neat rows up the hillsides and on the high, flat plains, as Bud and I had driven from the airport just a day earlier. We'd laughed about visiting a tequila tasting room together. Now, here I was, sitting in just such a place, with a group of murder suspects and a clock ticking in my head.

A lot can happen in a day.

After Dorothea had finished hugging Juan – a process during which I thought he was going to suffocate – she released him into Al's care.

The men spoke quietly in Spanish, then Al came to my side and whispered, "Our trip to Margarita's *hacienda* will have to wait, Cait; I'm going to take Juan to the mortuary, where he can see his daughter's body. On our way, I'll drop you at Rutilio's Restaurant, and I'll call Miguel…get him to meet you there. I prefer that you are with him or me all the time. You need to eat, and you can talk to Miguel and Rutilio about Margarita. I'm...I'm not sure how long I'll be gone, but I'll meet you there?"

I nodded my agreement, though I was annoyed that Al seemed to think I needed to be accompanied at all times. We exited through the main door, leaving behind the FOGTTs, who were all a-buzz about the latest emergency to blight their little paradisical community, and desperately trying to work out a plan of action for opening the tasting room that afternoon, and then the restaurant that evening.

Given that it was still early in the day, the brightness and warmth of the sun outside came as a shock to me; I hunted for my sunglasses in my purse. Al's police car was no more than two minutes' walk away, but even in that short time I started to sweat, and the humidity made it hard for me to breathe. I sat in the back of the car, as did Juan, and Al took off, with us looking like two people he'd arrested.

This is where poor Bud sat yesterday...covered in the blood of the daughter of the man beside me.

I gave myself a quick mental talking to, then said to Juan, "I am sorry that we are meeting under such sad circumstances."

The man's expression didn't alter, and he paid me absolutely no attention.

Maybe he speaks no English?

I hoped that a question would draw some response. "If we could have met at a different time, I'd have been eager to ask you about your work as a *jimador.* I understand it takes many years of practice to gain the skills you need?"

"I am the most excellent *jimador* in this State," said Juan harshly, and with pride.

Not too grief-stricken to be boastful. Good.

I pressed on with, "It must bring you great satisfaction to know that your plants are making such highly praised tequila. I understand that the *Extra Añejo Tequila Soleado* is doing very well indeed, and that this is just its first year on sale."

Juan turned himself on the seat to look at me with his raisin eyes. The folds in his face made it difficult to read him: few micro-expressions were visible, except around his eyes, and even there it was difficult to tell if he was smiling, squinting, or sneering. It took him a long time to speak, or so it seemed to me; I didn't feel very patient, and my tummy rumbled. Twice.

Eventually, he spoke, his voice graveled with age. "It is good if they make money. It is better if they make a lot of money. Then they can pay me more. I am very good. I work very hard. I deserve more than I get."

I tried to stop myself from being too judgmental; Bud's always accusing me of it, and I've been working on it. But – in my defense – being a criminal psychologist rather presupposes making judgments. As I looked at Juan, I "assessed" him as being selfish, and greedy; however, I countered this with the acknowledgement that he was clearly a talented and hard-working man, who'd probably had to scrape by his whole life without much of anything at all...eventually learning to not expect much of anything at all. Though, over the past several years, he'd managed to acquire some resources, having inherited land he'd then sold. He struck me as a very angry man, and I didn't get the impression that was because of his daughter's death.

Maybe a mantle he assumed when he lost his wife and sons?

Although I was pretty sure of the answer, I wanted to study his reaction to my next question very closely. "Did you see your daughter the day she died?"

Juan licked his thin, dry lips, then he smiled. It was a difficult smile for me to read because the contours of his face were impacted by his lack of teeth. But I was sure of one thing: it was not a kind smile. In fact, it gave me quite a chill. He wiped his rheumy eyes with the back of a desiccated hand.

"No. Not yesterday," he replied.

I reacted as naturally as I could. "I expect you were at church; it was Sunday, after all."

Juan seemed to chew over his answer, quite literally: his jaw moved up and down, and he finally said, "I said Mass early. I walked home. Then I went to be with my plants. Margarita, she was not the only one who loved plants. I love them just as much. But mine are not pretty like her roses." He gave that creepy smile again, then added, "My plants make more money than hers ever could."

Smug. Self-centered. Dismissive of his dead daughter.

Al pulled up in front of Margarita's store, and spoke to Juan in Spanish. "Do you want to go inside?"

Juan's gruff dismissal needed no translation.

"I'll pick you up at Rutilio's later, Cait," said Al, as I hauled myself out of the car. I nodded, and waved as he drove away…then headed for Bob's Bodega.

Bob was behind the counter, and Maria was arranging bottles of sunscreen on a shelf. They greeted me like an old friend, and I accepted their kind words with smiles and gratitude.

As we exchanged pleasantries, I cast my eyes about the place. There was a wooden double door in the back wall of the store; one door had stacks of boxes in front of it, the other was clearly kept free for access to the back lane. Other than the wooden ones at the back, and the glass ones in the front, there were no other doors in the place…meaning that the entire store was open to the public. So…there'd have been nowhere for either of them to have changed out of blood-soaked clothing, unless they'd done it in the lane behind the store…which Rutilio would have seen from his vantage point.

It was what I'd been afraid of, but – in a way – I was pleased; I didn't want either of these warm people to be on my list of possible suspects any longer…and now they weren't.

After complimenting them on the range of their offering, and the wonderfully inviting displays in their store, I explained that I'd just popped in to say hello before going to have something to eat at Rutilio's, and they waved me happily on my way.

As I rounded the end of the building, I decided to walk along the lane. I had no reason to creep…but I did. Margarita's van was parked where she'd left it. It certainly wasn't a hybrid, but it was a curious shape. Walking closer I realized it had a refrigeration unit on the roof.

Of course…she'd want to transport her precious flowers in a chilled environment.

I examined the entry-hatch at the back of her store: it sat flush within the wall. Its edges were a bit dented, and a few black scuff marks bore testament to its use. There was no lock, nor a handle, so no way of opening the door from the outside; it was clear that Margarita would have had to open it from inside the refrigerated unit within her store. This meant that it didn't present a security risk, but also meant that it didn't offer a viable entry point for the killer…unless the victim herself had opened this door from inside the store for her killer to enter by – which seemed very unlikely to me. So…the killer must have gone in through the front door.

But no one did…except Bud.

The little door was set into the wall about a foot off the ground, and was about four feet tall. As I'd observed the night before, it was narrow, no more than eighteen inches wide; Al had needed to duck, and turn sideways, to get through it. I guessed it was just about the right size to load in flowers without allowing too much cold air to escape, hence the step at the bottom – that's where all the cold air goes when you open a fridge door…it literally falls out, because it sinks. Again I saw evidence of Margarita's attention to detail at work; she must have had the unit specially designed.

I walked toward Serena Spa. The back door was wedged wide open, and the rear entrance was covered with a beaded curtain, which swayed in the ocean breeze. I peeped inside. The spa smelled awful – a mixture of potent aromas, none of which were pleasant. I could see through to the front of the store and could hear Serena singing to herself. To the left, against the back wall of the building, there was a small room with a massage table inside. I guessed that was where Dorothea had been at the time of the murder, though I wondered how the relatively small table had coped with her size. A narrow corridor led to the front, and I supposed that was where Ada had been. Either of them could have left without the other one knowing…if the door to the massage room had been closed, which I reasoned it would be when in use.

Finally, I turned toward the sea, heading for the front of Rutilio's Restaurant, and was rewarded with a waft of ocean air that cooled and refreshed me. Even my eyelids were sweating, so I took off my sunglasses and wiped them dry. I was glad I hadn't bothered with makeup that morning.

What's the point?

I took in the view: seagulls swooped in the luminous blue sky, the surf made its siren call as it caressed the shoreline about twenty feet away, and I could feel the healing and rejuvenating power of the ozone in the air.

I should be sharing this with Bud.

"Ah, Cait Morgan! Cait Morgan?"

I pushed my sunglasses on to spare myself from the glare of the sun, and spotted the man who was hurrying toward me.

Miguel was shorter than me, and wider. He puffed, ruddy faced, as he rushed along, and he was holding out his hand in greeting. Although he was a heavy man, his gun belt was buckled at the tightest hole, his pants were way too big for him, and the collar and shoulders of his shirt were loose.

You've lost a fair bit of weight since you started wearing that uniform.

"Hello, hello, I am Officer Miguel," he said, shaking my hand with both of his. "Come, come. Captain Alfredo said you would be hungry. My brother will feed us."

He waved me toward a table that was just outside the now fully opened glass front of the restaurant, beneath the shade of a jolly red parasol. I sat facing the glittering sea, delighting in the breeze and noticing, as yesterday, that clouds were gathering on the horizon.

The gaily striped tablecloths, the painted wooden chairs – and even the plastic lobsters on the restaurant's walls – looked so much more appealing in the sunlight. I also noted that the piped mariachi music was similar to that which had been playing the night before, but it seemed more tuneful by day…less dissonant, and mournful.

As soon as he spotted me, Rutilio declaimed, "You have returned! How wonderful!"

Seeing the two brothers together merely highlighted that there can be huge differences in terms of what can come out of one gene pool.

"This is my brother…my baby brother," announced Miguel proudly. "He is so handsome, so clever with food. He is a great businessman. He is the best little brother in the world." He beamed with genuine affection at Rutilio, who puffed out his chest and basked in the compliments. I noted that the expression on Rutilio's face exactly matched that of the huge neon sign that stood at the end of the building…though I imagined that the local fishermen might have had a point when they'd complained to Al that the giant fluorescent face frightened the fish after dark.

For the second time in less than twelve hours, I once again contemplated Rutilio's extensive menu; I was so hungry I felt I could eat everything listed. I settled for a snapper salad, which seemed to be the only item that didn't feature some sort of wrap, shell, or tortilla chip; I really didn't want to fill myself up with that stuff, even though I'd missed breakfast, and I supposed we were now into brunch territory. I also declined beer in favor of bottled water.

Keep a clear head, today, Cait.

Rutilio made himself scarce, after Miguel agreed with his brother that he'd have his "usual"…and I wondered what that might turn out to be. Keen to avoid chit-chat, and find out what Miguel knew about Margarita, it seemed the man was desperate to tell me about the "devil" that he and Al had arrested for her killing. Miguel had apparently been charged with keeping an eye on Bud earlier that morning, and he took great delight in describing how voraciously Bud had eaten his breakfast – and had continued to say nothing at all. This clearly infuriated Miguel.

I'm glad to know you've eaten, Bud.

I hoped that the arrival of the food would give me the chance to get Miguel to talk about Margarita, but I hadn't counted on Rutilio not just delivering our orders, but also deciding to take a break and join us.

Both he, and his brother, munched on massive *burritos*.

We all ate in silence for a few moments, then I said to the chef, "Al told me you were in the lane behind the flower shop yesterday, Rutilio. I expect you were glad that your brother was on the scene too, or you might have had to get involved yourself."

Rutilio wiped his lips with his napkin and smiled. Unfortunately, the refried beans from his burrito were still smeared across his huge teeth.

Yuk!

The he slapped Miguel on the shoulder. "Yes, my brother here captured the man. He is a hero. Me? I was here, in my kitchen, my other home. I could hear screaming, so I ran. What else could I do? My brother had done it all. By the time I arrived, he had the man. And we are all grateful for him. Our mother kissed him last night."

"Yes, she did," chimed in Miguel. "Usually she only kisses Rutilio, because he is the baby, but last night she kissed me too. It was as though I was the pretty boy, for once." He laughed and slapped his leg.

Interesting.

"So…you didn't see anything, before you heard the screams?" I directed my question at Rutilio, but it was Miguel who answered.

"What would he see? The devil was in the bodega, then he went to Margarita's store to kill her. He was never behind her store, only in the front."

"Yes, this is true," said Rutilio. "Why do you ask?"

I shrugged it off. "Oh, I'm just trying to get the full picture, you know? Who saw what…who was where when it happened."

"But why?" asked Rutilio.

I dared, "Because I wondered if the killer might have said something to someone that might explain his actions."

"He said 'No police' to Serena," said Miguel.

"He did?" Rutilio and I spoke in unison. We each sounded as surprised as the other.

Miguel nodded. "Yes, this is what she told me when I helped her. She said that he looked at her, with his evil eyes, and threatened her. When she opened the door and saw him there, he hissed at her, 'No police.' That is what she told me."

"So he speaks English?" asked Rutilio.

"At least that much," replied Miguel. "I told this to Captain Alfredo this morning when I remembered it, but he does not think that is much to go on. The man spoke in Spanish to Roberto…but Captain Al believes maybe he has just tourist Spanish. In case the man might understand English, we speak in Spanish in front of him, if we have to speak at all."

"So no one saw, or heard, anything that might suggest why this man killed Margarita?" I asked. I sipped my water. Both men shook their heads. Nothing. I added, "So what about Margarita herself? What can you tell me about her?"

"She was a good woman," said Rutilio.

Miguel nodded. "She was a hard worker."

Then they both applied themselves to their food, shaking their heads in disbelief at the loss of a woman I suspected they'd hardly known at all.

Timing Is Everything

I decided that I'd allow the brothers their chance to enjoy their food, but my mind was whirring as I nibbled my fish and leaves. The fish was well cooked – still moist and flavorful – and the dressing on the salad was zesty, which helped me feel revitalized. I took a moment to observe the other patrons and noted that wrapped, rolled, fried, and crunchy dishes were being eaten with gusto all around me. The same two girls who'd been serving the night before were chatting, and bringing food to the tables. I wondered who was preparing the food, given that Chef Rutilio was sitting right in front of me.

"Do you have an assistant?" I asked. I thought it was an innocent enough question, and I certainly didn't expect the reaction it drew from the brothers.

Rutilio stood, pushing back his chair so hard that it fell over, causing quite a stir among his customers. Miguel buried his face in his hands and started shaking his head. I was confused.

Rutilio waved his arms around, indicating his domain. He seemed incensed. He'd gone from cheery and chatty to incandescently angry in a heartbeat. He boomed, "I need no help. I am Rutilio. I make the menu. I make the food. I am this restaurant." I half expected him to start beating his chest.

Wow.

Other customers began to look as alarmed as I felt. The two serving girls giggled nervously and attended to their tables…fussing, and calming their patrons. Miguel motioned to his brother to sit and be quiet. I glugged my water.

Rutilio picked up his chair and sat with us again. He nodded at his brother, then said to me, "I am sorry, Cait. It is not your fault. You did not know what you said."

You're not wrong.

Miguel spoke in calming, conciliatory tones as he whispered, "My brother is finding the business difficult at the moment. It will pass. He is an excellent chef. The bank – they think he should close the place. Or else have somebody buy into the business with him. But he is a hard-working man, my talented baby brother – he will succeed." He smiled at his sibling indulgently. "He has a good plan. He is open here now for more hours than before, so he has more customers. The business, it is looking better…but our mother, she worries about him. He works so much, she thinks he needs help. Not just the girls to serve, but a helper in the kitchen. She has been...talking about it to him for a while, but he says he can do this alone."

Rutilio said, "It is true. Our mother has always loved me so much, but – sometimes – she forgets I am now a man."

Miguel smiled sadly. "Mothers worry; this is their role in life – to worry about their children. And our mother has always worried so much about Rutilio. All his jobs in the past have not worked out well. People did not understand that he needed to have authority, and to be creative – as he is here with his food – so they made life difficult for him. But now he has found his place. Of course, we have helped him all we can, and we understand that it takes time for a restaurant to work out. But the bank? They are not family. So now he must work even harder. My poor brother only managed to get to bed a couple of hours before he had to return here this morning. We all know how hard he is trying, but it has been very difficult for us all since my sweet Angélica Rosa was taken."

Throughout Miguel's loving testimonial to his brother's work ethic, Rutilio munched…and nodded his head sadly. I detected the smell of burning martyrs wafting across the table, and wondered about the extent to which the family had supported this much-loved son, who was, apparently, sadly misunderstood by all. I also wondered why he hadn't managed to get to his bed earlier the night before; all he'd had to do after Al and I left was brush down the grill, which couldn't have taken that long.

Our little group became silent, and the rest of the customers settled down again. It seemed that the normal balance had returned.

Rutilio finished his food, rose, took his leave, then returned with a tray of tequila bottles and glasses.

Oh no…you're kidding.

He beamed. "Last night, you were tired, and you had to rush off with Alfredo, Cait; it is understandable that you could not drink with me. But today? Today you are the Canadian on vacation again. Now we drink!"

Obviously Rutilio thought that being hospitable toward me and pouring tequila down my throat were synonymous.

I can't do it. Bud's depending on me.

I looked at my watch and stood, causing Miguel to look confused. "I'm sorry, Rutilio, you're very kind to offer, but I have to go to Margarita's store, and then to the police station. Until we discover who this evil murderer is I can't rest…nor relax."

Although he looked disappointed, Rutilio deflated with grace. "But of course. I know this is important to Alfredo. We can drink and celebrate when he has handed this devil to the *Federales*." He gave a little bow and took his tray of bottles and glasses back to the bar.

"There will be nothing to pay," said Miguel, as I hovered, uncertain what to do next.

"But I must pay," I said; I didn't want to be in debt to Rutilio for anything.

"He is my brother, you are my guest. It is normal. Do not question him about this." Miguel was being as firm as I could imagine it was possible for him to be. "You said you wanted to go to Margarita's store?" Miguel asked. I nodded. "Let us go. Then I will take you to the office, where you can meet up with Captain Alfredo."

I knew very well that Al had said he'd meet me at Rutilio's place, but I needed to get away from the man and his attempts to get me to drink, so I gathered my bits and pieces, shoved everything into my purse, and strode off toward Margarita's store once more.

I was glad to move; the shade of the red parasol under which we'd been eating had been helpful, but the humidity was beginning to build, and the sea breezes seemed to have died down. I felt less than fresh, and walking at least allowed me to move through the air, cooling me down a little.

It was only once we were standing in front of the door to the flower shop that it occurred to me to ask Miguel if he had a key. He looked hurt that I'd asked, unlocked the door, then pulled it open and stepped aside with a flourish to allow me to walk in. As soon as I did…I knew something was wrong. Even without the benefit of man-made lighting, I could see that the little shop – so neat and tidy the night before when I'd visited with Al – had been completely ransacked.

I gasped, which made Miguel panic.

When he switched on the lights, the destruction was painfully obvious: buckets of flowers and water, and unrolled spools of colored ribbon and tape were strewn about the place. The neat row of albums that had been on a shelf above Margarita's workbench had been flung onto the floor; the dead woman's photographs were all puddled with water, curled, and ruined. A copy of a local newspaper with the headline "BEWARE GIRLS" – warning of the next Rose Killer cycle – was crumpled in a corner, soaked and, ironically, strewn with roses.

"Who would do this?" Miguel spoke plaintively.

"I'm guessing whoever wanted Margarita's photographic equipment," I replied. I nodded toward the empty space beneath the workbench. "She had a lot of black cases and containers stored under there. I saw them when I was here with Al last night. Now they're all gone."

Interesting.

Miguel sounded alarmed. "I must tell Captain Alfredo. He will know what to make of this."

"Maybe you could also check if Bob and Maria heard anything?" I said, as Miguel pulled out his phone. He nodded, looking grim.

I wondered what Al *would* make of this; he believed he had Margarita's killer in a cell at his police station, so who might he think had stolen Margarita's cameras? I mentally added the search that had been made of my temporary digs, and the possible drugging of Tony and Callie Booth to my own list of puzzles to be solved. But I knew I couldn't tell Al about the break-in at my place. Not now. The only time to tell him would have been when he'd collected me that morning; that ship had sailed.

As Miguel stepped outside to make his call, I took my chance to survey the damage in more detail. I never want to interfere with a crime scene, but – as long as I didn't touch anything, and tiptoed between bits of debris – I didn't think there was much I could do to spoil this one.

The moment I'd seen the space where the cameras used to be, confirmed – in my own mind – the possibility that Margarita had seen and photographed something that had put her in danger. It made sense. And what if someone she'd photographed in a compromising situation had found out about that? Or…what if she'd taken such photos on purpose?

Margarita as a blackmailer?

Considering the scene again, it looked to me as though someone had been checking through Margarita's photographs, discarding them as their search turned up empty. The photos on the floor were clearly not going to contain any incriminating images, because they'd been left behind by the searcher, but – as I looked at the images she'd captured – it became clear that Margarita favored natural subjects over humanity. In fact, none of the photos showed any people at all…just seascapes, landscapes, the odd bird, and bunches of flowers.

But these photos had been discarded by the intruder…so had they taken the photographic equipment to access shots that Margarita hadn't yet printed out? That could be a possibility.

I returned to the question of blackmail: Bob and Maria had been quite convincing when they'd described how Margarita would say odd things to people. Maybe that was the florist's way of telling someone…obliquely…that she had something over them. Or maybe they already knew that, and she was being spiteful…pushing them as far as she could in public. The tragic loss of her family, estrangement from her father, terrible scarring, being bullied at school, and – if Bob and Maria were to be believed – an angry streak…these could all point to the sort of psychopathy that might lead a loner with a camera to become a voyeur with a fat bank balance.

Yes, it could be argued that Margarita's psychological profile bore all the hallmarks of a woman who could, quite easily, turn to blackmail. Or maybe she wasn't in it for the money…maybe power was her motivating force.

Without the opportunity to check through all the photo albums or take the cameras at the time of the murder – thanks to Bud's arrival – last night would have been the killer's first chance to get whatever they wanted out of the shop.

I wondered where those cameras were at that moment; being pored over by a person desperate to make sure they had, indeed, collected all the evidence against them? Or were they, maybe, at the bottom of the sea…having been tossed off a cliff somewhere along the coast.

I told myself I was running away with the theory that Margarita was a malicious person maybe a little too far, and too fast. I had little real evidence to support it, other than the psychological picture I'd built up of the woman. A woman driven to succeed in order to fill the void she'd created in her own life by not trusting people, or giving them a chance to really get to know her. Hmm…

"Don't touch anything!" Miguel was back.

I wouldn't, was what I thought; "I haven't," was what I said.

He added officiously, "Captain Alfredo says we are to lock up the store, and I am to take you back to your house."

"But I wanted to…" *quick, think, Cait*, "…take another look at his crime scene photographs, back at the station."

I need to see Bud again.

Miguel hesitated. "But Captain Alfredo said…"

I smiled. Beamed, in fact, and gently touched Miguel on the arm. "I'm sure that Al won't mind. He let me look through the case file last night, and he even read me his notes. He won't mind me taking another look, I'm sure. I'll wait there for him, at his office. It'll save you the trouble of having to drive me all the way out to the *Hacienda Soleado*. I'm guessing he wants you to go back to the station to check on the prisoner, right?"

Miguel hesitated. "You are correct. I have to give the prisoner food, and make sure that he is still secure." He puffed out his chest. It was clear he was proud that Al had put such trust in him. "If it was alright for you to see the file last night, I am sure it will be alright today. He has added nothing to it."

Having managed to get Miguel to agree to take me to the police station, I didn't want to waste any time – nor give him the chance to change his mind – so I stepped out into the dazzling sunlight once more, allowing him to lock the door behind us…for all the good that locking doors seemed to do in the area.

We walked toward the spa, which appeared empty, and there was Miguel's car…not a police car, but his own personal vehicle. At least, I assumed that was what it was. I must have looked puzzled.

Miguel smiled. "It is a good undercover car, yes?"

I smiled and nodded. To be fair, I would certainly never have guessed that the battered, aging, pale blue Honda Civic was being driven by a cop.

Miguel opened his trunk, rummaged about, then slapped a magnetic decal onto the passenger door.

"Now, it is not undercover anymore," he said, grinning like a magician who has just performed a spectacular trick. The badge on the decal matched the one on Al's white sedan, and Miguel appeared to be very proud of it. "This way we save money," he explained. "Captain Alfredo allows me to claim expenses for the miles I do when the badge is on – when I am on official business – but if I take the badge off, I can drive to collect my daughters from school in Bucerias…from wherever I might be."

Once we were on our way, Miguel pointed out the blue flashing light that he could put onto the roof of his vehicle if he had to drive to an emergency, but he explained that didn't happen very often…which appeared to disappoint him.

He was a careful driver, taking more time than Al would have done to deliver us to our destination, but I was glad for that little delay because it allowed me to observe Miguel alone, without his brother Rutilio's presence dominating him.

His car was full of symbols of his Catholicism: a rosary hung from the rear-view mirror, a little prayer card was taped to the dashboard, and a plastic model of the Madonna wobbled precariously above the glove box on the passenger side.

I observed, "You're a man of faith."

Miguel nodded. "It is my faith that sustains me. In difficult times, in happier times. I named my firstborn for the angels and the roses, and now she sleeps with the angels, and every week her mother and I place roses on her grave. She is with her God. She was a good girl. An innocent girl. I know she is with Him."

His faith might have been firm, but his voice trembled with emotion as he spoke.

I decided to follow the path I'd begun with. "Al told me that you revived a local custom and held a crucifix of Requiem Masses in your late-daughter's honor. That speaks highly of your dedication."

"This is true," said Miguel gravely. "We held them on December 7, the day before the Feast of the Immaculate Conception. Poor Margarita, she helped us a great deal. She made the floral arrangements for the church here in *Punta de las Rocas*, and she came with me to the Church of Our Lady of Guadalupe in PV to make her displays there. They were beautiful. Roses…of course. White ones, for the purity of my poor daughter. In all four churches. She sent the flowers with my wife and daughters for them to arrange in the church where they worshipped, and when my other brother – another brother, not Rutilio – came to collect our mother, to drive her to her home village, they had bunches of flowers to take with them."

How terrible. Death…and decay.

I felt the man's anguish, but knew I had to take my chance to build as deep an understanding of him as possible. "It must have been a very sad day for you all, Miguel."

"It was sad…though not as sad as the day we knew we had lost her. It was a day that allowed us all to remember her, and to celebrate that she was at peace with God. I, and all my family, discuss this often: my baby is at one with her Master…we should be happy for her. So it was also a happy day, in a way."

"I expect a lot of people took part in the services?"

"Oh yes…everyone in *Punta de las Rocas* attended one of the two local services. Margarita closed her store to be able to help me in Puerto Vallarta, and Rutilio even closed his restaurant for the night. He was so sad…so angry at whoever it was who had killed my baby. He lost interest in his business at that time. It is why he is still struggling now. It is why he had to give up his apartment in Bucerias and move in with my family. We love to have him, of course, because our mother is pleased to have her pretty baby boy with her. When God closes a door, He opens a window. It is always this way. We must pray to see His plan for us. If we pray enough, His Will becomes clear."

The poor man.

Upon our arrival at the unusual municipal building that served three purposes, Miguel let us in through the rear entrance to the police office, thereby avoiding the cells where Bud was housed. I was grateful for that because I didn't want Miguel to see Bud and I meet face to face – it had been difficult enough to mask my emotions in front of Al…I didn't want to have to go through that whole performance again.

I asked for directions to the washroom and found it to be clean and well decorated with dried flowers; I wondered if the arrangements had been supplied by Margarita. Refreshed, I rejoined Miguel in Al's office and sat down, picking up the case folder from Al's desk, as though to study it.

"If you need to get on with other duties, like feeding the prisoner, don't let me stop you," I said…as casually as possible.

Miguel thanked me, then headed off in the direction Al had taken when he'd gone to his apartment the night before. When he returned, sometime later, he looked at me and said, "I do not know why I am feeding that dog. He does not deserve it."

He's innocent, and I love him, was what I thought; "You must look after him properly, or the *Federales* will want to know why you didn't," was what I said.

Miguel laughed. "The *Federales*? They will show him no mercy. He won't be silent with them, as he is with us, for long; they have ways of ensuring they get the truth." His ominous words stung my heart. He might have been a religious man, but Miguel didn't seem to carry charitable feelings toward Bud. Maybe he was more the "eye for an eye" type of Christian than the "turn the other cheek" kind.

"There was a phone call that I answered," I lied. "I don't know who it was, or what they said exactly, but I heard the words '*niño enfermo*' and '*escuela*'. Does that mean something to you?"

Miguel looked panic-stricken. "My girls. The school. There must be a problem. I must go. You will come with me."

"Oh, no, Miguel…don't you worry, I'll stay here and work on this case file. You go and attend to your girls." He didn't seem keen to leave me. I smiled warmly. "I'll be fine. I'll just stay here and, if necessary, I know where the washroom is. I'll wait here for Al and tell him where you are when he comes to collect me. Don't give me another thought." I hated to trick him and cause him to worry about his daughters, but it was my only chance to get to see Bud.

It was clear that the poor man was desperate to get away, and I all but steered him to the door. As soon as I saw him disappear in his car down the track toward the road, I tried the handle of the door that led to the area where the cells were located.

It was open.

I pulled at it, peered inside, and saw Bud, sitting on his straw mattress on the floor, eating bread.

The most wonderful sight I've seen since yesterday morning.

I rushed in, causing Bud to look up…and drop his so-called "meal".

I whispered, "It's okay, we're alone," as I reached the cage.

Bud didn't move. He looked behind me, all around, and motioned that I should be quiet. We both listened. As I strained my ears, I noticed that he looked older, and much more gaunt, than he had the day before: his silvery beard had grown in a little and the stubble made him look haggard…almost sick. I know it's not possible to acquire prison pallor in a day, but I could have sworn he was paler than when we'd arrived.

"Are you sure?" he mouthed.

"Yes," I replied quietly. "Are you okay?"

Stupid question, Cait.

"I'm fine," he replied very softly. He pushed himself upright as he spoke. "You?"

Oh Bud.

I reached through the bars to touch him, and we held each other as best we could, just for a moment.

"You've been smoking," he said.

I pulled away.

What?

I hissed, "You're locked up in a Mexican prison, accused of a murder you didn't commit – about to be carted off to Guadalajara…where the cells are full of drug dealers who'd love nothing more than to see you dead in a matter of hours – and the first thing you want to talk about is me smoking? Are you nuts?"

Bud's voice was calm. "You promised you'd stop, Cait. I need you to be healthy, to be alive, to live with me. I need you,

Cait Morgan. That's what I'm saying. I've…I've been thinking about us – about life – a lot in here, Cait…so it didn't come out right. I love you." He smiled.

I smiled back. I could feel the tears welling, but I refused to lose control.

"Bud, I don't know how long we've got, so I have to tell you a lot of stuff – ready?" He nodded.

I filled him in. He nodded as he listened.

When I finished he asked, "So nothing by way of a name from Jack about who he might have gotten in touch with?" I shook my head. "And no one's approached you to make themselves known to you as someone who is working with CSIS, or the FBI, or the Gang Task Force?" Again I shook my head. He cursed under his breath. "What do they know, or think they know, about me?"

"You speak enough English to be able to say 'No police', and you're possibly a hit man working on behalf of someone else. That's it. By the way, why did you say 'No police' to Serena?"

"If you mean that woman who started screaming when she saw me, what I said was, 'No. Police.' I meant her to understand that I was the police, but she didn't get that, I guess. Then I thought it best to follow protocol and go silent. It keeps it out of the official channels that way, so thanks for getting hold of Jack, even though that might not have helped. Tell Sheila to tell him I hope he gets well soon." He looked…*thoughtful.*

Of course he's not panicking…he's Bud.

"I'm doing my best to work out who did it, Bud. I've got a lot of leads, but…there's something weird about this place. It's lovely, and it's got the normal tensions you find when there's a rich immigrant population rubbing along with a poorer indigenous one, but there's something under the surface. Something's not right. It reminds me of Alice in Wonderland, or

Through the Looking-Glass, where nothing is as it should be, or what it seems. At least, that's what it feels like at the *Hacienda Soleado*. It's all…off. Everyone seems so keen to help Al identify you before the *Federales* show up. He's a nice enough guy: bright, diligent, and ambitious…but I cannot fathom what it is about him that makes everyone want him to succeed in front of the *Federales*. It's weird."

We both sighed. I looked at poor Bud. "Bud, what can I do? I have to get you out of here. Are you sure you shouldn't talk? What about when Al ships you off to the *Federales*? What if I haven't been able to solve it by then? It could be terribly dangerous for you." My heart was pounding.

"As long as no one knows who I am, I'll be as safe as…anyone would be," replied Bud.

Was that a slight tremor in his voice?

He shook his head, almost like Marty does when he's been for a swim. "You're doing a great job, Cait. But, listen – I should tell you not to dig, because you're looking for a vicious killer. But…I also know that anything I might say won't stop you…so, have you got something you could carry as a…weapon?"

I pulled the flashlight that Tony had given me the night before out of my purse. "It's heavier than my hairspray," I said. I hadn't mentioned the break-in at the place where I was staying, because I didn't want Bud to worry, so understood why he looked confused. "I'll use it if I have to," I added, looking as fierce as possible.

Bud smiled sadly. "Cait, please be careful. I need you. Not just now, when I'm in trouble; I need you forever…"

"Hey – I told you there's to be no talk of marriage until September at the earliest, a year from when you first mentioned it. So don't start with it now. This isn't the time…nor the place." I grinned the best I could.

Bud hissed, "What's that?"

We'd both caught the sound of tires on gravel.

I said, "That's Al…parking up. Gotta go. Love you."

I took one last look, dashed out and hung a right, which brought me to the community hall area of the building. I was desperate to find a reason for being there, so stood in front of a large, framed piece of parchment that bore a huge red wax, beribboned seal. I gave it my attention, and read it through.

A moment later, Al was at my shoulder. I jumped. "I didn't hear you arrive," I said, feigning shock. "You seem to enjoy making a habit of startling me." I grinned.

Al smiled back. "You like it?" he asked, nodding at the framed parchment.

"The lettering is very beautiful, and it looks old."

"It is our charter from the Dubois García family, or, as you can see," he pointed at a portion of the writing, "the García García family. They were quite wonderful, and we have to thank them for all that *Punta de las Rocas* is today."

As he spoke I pretended to listen, but allowed my eyes to play over the delightful piece of history, which spoke of land ownership, of the unusual idea of property passing from woman to woman as well as from man to man, and of how all the García García offspring were to be treated equally. Clearly, as Al was telling me – yet again – the family had been well intentioned and farsighted in their plans for their municipality.

Finally, he asked, "Did you find what you were looking for?"

Careful, Cait. "How do you mean?"

"At Rutilio's, or at Margarita's, or here, in my office?" He seemed angry for some reason.

I considered my reply. "I think I'm beginning to understand Margarita a little better, and I think that the theft of the photographic equipment from her store is significant."

Knowing that Al had had feelings for the dead woman made it impossible for me to get an objective answer from him about whether Margarita might have been capable of blackmail, so there was no point asking.

"We had some luck on that aspect," he said.

"Really? What? Have you found something?"

"I think so." Al put his hand into his pocket and pulled out a digital memory card, of the type used in cameras. "I was on my way back from the hospital when Miguel phoned me about the theft at the flower shop. I wasn't able to speak to either Tony or Callie; they are both still in a dangerous condition, the doctors say, and Juan asked me to leave him with Margarita – which I don't understand...but I am not a father. Since I was alone, and had the time, I drove to Margarita's store, saw the damage, and had an idea: if someone stole the photographic equipment, maybe they just made the rest of the mess to make it appear as though they didn't know exactly what they wanted. I also knew that Margarita always kept some photographic supplies in her van. I got the keys and found this in the glove box. Would you like to see what's on it?"

"Absolutely. But do you have the sort of camera it's used in?"

"I do," replied Al. "It's an old one we used to take to crime scenes to take official photographs. Now we don't need to do that – we use our phones – but I am sure this will work in it. Let's go back to my office. It's in a cabinet there, somewhere."

Moments later we were head to head, looking at a small screen, showing expertly composed photographs of birds at rest, wild flowers on the cliffs, and waves crashing against rocks. The pictures were beautiful, but none of them showed an illicit embrace, a drug deal going down, or an illegal – or even worrisome – act of any sort. In fact there were hardly any photographs with human beings in them at all...as in the photographs I'd seen at her store. It was clear that Margarita had loved sunrises, and sunsets, because many of the shots were taken at that time. In a few, she'd used her bicycle wheels to frame an otherwise plain subject; with some it was the contrast of blurred images in the foreground with sharp ones in the distance that made a shot work…with others it was the reverse. She was a good photographer. As we clicked through her work, I could tell it was a difficult process for Al, but we kept going.

"Oh look, someone's got a van just like Margarita's," I said, as I clicked through several shots that had clearly been taken in rapid succession.

In the foreground of the shots were glittering waves, touched by the first light of day, crashing against the huge, pointed formation of reddish rocks which had inspired the name of the area. In the background was the winding coastal road, upon which there was a little white van, just like the one that Margarita drove.

I observed, "It's a shame it got in the way." Clearly the photographer had thought the same thing because she'd taken at least half a dozen more shots of the same scene even after the vehicle had driven out of sight…the effect of the light on the water slightly different in each one.

We soon realized we were looking at the first photographs we'd seen for the second time. "She was so good at this, but there's nothing out of the ordinary here," said Al sadly. "I had thought that maybe she'd seen something – or someone – she shouldn't have…" He struck his desk with his fist in frustration. "If only that man would talk!"

Clearly Al had considered the possibility that Margarita had known something, or had photographed something, that might have led to her murder. However, it was equally clear that he still firmly believed that Bud was the one who had killed her.

If I'm going to help Bud, I need to think.

"Al, could you do me a favor, please?" I sighed. "I know this is a difficult time for you, and I want to help with your inquiries all I can, but I could really do with some quiet time. Is there any chance I could just take half an hour, in a comfy chair, in your apartment? It would save me the trouble of going all the way back to Henry's place. I just need to think. I need to consider what the drugging of Tony and Callie and the break-in at the store might mean. Would that be okay?"

"You mean you have to work out who might have done those things, when that man is still locked up in there?" he snapped. I nodded. "Sure, let me show you through. I'll set you up with a beer, and you can have some thinking space."

"No, no beer, thanks, but a couple of bottles of water would be great. I'm finding that all this humidity, and the perspiring that goes with it, is making me thirsty, and I don't want to let you down by drinking beer and not being at my best."

A few minutes later I was settled in a corner chair, which was obviously where Al sat to read at night…given its proximity to a small table that was covered with books and papers, and a reading lamp. He opened the windows and turned on a ceiling fan, as well as a fan that sat on a table, and another that stood in the corner of the room.

I was grateful, because I had a cold bottle of water, a head full of information, an aching desire to work out what on earth was going on in *Punta de las Rocas*…and an excellent place to do just that.

Al paused before he left me. "I'll give you a shout if I get any news from the hospital. I'm hoping that maybe Callie or Tony can shed some light on who might have drugged them, and, of course, I'll let you know if my prisoner talks. You go ahead, Cait Morgan; I've read everything you have ever written, so I know that some of your methods are unusual. Give it your best…come up with an explanation, and then come tell me what it is. Okay?" He half-smiled, but concern played around his eyes.

"Okay, I'll do my best," I replied.

As he pulled the door closed behind him, he muttered – in Spanish, "It had better be good."

Odd.

Tea Time

I woke with a start when Al touched my shoulder. "You were tired. I let you sleep," he said quietly.

"What time is it?" I checked my watch. It was gone five. "What happened? I've been asleep for over an hour…I didn't mean to drop off." I panicked.

Bud hasn't the time for me to be napping.

I'd meant to do some deep thinking…to let my mind float in a technique I've used before called "wakeful dreaming", but my body had let me down. And I had let Bud down; I was keenly aware that his time in the relative safety of Al's cells was ticking away.

I jumped up, and immediately regretted moving so quickly. My mouth was parched; I drank from the bottle Al had given me earlier…it was warm, but at least it was wet. Somewhere on the edge of my consciousness was a sliver of a thought. A remembrance from a dream. What was it? It was a question I had to ask...who?

Think, Cait.

"I'm sorry, Al, I've let you down. I didn't mean to sleep. I've wasted time. I need to talk to the people from the *Hacienda Soleado* who were on the spot at the crime scene, and to Bob and Maria too. But I have no way of getting to either place. Could you help me out? Oh – and is there any news about the Booths? What have I missed while I've been asleep?"

Al looked at me and shook his head slowly. He looked tired. "The doctor at the American hospital says that Callie Booth has woken but has no idea what happened. She took Dorothea's sleeping pill, and from half an hour after that, everything was a blur. That is the good news."

Oh-oh…

He continued. "The sad news is that Tony has died."

"Tony's dead?" I grappled with the news that the young man who'd appeared to be so full of life the previous day was…gone. "What happened?"

"He never regained consciousness. I am partly to blame." Al's eyes were red-rimmed; he'd been crying.

"I don't see why you're blaming yourself."

Al shook his head slowly. "Last night, when you left to walk to Casa LaLa, I stayed with Tony and we had a few drinks together. The doctor says…he says it is because Tony had alcohol in his system that he died. Callie had not drunk anything, so she survived. Though…she does not see that as her good fortune – having been told that her husband has died…on top of her best friend being murdered."

"But…the blame falls upon the person who doped them both, not you." Al looked away from me. "Is there anything else?"

I hardly dare ask.

"The doctor at the other hospital, the Mexican hospital – where I left Juan this afternoon – has called me to tell me that Juan had to be ejected from the mortuary because he would not leave his daughter's body. He did not speak to her in life, and I know that this hurt Margarita a great deal – so his actions have…puzzled me greatly. I will also admit it has made me angry."

You look it.

He added, "Miguel has telephoned me from his girls' school to tell me that they are quite well, and to thank you for passing on the message, but to say you must have…misunderstood, because the school did not call the police station."

Al let that sink in for a moment, then added, "Other than all of that – as if it wasn't enough – I have been in my office attending to my normal duties, one of which, sadly, means I have to go out shortly. I need to visit a local family. A niece of theirs, who lives about fifty miles from here, has just been found dead. She ran away from home a few days ago, after an argument with her father. Her parents thought she would go to stay with a friend, then come home. The *Federales* found her body this morning, but they do not know exactly when she died. Maybe a day before she was found. It appears she was the latest victim of the Rose Killer. The news of the killing has broken, but the victim's identity has not been revealed to the public yet…and I must speak with her aunt and uncle. I think that someone in their family will have told them already, but – although this is a case for the *Federales* – I can perform my community duties and visit them, to show them respect."

Poor Al. Poor family.

"I'm so sorry, Al. That's good of you. Thoughtful."

"Duty…and care. The family lives in the village near the *Rocas Hermosas* Resort, so I propose that I take you to Rutilio's. I know that many of the people from the *Hacienda Soleado* will be there to eat this evening because, of course, *Amigos del Tequila* cannot open tonight without Tony, and it seems that the FOGTTs choose to eat outside their homes most days, so they have arranged to eat at Rutilio's tonight. Even an ill wind can blow good for some, it seems; Miguel says Rutilio is very excited because this group of people doesn't usually eat at his place. He has called his brother to say he's going to take his chance to impress them all." Al rolled his eyes. "Is that a good plan for you?"

His voice was flat, which wasn't surprising, but there was still anger beneath the sadness.

I agreed to his plan, so – once again – we sped off toward the sea. This time it was still light, and there was a strange greenish glow in clouds that had been bubbling on the horizon when I'd eaten brunch at Rutilio's, which now filled the sky. Layer passed across layer, some the palest greenish gray, some thunderous and blue-black…the fading sun streaming through fleeting gaps. The humidity signaled a probable storm, and I could almost smell the electricity building in the air. When we reached the resort, Al stopped in front of Bob's Bodega, and I got out of the car. As he pulled away, I walked toward Rutilio's Restaurant, where, sure enough, the full complement of FOGTTs was all present and correct. It was as though they operated like a flock.

A murder of crows?

My arrival brought mild interest but no cheer to the group, intent as it was upon discussing the terrible tragedies that had befallen the locality. Rutilio had pulled tables into a grouping so everyone could sit together, and there was a spare seat for me between Greg and Frank.

Oh joy.

I accepted the seat and Ada poured me a cup of greenish tea. It seemed incongruous, to say the least. I thanked her for her thoughtfulness, sipped at the tea – which tasted as disgusting as I'd feared – and I asked Rutilio for a bottle of water as quickly as I could get his attention.

He was red in the face and shouting at the two serving girls, who seemed to work the same hours he did. They all appeared to be rushing about without achieving a thing.

He's knocking himself out for the FOGGTs.

With the puzzling pots of tea finally giving way to cocktails, served alongside chips and salsa, I accepted a chilled *Pacifico* as well as my water from Rutilio, declined a glass, and sipped from the beer bottle…once I'd emptied the water bottle. Jean George didn't seem impressed by my presence – nor by my choice to drink beer – but impressing her wasn't on my to-do list that evening. In fact, given the stinky look she'd shot at me when we first met, it wasn't ever likely to be. I still had no idea why she'd been so snotty. After all, everyone else had been quite welcoming.

The conversations around the tables ebbed and flowed, as they always do within a group. Shock, disgust, sadness, worries about how *Amigos del Tequila* could continue without a chef – were all unsurprising topics. I managed to remain noncommittal, nodding when required, but not really participating. Frankly, I was impressed that these people – who obviously spent a great deal of time in one another's company – still had so much to talk about. And, boy, could they talk.

I paid attention to the dynamics within the group: I watched them chatter while I sipped my beer – *my first of the day, delicious!* – and gathered my thoughts.

At the farthest end of the table, I heard Dorothea banging on about how terrible it was that the horrible man in prison must have rushed in and killed Margarita without even taking the time to even talk to her.

Good grief…stupid woman.

Then I thought about what Dorothea had just said in a different way.

Context, Cait.

Of course – that wasn't how it happened.

I'd been focused on trying to work out who could have entered the flower shop while I'd been observing it. I'd become completely caught up in the idea that the whole incident had begun when Bud had left the apartment, because – for me – that's when it had begun. But all my thinking about the event had lacked true context – a context that included more variables than Bud's part in it.

You're the one who's stupid, Cait.

The entire series of events could have begun any amount of time earlier. There was no real reason to suppose that the killer had entered the store and killed Margarita immediately. Yes, her throat must have been slashed just a few moments before Bud entered her store, but the killer could have been in there with her for some time.

Why is this only occurring to you now, Cait?

My first visit to Margarita's store had presented me with a picture of an attack that hadn't involved much of a struggle. I'd interpreted this to mean that Margarita had been surprised by the attack…maybe hadn't even seen the knife coming, because it came from behind. But…what if she'd been in conversation with her killer…facing them, and not suspecting that they meant her harm? Yes…I had to reconsider the whole series of events leading up to Bud's discovery of Margarita's body from much earlier than just a few minutes beforehand.

Right…do that, Cait.

I felt compelled to remove Callie and Tony Booth from my list of possible suspects – given that they'd subsequently both been drugged – but that still left a lot of folks in the running.

Looking around the table I realized that maybe someone who'd been on the spot had seen something useful after all. They just hadn't been asked the right questions, about what they'd seen within the right time frame.

Purely by chance there was a lull in the conversations when I asked, "I don't suppose any of you saw anyone in the street, or going into Margarita's store, within the half an hour before she was killed, did you? And I mean anyone…even someone you didn't know or recognize." I heard Jean gasp.

Jean George glanced at her husband. "Dean and I had been walking on the beach together for at least an hour before we arrived at the flower shop, hadn't we, honey-pie? So we couldn't have seen anyone go inside the store at all."

Dean nodded, but no one else answered, because, at just that moment, Al arrived.

I was annoyed that Al's arrival meant that seats were rearranged to accommodate him – allowing folks the chance to shift the topic away from my question – and then the food appeared. We all sampled different items from the large platters that Rutilio had decided to serve to us family style. It wasn't bad food…it just seemed as though it was all made from roughly the same ingredients encased in different things: chicken and pork; red, yellow, and green peppers; refried beans; onions and tomatoes…all served in different proportions but all – basically – tasting the same. To be fair, despite the fact that I was rethinking the entire case, I enjoyed everything I ate, and some of it was very tasty indeed.

Maybe Miguel had a point when he said that his brother prepared good food. Though I suspected that Rutilio had taken the decision to cater to the tourist palate just a bit too far, and we were missing out on many wonderful local flavors, sauces, and exciting dishes.

As I ate, and thought about the people I was sharing my meal with, I caught a snippet of something that Dorothea was hissing at Greg in a whisper. "…color looks great in the bottle…never know," she said. My mouth was full of chicken fajita when it came to me in a flash.

Of course, maybe that's what you're up to…bottles versus barrels. Callie's notes…the calculations.

"I'd like to make a toast," said Al, breaking across my train of thought. He was standing at what had now, de facto, become the head of the table. He cleared his throat. "This isn't going to be a normal sort of toast, but I think you'll understand why I'm doing this if you'll give me a moment." There were shufflings, and a couple of nods and smiles. "When I first met Professor Cait Morgan, I spoke very highly of her." Smiles and nods were directed at me. "I was delighted when she said she'd help me look into the identity of Margarita's killer, because I have developed an admiration for her work as a part of my studies. I have read everything that she has published, and she is an excellent thinker and researcher." I was beginning to feel a bit embarrassed. "As some of you know, it was I who recognized her for who she is, because I had seen her photograph on her university's website." Nobody, myself included, seemed to have any idea what Al was rambling on about, and I wished he'd get to the point. "I visited that same website when I was in my office earlier today, and it was then I found out that at the end of the last academic year Professor Morgan was elected to her university's Roll of Honor for a second time."

I had no idea what was coming next, but I was squirming in any case because I hate being praised in public.

Al continued, undaunted. His expression was complex: a mixture of determination, anger, and...*sadness?*

Odd.

"To mark this, she was invited to a luncheon, which was followed by a ceremony where she was presented with a framed commemoration of her achievement." He pulled a roll of paper from his pocket, smoothed it out, and held it up for us to see. It was a color print of a photograph of me being presented with the item he'd just described. He turned the photograph so that everyone had a chance to look at it, which they did, most smiling in my direction afterwards, and trying to look gracious.

"I've also made an enlargement of a figure standing behind Cait Morgan."

Oh...no...

He unrolled the second photograph and held it up. I didn't need my glasses. I knew what it would show. There was Bud, smiling proudly and clapping, as I beamed into the camera.

Frank shouted, "That's him! The killer. In that photograph."

He was speaking on behalf of the entire group, and all eyes turned to me. I could feel my whole body tremble; I'd only ever felt that way once before in my life – when the cops dragged me out of my home, as the corpse of my ex-boyfriend lay on my bathroom floor.

I wanted to stand. I wanted to run away. I knew there was no point trying to hide my terror. I was rooted to the spot.

"Cait Morgan, you know the man in that cell, the one who killed Margarita. You have known his identity all along." Al's voice was as deep as when he'd been speaking Spanish. He was righteously angry – shaking almost as much as I was. "That man asked for flowers in the bodega – for you, I believe. You have inserted yourself into this case with the sole purpose of preventing us from discovering the identity of your murderous partner. I accuse you of drugging Tony and Callie Booth when you were at their home with me last night and, thereby, of killing Tony Booth. I accuse you of stealing Margarita's photographic equipment, which you spotted when you insisted upon visiting the crime scene with me last night. And I accuse you of doing all this to cover up your partner's vicious slaying of Margarita Rosa García Martinez because she could identify him as the Rose Killer." There was a table-wide gasp. "You have used me, and you have used and abused the friendship you have been shown by this community, to shield a merciless serial killer from the law. Please stand. I will now take you into custody, and you will be turned over to the *Federales* when they arrive tomorrow to collect your partner…in crime."

Oh…no…

I still couldn't move. My brain was struggling to process everything Al had said. He'd taken the step from truth to untruth without effort…and I could understand his reasoning – up to a point – but why on earth would he take the leap to believing that Bud was the Rose Killer?

People at the table were moving away from me so fast you'd have been forgiven for thinking I'd developed a highly contagious form of leprosy. Within a moment, I was the only person still seated.

Unfortunately, I knew there was enough truth in what Al had said that it might be impossible for me to prove the untruths.

I'm trapped. Literally, and figuratively.

There was only one thing I could do. I stood, picked up my purse, and said, "All I can say is that you are wrong, Al. Very wrong. About so many things. I won't say more than that for now."

As he led me to his car, I knew it would be a very different journey to the police station for me this time, and I wasn't at all sure what would happen when we got there.

Doing Time

Al drove from Rutilio's to the police station in record time. He didn't speak, nor did I; he was fuming, and I was terrified. The atmosphere was strained, to say the least. The silence continued when we arrived. Upon this viewing, the floodlit building looked forbidding rather than whimsical, and I wondered where Al would put me – the only cells I'd seen were where Bud was incarcerated, so I dared to hope I might at least be close to him. This thought sustained me as Al unlocked the doors to the main part of the police station.

Bud was up on his feet as soon as he saw us. His face conveyed almost nothing when he spotted my handcuffs…but one blink that lasted twice as long as it should have done betrayed his feelings to my trained eye.

"There's no way any charges will stick," I said loudly, as Al pushed me forward. "This man is not the Rose Killer, and you cannot prove otherwise. He did not kill Margarita, and he certainly didn't kill eight innocent young women over the last eight months. I know for a fact this is the first time he's been on Mexican soil for many years."

Al stopped pushing me. He looked me up and down and did the same to Bud. "I understand that you are trying to communicate a plan of action to your partner in crime, Professor Morgan. Once we leave this room, I will make sure to put you somewhere that will not allow you to confer and develop your cover story. So stop talking now!" His voice was rough with anger. "You have been very clever to encourage me to work out who this man is alone, without involving the *Federales*, and I have achieved that. You do not realize that I have people I can call upon. Others who, like me, are using their time to study to be able to better their careers: I have a friend who works in airport security who will one day have the qualifications that will allow him to advance. In the meantime, he's prepared to help a fellow student. I sent him this man's photograph – the one I found on your university's website. He is able to look at old information on the system, and he has found several photographs of this man. My friend has informed me that your partner has visited Mexico almost every month for the last year, using several different names, and traveling on several different passports. Why would a man do this? It cannot be for a good reason. I believe he's come here to kill, and kill again. He is the Rose Killer. That is why he asked about roses at the bodega. I am even beginning to wonder if poor Angélica Rosa was his first victim, or whether he has killed in other states before he began to visit ours. So there you have it, Cait Morgan. I know he's been in and out of Mexico, whatever you might say. As for what he's told you, or why you are with him on this trip – other than to cover for him, and to commit crimes on his behalf – I do not know. You can take that information to your cell with you, and make of it what you will. You will be taken to Guadalajara tomorrow afternoon. That's when they'll be coming for you both."

I didn't reply, because I was so shocked. Not just because of what Al had said, but because of Bud's reactions when he'd said it. Bud had dropped his shoulders. It doesn't sound like much, but it told me he was feeling…defeated.

It's all true – Bud's been secretly traveling to Mexico on a regular basis.

Al pushed me toward the main hall. Once there, he slammed the door between Bud and me. It was a horrible sound. So final. I suspected that the next time I saw him we'd both be in shackles and being hauled off by the *Federales* to the danger of a jail in Guadalajara.

Meanwhile, I was in the comparative safety of the municipal hall of *Punta de las Rocas*. Al locked me in a little room that looked more like a large confessional than a jail cell. Its wooden construction didn't suggest it would be impossible to escape, and the door had a metal grille in it, meaning I could look out into the great hall. Inside my cell, a cushioned bench ran along the outside wall, beneath a window, which I could tell was covered outside by a decorative iron cage. A table and chair stood against another wall. There was a large plain wooden crucifix on the wall above the table. That was it.

When Al had secured the door, he spoke to me through the grille. "I will bring you water later on. You'll be able to use the bathroom in my apartment, but I will accompany you and stand outside the door. There is no way to get out of my bathroom. I will treat you well while you are in my care. You're not going to have anything to complain about to the *Federales*. They'll be here after noon, tomorrow – hopefully by two. I suggest you get some sleep." He was addressing me more formally than he had done since we'd met, and his anger hadn't subsided.

"What is this place? This room I'm in?" I asked. Despite my circumstances, I couldn't help but be curious.

Al turned. "When he returned from his travels in America, when he was still quite a young man, this was the place where Juan Carlos García García lived, the eldest son of the Dubois García family, the man who granted lands to his family and made sure the community was well served. The true father of *Punta de las Rocas*. He was a simple man. This was all he needed."

How strange that he's so passionate about this man…even at a time like this.

Al walked away, turning off lights as he went, until I was completely alone in the dark. I allowed my eyes some time to adjust: there was no moonlight coming through the window, so it took a few minutes. I peered at my watch, but it was just a blur. I didn't have my glasses, because they were in my purse, which Al had taken from me. I told myself that it didn't really matter what the time was because I wasn't going anywhere…not until the following afternoon.

I was wide awake, adrenalin pumping around my system, and I couldn't do a single thing to help Bud, or myself. How had this happened? I gave it some thought. I could understand why Al – after discovering that Bud had been entering Mexico on a regular basis, using pseudonyms – would suspect him of being involved in something illegal…but why had Al decided that Bud was the Rose Killer? What was it about those cases that made him jump to that conclusion? Maybe the dates when Bud had been in the country tallied with the dates of the murders? Would that be all it would take? Not that it was an insignificant factor.

I sat at the little desk, held my chin in my hands, and recalled the online reading I'd done about the Rose Killer case. I closed my eyes a little and hummed…which helps with my recollection process. In my mind's eye I reread the newspaper articles, and quickly realized that the times of death – as well as the dates of death in some cases – had been set within pretty wide parameters, which, in this day and age of advanced forensic pathology, was…odd. I didn't know much about the Mexican system of coroners or medical examiners, nor anything about the sophistication of their techniques or equipment, but I assumed that once it had been established that they were dealing with a serial killer, they'd have put their very best people and resources on the case. Ascertaining time of death is one of the most basic requirements of most autopsies. I gave some thought to the factors that can adversely affect estimating an accurate time of death; I might not be an expert, but I know the basics. And that was the point: this was all very basic stuff.

If I'd had a pen and paper, I'd have made a list. But I didn't have those luxuries, so I made mental notes instead.

There are many ways of working out time of death.

Body temperature is one: the human body cools at a constant and predictable rate after death – 1.5 degrees per hour – until it reaches the temperature of its surroundings, which is why a rectal or liver temperature is taken as soon as possible after a body is found. Factors like ambient temperature will, of course, impact the calculations made, but, eventually, the body's temperature becomes less informative, because it's just the same as its surroundings.

That's when the reference point of rigor mortis is used: rigor also works in a fairly predictable manner, affecting different parts of the body at different times. Unfortunately, hot or cold conditions influence the onset of rigor…as does the amount, or type, of physical activity undertaken by the victim immediately prior to death. Also, rigor is of little use after thirty-six to forty-eight hours, because it's worn off by then.

That's why they'd had to use an analysis of stomach contents to work out when poor Angélica Rosa had died. It was their only reference point, and it showed that she'd died shortly after eating, which – according to her uncle Rutilio – had been about half an hour before she'd set off to walk home after work.

In the case of the second victim, they'd been able to use rigor mortis to work out when she'd died, but they'd come up with a very confusing result: the girl appeared to have died earlier than the multiple sightings of her.

Why am I worrying about the time of death of these girls?

Because you need to prove that Bud didn't kill them, and when they died might be critical.

Unfortunately, critical or not, the newspaper articles that dealt with victims three and onward hadn't revealed their time of death at all…only the presumed date of death.

If Bud had been in the country on those dates, then Al had a point – Bud had the opportunity to kill those girls. That's why the first two were so important: they were the only murders where I had access to more detailed information.

Angélica Rosa had been killed on November 1st and found on November 4th; I'd been up to my ears in grading at that time, and hadn't seen much of Bud at all.

Not helpful.

The second victim had been killed on Friday, December 7th, the day of Miguel's family's crucifix of Requiem Masses.

What a relief.

Bud and I had been at my School of Criminology Christmas party on December 7th. I'd taken photographs…I could prove to Al that Bud couldn't have been killing a girl in Mexico, because he'd been sipping warm beer in BC.

Yay!

The dates of the other murders had all been very general, which took me back to the issue surrounding times of death. So…I had to concentrate on getting Al to understand that Bud hadn't killed Margarita, and that meant working out who had.

I had to make the most of what I already knew. I could eliminate some people from being in the frame for Margarita's murder, but now I also had to consider whether Tony's killing had anything to do with Margarita's death, or if that was to do with the barrels and bottles issue…which I'd worked out in Rutilio's Restaurant.

It was confusing, to say the least. I needed a smoke…but I didn't have my purse. If I was going to make the most of my time, it would be a good idea to first use Al's washroom, then settle in for the night. I called out to my jailer, hoping he would hear me.

"Hello, Al? Could I use the washroom, please?" Nothing. I waited. And waited. Having decided to go, I really needed to go.

"Al? Can you hear me? I need the washroom, please." Still nothing. Eventually, I heard some clattering within the darkness of the municipal hall. "Is that you, Al?"

"Yes, who else would it be? What do you want?" Al sounded…yes, still angry.

"I really could do with using your washroom," I replied, sounding as desperate as I felt. "I called and called, but you didn't answer."

Clicks in the distance led to the hall being illuminated, then Al was outside my door. "I was speaking to the *Federales*. It was an important call. I'm here now." He placed the big, old iron key into the lock of the door. It squealed as it turned. "I will accompany you to my bathroom. Do not even think of trying to run away – the whole building is locked. You have nowhere to run. Just follow me." He pulled the door open, and I rushed out.

"I really need to get there quickly," I pleaded. Al picked up on my genuine distress and marched quickly to his apartment's bathroom, flung open the door, and ushered me in.

As I eventually ran the water to wash my hands, I looked around the room for anything that might be of use to me, or Bud. This being Al's own bathroom, I even dared to peep inside his medicine cabinet. Caffeine pills – possibly to help with late nights spent studying; a fair stock of Band-Aids – it looked as though he was as clumsy as me; a couple of bottles of over-the-counter antihistamine pills…that was it. I took stock of myself in the mirror. I was a blur, but basically a pasty blob, with tiny eyes. Cait Morgan…stop thinking that you're living in a looking-glass world and make some sense of all this stuff. I turned off the water and opened the door.

Al was right outside. "Use quite enough water, did you?"

I blushed, recalling his point about how all we visitors use too much of the precious resource.

Water…of course…

I dared, "The water supply for the *Hacienda Soleado* tequila-making plant, where does it come from? Who runs the manufacturing, or I suppose it's the distillation, operation? Is it Greg?"

Al glared at me. "He oversees it, with Juan, though it's none of your business." Any sense that Al and I were on the same side had clearly evaporated. I needed to make the most of the short walk back to my cell.

"Al, I know you're angry with me, but all I can do is ask that you believe me when I tell you that neither I nor the man you have incarcerated had anything to do with Margarita's death, let alone the Rose Killings. And, of course, I wouldn't even ask to be allowed to smoke in that wonderful, historic room you've put me in, but…is there any way I could please have the nicotine gum that's in my purse?"

Al stopped in his tracks and gave my request some consideration. I hoped that, as a smoker himself, he'd help me out. He shrugged. "Can't hurt," he replied gruffly.

"Oh, thanks ever so much, Al," I gushed. "It'll help me relax. If you dig around in my purse, you'll find it. You'll also find some notes I was making about Margarita's death and my phone, which has photos on it that can prove –"

He snapped, "Stop it, Professor Morgan. I will give you your precious gum to assuage your addiction – you won't be so lucky when the *Federales* are in charge of you, of course – but that's it. I will not buy into your 'tales' anymore. Now come on, back to your…accommodations." He grabbed my arm and more than steered me back into the little room, where he slammed the door and locked it, violently.

A few moments later he returned and pushed a pack of gum through the grille in the door. "Here – chew your jaw off. You'll be pleased to know that the *Federales* will come early; they will be here to collect you both around nine o'clock, tomorrow morning. I have spoken to the officer heading the Rose Killer case, and he will be coming here himself, straight from the place where they found the most recent victim. Make the most of your last few hours of comparative 'freedom'. It won't be long now until I can prove my worth as a detective."

When I'd checked my watch by the light in the bathroom, I'd seen that it was midnight.

Nine hours…that's all you have, Cait.

Nine hours to use my brain to work out what had really happened since Bud and I had arrived in *Punta de las Rocas.* I popped out a square of nicotine gum and chewed furiously. Within a few moments the craving for a cigarette had passed, and I knew that I'd be able to concentrate better without feeling the terrible pangs of my addiction, which had become very strong again, very quickly. I chastised myself for having given in to buying cigarettes at the airport – *was that just yesterday?* – and I saw again, in my mind's eye, the picture of the wonderful "In Search of Reason" on the *Malecón* in Puerto Vallarta. As I visualized myself clambering up Bustamante's unsupported ladder, the first clap of thunder boomed above my head. Seconds later I could hear fat drops of rain slap against the metal bars that encased the window. I opened the casement just a little and drew in deep breaths of the metallic air: rain on sunbaked dust smells wonderful, but it was all I had to smile about.

I lay on the cushioned bench in my little room and closed my eyes, releasing my thoughts to form themselves into a reasonable explanation of all the facts I'd gathered and observations I'd made. The answer had to be in there…somewhere.

Usually when I'm using the wakeful dreaming technique, my thoughts whirl about in no particular order to begin with, then various aspects of my findings gather themselves about a person or a place. This time, things went a little differently. I allowed the process to take the path it had chosen for itself, because, after all, that's the whole point, but it seemed to be leading me into a world where Edward Lear had laid his hands on everything I saw, and I felt uncomfortably like a very confused Alice.

First I see Bud…dear Bud. He's running around in his cell with a giant watch face hanging about his neck. He looks panic-stricken and shouts, "I'm out of time, I'm out of time!" He keeps bouncing off the bars of his cell, and, as he does so, they transform into giant rose stems, the thorns cutting into his flesh until he's covered in blood. But he doesn't stop running…around and around…bouncing and bleeding. I feel sorrow, and anguish, gripping my stomach.

Dorothea appears next, popping out of an exploding barrel, she's a red-cloaked giant, with a face painted green. She swooshes into the municipal hall demanding that Bud be hanged. Her voice makes the walls shake. She pumps her fists at the roof, which blow away to reveal dark thunderclouds. "Hang him, hang him!" she bellows, and a gallows appears in the corner of the hall, looming ominously, and growing by the minute.

Now I see myself pop into existence in the middle of the hall, surrounded by a group of menacingly tall men. Al, Frank, and Dean crowd around me. As they grow ever taller, I feel as though I am shrinking. The foliage on Dean's Hawaiian shirt springs to life and starts to grow independently of the man. Sinuous vines creep across the floor of the municipal hall, which disappears and transforms into Margarita's flower shop. Suddenly the vines blow apart, and the insubstantial flower shop is full of living blooms which are singing and weeping for

Margarita, who lies among them, broken into pieces…but alive. "My children, I love you all," she says, as she gathers as many of the living, singing, weeping flowers into her arms as she can.

I reach toward the woman, who I see has a golden scar running across her face, which she strokes proudly, but she turns away from me and screams to Al that he has to save her…he has to make her whole.

Al runs to her, his chest puffed out in his glittering dress uniform, which I somehow recognize as an ancient French general's style. He gathers the scattered pieces of Margarita together, but they keep slipping through his arms. He calls, in French, for Frank to help him…but Frank is drinking tea with Ada. They seem completely oblivious of everything that's going on around them…content to be in their own little world, with Ada pouring tea and Frank telling her how useless their children have turned out, but how much he loves her. Ada keeps pushing his hat off his head, telling him it's rude to wear it indoors.

I see a cigar in Frank's hand, but I can't smell the smoke, because all I can smell is an overwhelming scent of dampness…mold. I turn from the scene where Margarita had lain to see Greg Hollins curled up on a big, moldy cushion on the floor in front of me. He's leering up at me and offering me a pack of cigarettes…that I somehow know are made of rose petals dyed brown, not tobacco. "You'll enjoy them; they are exactly what I tell you they are...you know you want them." He speaks…greasily, with a sly look and a crooked smile. I push the packet, and him, away, and I turn again to try to…escape.

Jean George springs out of the ground in front of me. She scowls "We don't want you here!" She's screaming, but her voice is drowned out by another, more piercing scream. I know it's Serena. I'd recognize her scream anywhere. She flies into the room, a bird with a giant female head and a bill that's wide open.

She lands on top of Bud's prison cell, and her claws and beak try to reach him inside it. I run to chase the woman-bird away, but Al grabs me, drags me back to Henry's house in an instant, where he pushes open the front door with one finger and says, "You should lock your door, Cait. It's too easy for people to get inside."

"Leave her alone," shouts Ada Taylor, suddenly beside me. "She's a Canadian; she can't have done anything wrong."

"She is not Canadian," shouted Al. "Like me, she is nothing, she is no one. We have no home, people like us. We are not one thing, not another. Look," he points at my face, "she has no face. No identity. Look around – no one has a face!"

I look around, and I can see that Al is right; no one has a face. They are just blobs, with no bodies, no faces, no identities. One blob moves, and it immediately becomes Greg Hollins, but a new version of the man: this version is wearing a hat with corks dangling from it, and has the legs of a kangaroo. Now, instead of holding a pack of cigarettes, he's holding a bottle of tequila toward a blob I know to be Dorothea. "G'day Dotty, strewth, you're fair dinkum. Have some of this…" he says, in a comedic Australian accent.

Tony Booth appears next. He's in his chef whites, but instead of a head he has a *Día de los Muertos* skull, like the one popularized in the etching *La Calavera Catrina* by José Guadalupe Posada. His body is elongated in the same style, and he's tossing pepper around his kitchen and wailing, "I am going to ride the surf forever!" Beside him appears a weeping Madonna, who I know, instinctively, is his wife, Callie. She showers her dead husband with yellow sticky notes as she sings, "The numbers always tell our secrets."

Dean and Jean George rush past on a white horse, being chased by Juan Martinez in his blue pickup truck, which trails blood and water rather than exhaust. His arm is hanging from the window of his truck, and I can hear him screaming the name of his dead daughter.

Margarita magically appears, alive and whole, filling her little white van with gas at a gas station, but the tank is overflowing, gas pouring down the hill, which is, I somehow know, the hill upon which the municipal hall is built. Then her white van transforms into a horse, which is still white because it's made of ice. It rears up and gallops away, and I am now on its back. We pass grave after grave along the roadside until we reached Rutilio's Restaurant, which is floating on a pontoon out at sea, with fish swimming away from it in all directions.

I jump off the frozen horse and find myself behind Margarita's flower shop, inside a tiny box that's so small I can hardly move. Rutilio stands above me, pouring tequila into the box from a tiny little bottle that seems to pour forever. "Drink, drink, it is the good stuff – see, it is dark; that shows it has aged in the barrel."

"I don't like tequila – I hate it!" I cry as I burst out of the little box and stand in front of Rutilio, who's holding a giant bunch of white roses.

"For my dead niece, and for my dead friend." He weeps.

Bob and Maria are now beside him, their individual faces mixed in my mind into one. They are twins, male and female. Then Miguel appears, so very different from his brother. He slaps a big badge made of mirrored metal onto his brother's puffed chest. "Now he is my pretty baby brother policeman," he says. They all carry white roses.

Dorothea, appearing as a red cloud above us all, blows at our little group like a fierce wind, scattering the others away so that only Rutilio and I remain. The roses he clenches are white, his shirt red, and he's grinning so widely I think his head might split open. Then he begins to disappear…in a series of blinks, he and I are at his niece's grave, then at a church in *Punta de las Rocas*, then at a church in Puerto Vallarta, then back inside Margarita's flower shop. As we move from location to location he gets dimmer and dimmer, until all that's left is his chef hat, his teeth, and the white roses, all hanging in the air. Margarita's store evaporates, leaving Rutilio standing in front of the rear wall of his restaurant, where his remaining features disappear completely against the white of the wall.

I jumped up from the cushioned bench with a start. Of course! White roses, yellow roses, red roses, blood spatter, too much gas, the frozen horse, the flowers for four masses, and the Cheshire Cat. I was sure I knew who had killed Margarita, and why…except that – if I was right – they'd been in two places at once. I was so close…but…there seemed no way that I could be right about it all.

Time's Up!

With the morning light streaming through the window of my cell, and by screwing up my rested eyes to peer at my watch, I could make out that it was gone nine in the morning. Obviously my wakeful dreaming had become a full night of sleeping dreams…no wonder everything had seemed so complex and detailed – I'd been asleep for hours.

It dawned on me that the *Federales* should have already arrived. So…what was going on? I wondered if, maybe, the Mexican attitude toward timekeeping applied to the police force as well. Besides, it wasn't as though I was looking forward to their arrival. But…I needed to get to the washroom. Fast.

I popped a piece of gum into my mouth.

That's a bit fresher, but not much.

"Al. Al? Any chance of using the washroom, please?"

Al was outside my door immediately.

Good grief, he is always so stealthy.

"I wondered when you'd wake," he said thickly. "Though I don't know how you could sleep at all. You and…that man…have no shame. You don't seem to feel the weight of your guilt at all."

A riposte of any sort was beyond me, let alone one as acidic as I'd have liked, so I just contented myself with heading toward his bathroom as fast as I could.

When I was as cleaned up as I could be, I opened the bathroom door and said, "Is there any chance I could use the brush that's in my purse? And maybe the lipstick?" Al was about to explode, I could tell. "I don't want to use the lipstick to make myself look better. I don't think that's possible. But my lips have dried out, and they're cracking." I licked them as I spoke. "It would help. Please?"

Al tutted loudly, slammed the bathroom door, and shouted, "Don't move!" as he stomped away.

I looked at the woman in the mirror, and my mother looked back at me. I shook my head at my mirror-self. When had I become my mother's age? I didn't have my glasses on, but my eyes were rested enough that I could see many wrinkles…most from laughter, some from frowning at students, or worrying over grading. Probably many of them from smoking too much, for too long. As I chewed my nicotine gum and thought about how I yearned for Bud and I to be together, I promised my mirror-self that if we got out of this, I'd never smoke again…and I'd stop drinking…and I'd lose fifty pounds.

I can do it.

Al knocked on the door and opened it a crack. "I'm passing things to you," he announced. He handed me my hairbrush and my lipstick.

"Can I have my specs too, so I can see what I'm doing?" It seemed reasonable. I could hear Al rooting about in my purse, and my glasses appeared. "Thanks," I said.

Five minutes was all it took, but I felt like a new person when I emerged – ready to face my accusers and the rest of the world. Which was just as well, because when Al and I walked back into the municipal hall, all the FOGTTs were there.

"Good," said Al, unsurprised. "You're early."

I was puzzled. My watch clearly said it was ten minutes before ten; if the *Federales* had been due at nine, what exactly was it that the FOGTTs were early for? I couldn't help but speak up.

"What's going on, Al? Why are these people here, and what's happened to the *Federales*? They should have been here nearly an hour ago. Aren't they coming?"

I can hope.

"They have ten minutes," snapped Al. "They'll be on time."

Am I losing my mind? was what I thought; "But my watch says it's ten to ten," was what I said.

Dorothea boomed, "Haven't you changed it?"

Whatever my situation, I wasn't going to take that from her. "Yes, Dorothea, I have changed my watch. I changed it when I flew into Puerto Vallarta. They announced the local time, and the temperature, on the flight. We're two hours ahead of Vancouver here."

The bossy woman snapped, "No, we're not. You don't know anything, do you? You come here, poking your nose into our business and doing terrible things, but you have no idea how the world really works." She puffed out her chest – encased this time in magenta – and announced, "Here in *Punta de las Rocas*, we're in Nayarit. And Nayarit is an hour behind PV. Everyone knows that."

I could see Ada and Frank Taylor, and Dean and Jean George, nodding in agreement with the annoying Dorothea. Greg ignored her. I sensed that something had happened between him and Dorothea – something had made him angry with her.

Not unusual, in all probability.

At least now I understood why Dorothea had said that Margarita's murder had taken place at eleven…I must have heard a clock from outside Nayarit chime twelve just before I heard Serena screaming…and I also understood how the Rose Killer could have been in two places at the same time.

What a relief! Gotcha!

I snapped, "Whatever the time is, why are you all here?"

I think that's a fair question.

"I invited them," replied Al gruffly. "I want everyone who has been touched by the death of Margarita to be here when the *Federales* come to take him, and you, away."

You want an audience, so you can show off.

He added, "You can wait in your cell until the Federales arrive. I have put bread and coffee there for you. I must make myself ready."

After Al locked me into my little room once again, I consumed my breakfast with gusto. Still glugging coffee, I peered into the hall, where I could see Ada and Frank with their heads together. They – more than anyone else – seemed to be feeling very uncomfortable about the whole situation, and I wondered if they'd stick it out. Meanwhile, from my vantage point behind the grille, I could see Dean and Greg hauling chairs into a semicircle facing the end wall of the municipal hall. Ada shooed Frank away to help out, and she sidled toward the door of my personal prison.

Once she was nearby, Ada whispered, "How are you doing?"

How on earth do you think I'm doing? was what I thought; "Not too bad, considering, thank you, Ada," was what I said. It wasn't poor Ada's fault that I was in this state…I couldn't take it out on her. That wasn't fair.

She continued, speaking rapidly, "I talked to Frank last night about whether we should get in touch with the Canadian embassy – or someone like that – about you being arrested. I even talked to my son about it, you know, on the internet. They both said I should leave it up to Al. But I'll do it if you like. I could go outside and phone them right now. I put the number into my cellphone. Would you like me to do that?"

My heart softened even further toward the woman. "Let's see how things go. If I shout out to you for help as they drag me away, maybe you could make that call?"

Ada nodded nervously and scuttled away. I wondered, just for a fleeting moment, if she was the operative in the area that Jack had referred to. He would likely know her from his time in the area, and – if she was undercover – she was making a good job of it. I could tell from Ada's body language as she made her way back toward Frank that she hoped no one had seen her, but I also noted that Al's eagle eyes hadn't missed a thing. He cast a suspicious glance toward Ada as she began to help out with the chairs. While the seating arrangements were being made in the hall, as if for a civic meeting, the rest of the gang showed up. By the time the *Federales* arrived, everyone was there: the FOGTTs had been joined by Bob and Maria, Rutilio, Serena, and, of course, Miguel and Juan, who arrived together.

Everyone looked grim, but none as grim as the *Federales.*

I hadn't been sure what to expect; what I saw was an intimidating sight. As Al greeted their arrival by saluting and fussing about them, I could see him – more clearly than ever – as a relatively young man, with the softness and eagerness of the graduate student who loves art, literature, and poetry etched on his face. His federal colleagues, however, were a different breed altogether. Militaristic in appearance, they were dressed in black, wearing ball caps, Kevlar vests, and gun belts that dwarfed Al's. Several of them had automatic weapons slung over their shoulders, as well as pistols in holsters. They were all business. Five of them surrounded a shorter man, who looked as dapper as he did forbidding in a more formal, but still highly militarized, uniform. If the number of gold stripes on his uniform, and the uprightness of his stance, were anything to go by, this man was pretty high up the food chain. I guessed he was in charge, and the way that Al, Miguel, and the other cops were deferring to him made that clear.

What was also clear was that Al was setting the stage in such a way that he would be the star. The body language among the *Federales* told me that they were being faced with a situation they had not expected. They'd marched through the main entrance to the municipal hall, so they hadn't seen Bud in his cell, and no one seemed to have noticed the room I was in, let alone me in it. Unfortunately, I couldn't hear anything that was being said, because everyone was way down at the far end of the hall.

Al came to the door of my little room, unlocked it, and said pointedly, "They are here. Don't make a fuss, or they'll probably shoot you."

Lovely.

He put handcuffs on me, with my hands in front of my body, led me to a chair set to one side of the main group, and sat me down. Miguel was next to me, so close I could smell the tobacco on his clothes. I chewed my gum and wondered if I usually smelled that bad. Al brought Bud from his cell. Upon Bud's arrival, two of the *Federales* stood beside him, one on either side, as he slumped onto a chair.

I looked at Bud, now no more than ten feet away from me. He looked awful. Al stood and cleared his throat. This was obviously an important moment for him, and he looked nervous. He began in Spanish, translating into English.

He introduced the cop with all the braid on his jacket as the man who'd been heading up the Rose Killer case. He also introduced the head guy's right-hand man, who was the slyest looking of the bunch. With this man by his side, his boss could afford to sit and look imperious, which he did very well. The man with the most stripes was Captain Manuel Enrique Herrera Soto. The way Al introduced him made it quite clear that being a captain in the *Federales* was quite a different thing to being the captain in a tiny municipality.

Context.

Al's introductions were over, and he was about to begin his explanation of why Bud was the Rose Killer. For his own sake, as much as for Bud and myself, I decided to try to stop him.

Before Al could begin, I shouted, "Al, please don't. Don't do this. You've really got it all wrong, and I can prove it."

All eyes turned to me. The *Federales* didn't know the story yet; they just saw me and Bud in handcuffs and presumably assumed that "we" were the "Rose Killer". Why would they be there otherwise?

Captain Soto ran his beady eyes over me, and I clearly heard his right-hand man say in Spanish, "She'll be able to live off her waistline for a while in prison." He smiled conspiratorially at his boss.

"I'm not listening to you anymore, Professor Morgan," replied Al. As he used my professional title I saw a look of surprise cross Captain Soto's face.

Not expecting me to be a professor, were you?

I looked directly at Captain Soto and spoke to him in English. "Please Captain Soto. Captain Torres has misunderstood some facts, and I am sure I can explain everything to your satisfaction."

Now everyone turned their attention to Captain Soto, a situation with which the man seemed perfectly comfortable. He didn't stand; he didn't need to. We were all waiting for him to speak. When he did, it was in a surprisingly deep voice for a man of his stature, and, even more surprisingly for some there, it was in very good, if heavily accented, English.

"I have been invited here by Captain Torres of the municipality of *Punta de las Rocas* with the promise that he can reveal the identity of the Rose Killer, as well as the person who killed a florist in this area, and poisoned a local chef. I have set out early and have traveled many miles to listen to his evidence and to take charge of his prisoners. This is not a court of law. This is simply one officer being courteous to another, and allowing him some latitude to tell us how he arrived at his conclusions. I have been told that Captain Torres is interested in a career with the *Federales*. Let's see if he's up to it. You, Professor Morgan, will have your chance to tell your side of the case in a courtroom. Captain Torres, please continue. You may do so in English; as you can see, I speak it very well. I am sure that Professor Morgan will not interrupt you again." His look told me it would be unwise to respond.

As motes of dust danced in the shafts of sunlight that streamed through the small, high windows, and old wooden chairs creaked in the tense atmosphere, Al cleared his throat again and spoke. It quickly became clear that Al wasn't just bright, he was observant, logical, and ruthless. Just what you want in a cop…but not one who's trying to put you in prison.

"This man," Al waved toward Bud as he spoke, "was found with his hands around the throat of Margarita García Martinez on Sunday morning. I took him into custody, and he has remained here since, refusing to say one word. I have been able to use informal resources, without breaking any laws, sir," he nodded at Captain Soto, "to discover that this man has entered Mexico on numerous occasions during the last year, using different names and passports. I have been able to find thirteen visits where he flew into various Mexican airports. Here are the dates, his aliases, and the countries of origin of the passports he used." He approached Captain Soto, who motioned for his aide to take the file Al was holding, which he did, passing it to his boss, who impassively ran his eyes over its contents.

Al moved back to his original spot. "As you can see, sir, he has represented himself as Canadian, Swedish, and American. He has used various names. I found this passport in his accomplice's purse," he held up Bud's passport, "which names him as Bud Anderson of New Westminster, British Columbia. I suspect it's a fake, as are all the others he's used."

Captain Soto motioned to Al, who handed Bud's passport to the slimy sidekick. The captain whispered some instructions to the man who then took Bud's passport, and the file, and left the municipal hall.

I saw Bud's shoulders sink, and he shook his head ever so slightly. I knew that seeing his passport fall into the hands of the Mexican police was breaking protocol for him – I'd gathered that much from Jack before he'd upped and had a nasty fall, and possible heart attack.

Captain Soto motioned for Al to continue, which he did. "Once I'd established that this man had been making illegal entries into Mexico, I, of course, began to wonder why that might be. I also wondered if the reason for his trips here was what had led to him kill Margarita Martinez."

I noted that Al kept things formal when talking about the woman for whom he'd had feelings – obviously wanting to look professional in front of a man who would probably be able to influence any future career advancement Al might hope for.

Captain Soto nodded as he listened. Al pushed on. "Once he was arrested, I knew I had to try to find out who he was, but I was sidetracked from that endeavor by the arrival of Professor Morgan." Al waved toward me. I nodded and smiled at Captain Soto. He didn't smile back. "I knew Professor Morgan by reputation. She is a criminologist, of sorts, from Vancouver."

You cheeky so-and-so.

"I was suspicious of her immediately, so I courted her company, to keep an eye on her."

Yes, you tried to make sure that either you or Miguel were with me at all times, when possible.

"As I said, I knew of Professor Morgan by reputation, and I have read what she's written about observation techniques when building a picture of a victim. I have also studied such techniques as part of my advanced interrogation training, which I have already completed at the police training facility in Guadalajara."

Now you're really sucking up to Soto.

Soto's body language told me that he was curious, but not impressed. If Al's skills were as good as he claimed, he, too, would have noticed this…and it seemed that he did, because he went in for the kill. "When I first met Professor Morgan, at a local bar and restaurant – in fact, the site where the killing of Tony Booth took place – she had a sunburned nose and had clearly been in the sun for some time. I knew immediately that she could not have arrived in Puerto Vallarta only an hour before I met her, on the day of Margarita Martinez's murder. Also, when I helped her with her luggage I noted she had two suitcases, which, even for a woman, is a lot for a week's vacation. Furthermore, one suitcase – battered and ugly – was hardly filled, whereas the other – better cared for and more elegant – was stuffed. That is not how one person packs luggage – in two very different bags and with such variances in weight distribution."

He had me on both those points, and I saw Bud glance around at me.

Al continued, "As I said, I tried to be with the suspect at all times. I knew that something wasn't right, but, at that time, I didn't know what. I didn't connect her to the slaying at the seafront, nor, at that point, did I connect the death of Margarita Martinez with the Rose Killer at all. As a good detective must, I persevered. I took Professor Morgan into my 'confidence' and invited her to work the case with me. She accepted eagerly. Too eagerly for someone trying to take a break from work. I could tell from her approach to the case that her agenda differed from mine; I wanted to discover the identity of the man in my cells – she was trying to hide it, throwing up a smokescreen of useless lines of questioning about the locations of different people at the time of the slaying…about the crime scene…about many things that were not relevant. She was transparent and foolish to think she was leading me astray. When she saw the man I had in my cells, she was shocked. Immediately I saw the way they looked at each other, I had no doubt that she knew him. With that lead, all I had to do was follow through."

Oh Cait, you're obviously hopeless at hiding your emotions.

There was a general rustling around the room at this observation, and folks shifted on their chairs. I suspected they were running through their interactions with me in their heads, thinking back on how I'd spoken to them, what I'd asked, and how I'd used them in my ruse to lead Al away from learning Bud's true identity.

Al looked pleased with himself. "As someone trained in these matters, and as a student of criminal psychology at Guadalajara University, I decided that I needed to find out what Professor Morgan was really up to. So, when I left Tony Booth at *Amigos del Tequila* that evening, I entered the house in which Professor Morgan was staying, and searched the premises."

Captain Soto held up his hand. "You broke into the place where she was staying to gather evidence?" He sounded annoyed. I wondered what the Mexican rules of evidence were.

Al sounded proud as he replied, "The owner, Henry Douglas, is known to me. I had telephoned him to explain that I was deeply concerned that the tenant he had at his house was not quite what they claimed to be, and asked his permission to use the key that we hold at the police station to gain entry to his home to check that all was well. He agreed. I have his number for the records, sir." Soto nodded, and Al preened just a little.

You sly old dog, it was you who crept around me as I slept. I bet you never knew you'd put my shoes back the wrong way up.

"Upon searching the premises, the only thing I could find amiss was that Professor Morgan's second suitcase did, in fact, contain male clothing. I couldn't find her purse, so I was unable to learn anything else about who the clothes belonged to, but, having witnessed their meeting, I was in no doubt that it was the man in my cells. The man who had ruthlessly killed Margarita Martinez." Al paused for effect, and he got what he wanted, because all eyes followed his to Bud, who sat with no emotion on his face, looking at the floor.

Even though your secret's out, you're keeping quiet, Bud?

Al almost snorted when he said, "Yes, Professor Morgan was in her bed, asleep, when I searched her temporary accommodation, but I believe she left later that night to carry out various nefarious tasks, to cover the tracks of her murderous partner. I believe she returned to *Amigos del Tequila*, using some excuse, and talked Tony Booth into drinking a beer she had dosed with a sedative. Once he had succumbed, having gone to bed not knowing he was drugged, I believe she roused Callie Booth from her already drugged state and made her drink from a glass laced with a sedative, on top of the one already given to her by Dorothea Simmonds. It wouldn't have been difficult for Professor Morgan to gain entry to the premises as the Booths were not good at remembering to lock up, and she knew this. Also, Tony Booth was a good man; he was very hospitable. She would then have had access to the keys to Tony Booth's truck, which I believe she drove to the scene of the morning's murder, where she ransacked the flower shop and stole all of Margarita Martinez's photographic equipment – which she had noted and remarked upon to me when we had visited the flower shop together earlier that night. I saw her eyeing up the equipment, but she tried to sidetrack me with a pathetic story about her mother's wedding bouquet – a lot of rubbish designed to mislead my thinking. I saw what she saw, and she returned later that night to steal it, which made me wonder what it was she thought Margarita Martinez might have captured on her cameras. Professor Morgan had been asking everyone about Margarita's interest in photography, and I began to put the pieces together: if Professor Morgan had arrived with the man who'd killed Margarita, was Margarita's death, and the theft of her photographic equipment, all because she had seen something she shouldn't have? Was she dead because she knew something so damning, so bad, that she couldn't be trusted to not tell anyone? What could be that bad? Nothing bad happens around here…nothing except the Rose Killings. I put those facts together and worked out what had happened. Margarita had, somehow, spotted that this man was the Rose Killer, and she'd had to be silenced for knowing that."

A wave of "Oh no!" and "How awful!" swept through the audience. Heads were shaken at Bud.

I noted that Dorothea was clearly desperate to speak, but everyone could see that Al wasn't done. "I decided to apply Professor Morgan's investigating techniques back onto the woman herself: I knew she'd drugged the Booths, and I knew she'd raided the flower shop, but no one had seen her, and she had good reason for her fingerprints or DNA to be at both sites. I turned to her background. I checked out her university's website, and I found a photograph showing the man in my cell standing right behind her. I had proof they knew each other. It was the break I needed. When I asked for the help of a friend, the one who discovered the information about Bud Anderson's aliases and passports, I was able to match several of his trips to the times of the Rose Killer murders. I am sure that when you get involved, sir, and have full access to all our immigration data, you will find that he was here on every occasion."

Captain Soto waved an imperious arm as if to say, "Maybe," but didn't strain himself by actually speaking.

Al added, "To be fair to Professor Morgan, I think I know why she has done what she has done. She is a criminal psychologist. She studies deviant psychological behavior. I am sure she has studied many cases about serial killers, and I believe that she met this man as part of her studies, or that he targeted her as someone he could bend to his will, and he has brought her under his power." I found it hard to imagine Bud as a Svengali-figure, but I understood what Al was trying to say. "I do not believe that she meant to kill Tony Booth, only to drug both him and his wife so that she could gain access to their truck to be able to do what she needed to do at the flower shop, and then dispose of the photographic equipment, which she has clearly done. In fact, Captain Soto, I have to admit that maybe if I had not stayed for a few drinks with Tony Booth that evening, he might have survived the drugs she gave him. I will always feel guilty about this. But I have brought you the Rose Killer, who is also the man who killed Margarita Martinez, and I have brought you his accomplice – at least on this visit to Mexico – who has, albeit unintentionally, killed Tony Booth." He saluted and bowed.

Oh dear…you don't know the half of it, Captain Alfredo Jesus Beselleu Torres.

"Very convincing," said Captain Soto, tapping his chin. He spied his right-hand man hovering, and called him over. He waved a hand to dismiss Al, who took a seat, and we all waited while Soto listened to what seemed like a very long speech, whispered into his ear.

I couldn't hear what was being said, but Captain Soto's face, and body, spoke volumes: his eyes gradually hooded over, his breathing became labored, his fingers began to drum on his armrest, his blinking increased. He didn't like what he was hearing, and the way he was looking at Al, who was glowing with pride and happily acknowledging the silent nods, grins, thumbs up, and attaboys from the locals, wasn't good...for Al.

I hope it's good for Bud, and me.

Eventually, Captain Soto gave a couple of instructions to his slimy sidekick, who retreated outside again. Then the small, powerful man looked right at me and indicated I should rise. I did.

He cooed, "You have heard what Captain Torres has to say. I think I am right in believing you would welcome a chance to put forward your version of events."

I nodded, and replied in Spanish, "Very much so, sir. Would you like me to address you in Spanish or English?" There were surprised glances all around.

Soto mouth smiled. His eyes didn't. Again, he tapped his chin. He smacked his hand on his leg and said, "Very well. Speak. I will listen. English, please."

I suspected that my Spanish accent was terrible.

I turned to Al and said, in English this time, "Al, I'm sorry about this. You're a good police officer, and I tried, several times, to warn you that you had this all wrong, but you wouldn't listen. Now that you've made these accusations against Bud and me, I'm sure that everyone in this room understands that I'm fighting for our lives." I turned to Bud. "Before I begin, Bud, I have one question for you. Is there a name you can give Captain Soto, so he can get you checked out? There's no point sticking to protocol now. You know that."

Bud nodded. He cleared his throat – it had been a long time since he'd spoken. "Captain Soto, sir. If you contact Fernando Ramirez at the Ministry of the Interior, he will know me. Use the name Bud Anderson. It's the one he knows me by."

Soto nodded, held up his hand to indicate I should wait, pulled out his cellphone, spoke rapidly, listened, then put it away again. He looked at Bud as he spoke. "I know of Señor Ramirez, of course, though we have not met. His role in government is such that he does not mix with a mere captain of the *Federales.* Thank you, Mr. Anderson. Continue Professor Morgan." As he nodded at me, quite graciously, I caught a look of total confusion cross Al's face.

Oh boy – you ain't seen nothing yet, Captain Al.

Time for the Full Story

"Would you mind if someone took these off?" I asked, indicating my handcuffs. Soto nodded and Al did as he was told. I didn't dare ask them to do the same for Bud.

I began, "Captain Torres has examined the facts and come up with a plausible hypothesis," I began. "But I'm afraid he gets an F when it comes to proving it. He has no proof that I drugged the Booths, stole their truck, burgled the flower shop, and disposed of the photographic equipment, nor that Bud Anderson is the Rose Killer…because none of it is true."

Meaningful glances were exchanged, though the messages were mixed.

"Here's the truth. Bud and I arrived to stay at an apartment at the *Rocas Hermosas* Resort on Sunday morning. Bud popped out to get some beers, and the next thing I knew, I was looking out of our apartment window to see him covered in blood and being hauled off by the cops. That's the short version. The fact of the matter is I saw the whole thing, pretty much from the moment Bud left our apartment, until he was driven away to this very building. As I explain, I'll have a few questions to ask – is that alright with you, Captain Soto? I don't want to cross any lines."

Soto nodded. "Remember, this is not a court of law. I am being…polite, by letting you do this."

I nodded and continued. "Al, you were right about some of the facts: I did arrive here, in Mexico, earlier than I said I did, and I was in possession of luggage for two people. You did well to spot that, but you drew the wrong conclusions. Bud, I'm guessing you went into the flower shop and Margarita was bleeding out on the floor?"

Bud nodded.

"You tried to save her because your training kicked in."

He agreed.

I heard a loud whisper from Dorothea. "What training?"

I pounced. "Oh, of course, I didn't tell you how Bud and I met. You were right about that too, in a way, Al; it was through my work." Al looked smug. "Bud is a retired, decorated homicide detective, who was heading up the Integrated Homicide Team in British Columbia when we met, and he hired me as a consultant. His training as a law enforcement officer kicked in, and he tried to save Margarita."

Al blurted out, "Why did he not say this…speak up?" He was visibly shaken.

I said, "His last job was as a Canadian liaison for an international gang-busting task force, and there are certain protocols you follow when you're representing your country."

Eyes were widening around the room; Soto didn't look surprised…I guessed his guy had already told him who Bud really was, and was now checking with the high-ups in the Ministry about how they should handle things.

I noticed that Al was sweating.

I continued, "Just because Bud's a cop, and a very well-respected one at that, it doesn't mean he absolutely couldn't have done it – but you have to understand that I knew he wouldn't have done it. Bud – did you see anyone make their way out of a tiny door in the back of the store?"

Bud shook his head.

"Okay. So, you all thought Bud was the killer, whereas I knew he wasn't…which gave me an advantage. While you were focused on Bud, I was working out who the real killer was. I learned where pretty much everyone was in the few moments leading up to – as well as at the exact moment – when Bud was discovered. I knew no one had entered the flower shop, except

Bud, and no one had left it within the critical timeframe of about three minutes. I was able to discount certain people as viable suspects, but I was left with quite a few possibilities, all of whom had opportunity. Of course, there were two critical points I had to consider regarding opportunity, the first of which was: How did Margarita's murderer get into and out of the flower shop? Who could have walked right in through the front door of the flower shop without being noticed…and who could have then made their way out through the little door that Margarita had built into the back wall of her building, inside her refrigerated units?"

I turned and looked at Margarita's grieving father first. "Juan, I had to consider the possibility that you might have killed your daughter – to be able to inherit her land and her water. I saw your blue pickup truck at the crime scene, at the time. You could easily have been inside it…but – to be fair to you – it could also have been driven by either Tony or Callie Booth…or, maybe, even by Greg. None of the folks I just listed had a watertight alibi for where they were at that time. Dean and Jean? No one knew exactly where you two were, either. Rutilio said he was in his kitchen; Dorothea was out of sight in Serena's massage room; and Ada was unattended in the salon."

"Now wait just a minute, dear…" began Dorothea, about to launch into full attack mode.

I held up my hand. "Don't start, Dorothea. I've had quite enough of your bluster. Your attitude toward the people whose homes you live near has rubbed me up the wrong way. You have no sense of how tough it is for some folks here. You rail about being 'ripped off' without the slightest comprehension that people who rely upon income from tourism have to make their money while they can, in a short season, so they can live all year long."

"Exactly," shouted Rutilio.

I turned on him next. "And you? You're just as bad as Dorothea. You see people on vacation, spending lots of money, and you seem to assume that's how they live all year round. You don't consider how hard they might have had to save up to be able to enjoy a couple of weeks of spending as though it doesn't bother them. Bob, Maria – I think you get it. And, Al, I have great sympathy for the points you've made about how visitors don't respect the local issues, like water usage. You all live in an area that balances on a knife-edge: tourism changes everything – sometimes for the worse, sometimes for the better. But if an area has decided to embrace tourism, it must then work within that changed environment. I see some of you resolving this, and some of you not. It generates tension between almost everyone. And that tension contributed to this crime. Or, I should say, these crimes. I believe that the killer was under tremendous pressure, which might have contributed to their actions. But it doesn't excuse them. Another thing you were right about, Al, is that there are links between the Rose Killer, Margarita's killer, the person who drugged the Booths, and the one who stole Margarita's photographic equipment. So, Captain Soto, you will get to take the Rose Killer into your custody today – it's just not Bud Anderson."

Captain Soto smiled. I saw a gold tooth glint. "So, Professor Morgan, who is the Rose Killer?"

"I'll get there," I promised. "But, first, a couple of sidebars. When I was at the Booths' home, awaiting the ambulance to take them away, I found some notes that Callie Booth had made about accounts she was working on. A couple of them were crossed out, as though they'd been dealt with; one looked as though it had yet to be addressed. One of the 'canceled' notes related to the price of wax at your spa, Serena. Callie had noticed that your costs for wax had decreased considerably in recent months. I am guessing you've found a new supplier and decided to, shall we say, compromise on quality?"

Serena blushed. "You are right," she replied. "People do not spend as they used to. Even when there is a big wedding at the resort, not all the women come beforehand for treatments, to make themselves look nice. These are difficult times. I have to save on what I can." She smiled at Ada and Dorothea, who were, as I knew, good clients of the spa.

I nodded. "Thanks, Serena, that clears that up. Another of Callie's notes related to the extraordinarily good mileage that Margarita was getting from her little van" – puzzled looks were exchanged – "and the third, the one that looked as though it had not yet been dealt with, mentioned 'barrels and bottles' at *Hacienda Soleado*. Would anyone like to comment on that?"

Dean spoke first. "I'm sure it's nothing, Cait. Nothing. It's probably an oversight." I caught a glance he threw to me, and me alone. It was a warning. He was trying to threaten me into silence…I wasn't going to stand for that.

"But it's not 'nothing', Dean," I replied, staring him down. "Callie Booth discovered that the tequila production facility run by the FOGTTs doesn't own enough barrels to contain the number of bottles of 'aged' tequila it sells. I first suspected that it was this discovery that might have led to Margarita's death, and to Callie's and Tony's poisoning, but—"

I couldn't say more, because, at that point, Dean George stood and bellowed, "Enough!" He had an amazing voice; I could almost feel his deep bass resonate around the hall.

With all eyes on him, and the nearby guard dwarfed by his huge mass, Dean George turned to his wife, looked down at her, and whispered, "Sorry, my dear." He then turned to Captain Soto and said, "Captain, your indulgence, please. You need to take a look at this." He held out something that was small in his huge hand; the guard took it from him and passed it to his boss. The man with all the braid looked at what he'd been handed, puffed out his cheeks in surprise, rolled his eyes, and allowed the guard to return Dean's property.

"Professor Morgan, you need to let this gentleman speak." Soto waved me into submission. I knew when it was time to cede the floor.

As someone who reads people, I should have been able to interpret Dean's glaring at me better than I had. But in my defense, I'd been focused on clearing Bud, rather than on picking up on micro-expressions. That said, as Dean stood in front of our group, I saw a different person emerge from beneath the folds of his Hawaiian shirt. Jean rose to stand beside him, they held hands, and Dean addressed his expectant audience. Just before he spoke, a light bulb came on in my head. A retired government employee? Evasive when questioned? He and his wife giving each other a cover story? Dean wasn't the person I'd thought him to be. His larger than life persona was just that, a personality he'd adopted to keep his true identity safe.

Of course…Dean and Jean. What damage have I done?

Dean commanded our attention, and his voice – softer now, but still as powerful – filled the chamber. "My name is not Dean George, and, although this wonderful woman is my wife, her name is not Jean George. Juan García Martinez, Dorothea Simmonds, and Greg Hollins – I'll call you that for now, Greg, though I do know your real name – you are all under arrest for multiple counts of fraudulent trading of falsely labeled tequila in the USA. I represent the US government, and before you leave this room – no, don't try to run, Juan, I'm sure that Captain Soto's troops will have something to say about that – we will be joined by members of the Mexican authorities responsible for the examination and certification of tequila, who will escort you all into custody, where you'll find that a long list of charges are due to be brought against you."

Frank and Ada Taylor couldn't have looked more shocked, Bud clearly had no idea what on earth was going on, and – of all the faces in the room that displayed disbelief – it was Al's that drew my attention: he looked as though he was about to burst into tears. I could sense the confusion that must have been running through his mind at that moment. Not only was I undermining him, but Dean George was doing the same.

Dean continued, "Captain Soto, I need to make a couple of calls, with your permission?" Soto nodded. Dean looked at me. "Don't worry, Cait, this isn't your fault. We were almost ready to scoop everyone up, but your comments about the FOGTT accounts mean we'd better do it now, before these three can get word to anyone else and spoil our entire case. I had no idea that the FOGTTs had given their accounts to Callie Booth – they've always had a guy we know about in PV do them before. With that information out there, it's best we do it this way, now. I only hope it wasn't this case that got the Booths into trouble and Tony and Margarita killed. I knew we were dealing with international criminals, but I didn't think for one minute they were killers. By the way," he added, "just so you know, Captain Soto, word has come down to me through…various channels…that this man is on the side of the angels." He nodded toward Bud. "I've been ready to get your back, sir," he said directly to Bud, who nodded in response.

Dean didn't sound like a lower-ranked official for whatever agency he represented, and I wondered if his reference to Bud as "sir" was anything other than a general politeness.

"We had nothing to do with Tony's death…nor Margarita's," shouted Dorothea.

"Shut up, you stupid woman," spat Greg Hollins. "This is all your fault. I told you to wait with those accounts…wait until our regular guy in PV was back from his vacation, but you had to do it, didn't you? You had to give them to Callie. Why couldn't you wait? You always have to have everything done the way you want it, damn you."

Greg's accent wasn't Australian anymore. New Jersey was nearer the mark, to my ear. Juan Martinez threw out some choice phrases in Spanish…which certainly didn't need to be translated in order for Dorothea to know what he thought of her. Then all three of the culprits sat silently, glowering at each other, as Dean George walked toward the exit with his phone clamped to his ear, his hands waving, and a lot of "Sorry, ma'am" and "Yes, right now, please, ma'am" audible to the room.

Captain Soto motioned that I should continue, which I did, though I could tell that I didn't have everyone's undivided attention anymore.

That doesn't matter as long as I have Soto's.

"So, there we have the explanation of Callie's note about the FOGTT bottles and barrels," I said…maybe a little too brightly. "Let's get back to Margarita's gas mileage, which was something else that the eagle-eyed Callie Booth queried. How many of us get into our vehicles and notice the mileage? Not many, I'm sure. But what about how much gas we have? Pretty much everyone. Margarita cycled almost everywhere, using her van only when she needed it. She was careful with money, she had to be, and she'd have noticed if, on any given morning, she'd climbed into her van and there was less gas in it than there had been the night before. Margarita was a woman who paid great attention to detail, but she might easily have missed the fact that hundreds of miles were being added to her odometer. Which they were. You see – cleverly – the person driving her van without her permission, or knowledge, was refilling it with fuel after they used it. So when she gave her mileage and her gas receipts to Callie, the accountant was puzzled, and made a note to speak to Margarita about the anomaly – that she seemed to be driving a lot of miles for the gas she said she was putting in. The notes were near Callie's phone, and the chances were that Callie had spoken to Margarita about this matter already, then crossed through the note to herself."

"Who borrowed Margarita's van and filled it with gas?" asked Frank, his hand raised. Ada pulled his hand down and tutted.

"Well, Frank, to answer your question, the Rose Killer was borrowing it, to transport and dump bodies. The same person was driving it the day that Margarita took photographs of her own van – not one similar to it, but her actual van – when she was out taking daybreak shots of the surf. I don't think she knew what she'd seen, or photographed, at first. But she finally put it all together yesterday morning when someone came into her store to buy two red roses…and she suddenly realized she was looking at the person responsible for killing Miguel's daughter and all those other girls. The killer's response, knowing they'd been found out, was to act instantly. That's why Margarita died."

"So who is it?" asked Ada plaintively. "Is it one of...us?" She looked around the room, wide-eyed. And she wasn't the only one.

"Preposterous!" exclaimed Dorothea.

"No, it's not," I said quietly.

The body language being displayed by almost everyone in the room was spot on for the situation: anxiety, and heightened awareness, as well as a sense of…expectation.

I looked at Captain Soto and said, "Ready?" He nodded and signaled his men with his fingers; anyone thinking of making a run for it would have several automatic weapons to consider.

"I think that the death of Miguel's daughter was an accident: a heavy drinking session resulted in her death, and the person she'd been drinking with panicked, identified Margarita's van as a convenient way to get the body out of the vicinity, and thought they'd got away with it. But the police pulled in Miguel as a prime suspect. A month of having the *Federales* buzzing about the area didn't go down well in many quarters for...many reasons – not the least of which would have been the illicit tequila trade some of you were engaged in. So – despite the tragic aspects – there was general relief when another girl was killed and everyone around here had an alibi: they were all attending one of the crucifix of Requiem Masses that Miguel had arranged. Captain Soto – I assume you had all the men in this area under observation at that time?"

Soto nodded. There were a few surprised expressions around the room. Ada patted her husband's hand – to stop him from blowing his top, I assumed.

I asked Soto, "But that day, with everyone heading off in different directions for religious observances, did you ease up a little?"

Again, he nodded, ruefully.

I explained, "The one day that Margarita's van was available in the daytime – because she'd closed her shop – you saw the only daytime abduction of a girl who was killed. Unlike Angélica Rosa, the second girl was drugged. Her exact time of death was suspect, though you knew she hadn't been dumped before a certain point in time. Now, let me pose this question: If a young woman was alone, who would she trust enough to accept a ride from? What type of vehicle would she willingly get into, if she were offered a lift, by a stranger?"

There were shrugs around the room.

To be expected.

I answered my own question. "I would suggest a police car. Despite rumors about the trustworthiness of the Mexican police force – and I'm sorry, Captain Soto, but even you have to accept that the evidence for some corruption is pretty clear – there are places where people still trust their local cops."

Soto shrugged, and there were nodding heads, and glances in the general direction of Miguel and Al.

Good.

I pounced. "But how could Margarita's van ever be mistaken for a police car? It's white, which helps…and I discovered that Miguel has a magnetic decal that can be attached to any vehicle, thereby transforming it into a 'police car' containing a person a girl might, psychologically speaking, trust. And that's exactly what the killer did: placed Miguel's decal on Margarita's van and used it to lure girls. Those girls would then be plied with drugged alcohol and allowed to die."

I heard a little gasp from Ada.

I ploughed one. "Given the nature of the victims' backgrounds, I suspect that the alcohol and drugs were disguised in some sort of seemingly innocent beverage, which they accepted without question, as a friendly gesture from a trusted person. But why? There was no sexual interference; no apparent sexual motive at all. Was the killer doing it for the simple pleasure of watching these poor young women die? If so, why lay them out with such reverence, wrapped in a sheet, their hands in prayer, holding roses?"

There were mumblings. I turned and looked directly at the Rose Killer.

"Because that's what you felt it was right to do for your poor little niece, wasn't it, Rutilio? I've seen how you like to pour your drinks; I'm betting you gave Angélica Rosa just one too many strong drinks the night of the *Día de los Muertos* celebrations, she passed out, and you found she'd died. You panicked, loaded her body into Margarita's van which was always – conveniently – parked overnight in the lane behind your restaurant. I'm sure you knew where Margarita kept her keys, and how to get to them. Then you drove your niece's remains far away where you…well, at least you showed respect for her after death, in the way you laid out her body – wrapped in white, and with roses pressed into her hands."

Miguel stared at me as though I'd lost my mind…then stared at his brother, his eyes wide.

Keep going, Cait.

"It didn't occur to you that your brother would be suspected of killing his own child. It was during that period that your business suffered – I suspect you were racked with guilt…but how could you help him? Then you came up with a plan: on the day of the Requiem Masses you took Margarita's van, and, once you were away from this area, added your brother's police decal. You might even have 'borrowed' one of his spare uniform shirts to complete the look – it would have been easy enough for you to gain access to one. You drove around until you picked up your second victim, then you made sure you dumped the poor woman's body in a place where the time after which she was dumped – six o'clock in this case – would be known. Maybe you followed a cop car on its rounds, or possibly knew their schedule – however you managed it you knew there'd be a clear, unequivocal timeframe for the dumping of the body…because that was the vital part of your plan. Then you returned to *Punta de las Rocas* for the service here, assuring that both you and your brother, in Puerto Vallarta, had watertight alibis for the critical time period, and – because you stayed with him – throughout the night, until the body was discovered."

Miguel shot to his feet, and got everyone's attention.

He shouted, "My brother could not have done this. I was cleared because I could not have had time to drive from the place where the poor girl was dumped to the Mass I attended in Puerto Vallarta – where many people saw me. But my brother has the same alibi: he was at another service here." Miguel looked terribly distressed.

"What time was the Mass said here?" I asked Al, who I knew had attended with Rutilio.

Al looked puzzled. "It was at seven, the same time as in Puerto Vallarta."

I nodded. "But *Punta de las Rocas*, and the whole of Nayarit, is an hour behind Puerto Vallarta. When it was seven o'clock in Puerto Vallarta, it was only six o'clock here: Rutilio had a whole extra hour to get back here from the dump site, and still be at the church in time for the *Punta de los Rocas* seven o'clock service. You're all so used to the difference it didn't occur to you. I didn't even know about the time difference until this morning, which was why I was stuck…I couldn't work out how Rutilio could have been in two places at once that day, though I knew, by then, that it was him who'd killed Margarita."

"This is rubbish!" shouted Rutilio, leaping up from his seat. "I would not kill my niece. I would not kill all those other girls. Why would I do that? You have no proof. There is nothing that points to me." Rutilio grinned at me with his big teeth.

Look out, Cheshire Cat – here I come.

One of the cops motioned with his weapon that Rutilio should sit, and he did, grumbling.

I sighed. "Rutilio, you're a classic narcissist with sociopathic tendencies. The giant sign you have of your own face? The way you present yourself as the star of your own show at the restaurant? The roses you like to give the women with their checks, so that you can flatter them and have them focus on just you? By the way, I know that's why, for the first time, you had to try to get the red roses from Margarita for this latest kill: you mentioned to Al – when the two of you chatted in your native tongue, believing that I couldn't understand you – that you don't have your own roses during the summer months. For the rest of the kills, you used the ones you already had in bulk at your restaurant. And I know you used Margarita's van…because it's refrigerated. It was the refrigeration that threw off the coroner's ability to come up with an accurate time of death for the second killing – it messes with the onset of rigor mortis. Sometimes rigor sets in more quickly because of it, sometimes it's delayed. After all the press coverage about the confused time of death, you might have put two and two together and worked out that, somehow, the refrigerated van could help you mask when you were really killing."

Ada burst out with, "But, Cait – those poor girls…many of them were from places far away from here; how could Rutilio have known them all?"

I replied, staring directly at Rutilio himself, "You didn't target specific girls; you'd just drive until you found one who was ready to accept the offer of a ride home from a man driving a cop car. Enough young people walk in these areas, because they don't own a car or even a bicycle, so it wouldn't take too long. Your niece's death was an accident. You covered it up. Your first 'real murder' was when you resorted to plying a girl with drink and drugging her, so as to clear your brother, and you, of suspicion."

This time it was Frank who cried out, "If he did do what you're saying, maybe I could see why he killed second time…but…but why didn't he just stop, then?"

I acknowledged Frank. "Good question. Why more deaths, Rutilio? Why continue? My assessment would be that you did it just because you could…and because you liked it. It had become 'your thing'…and you don't have many of those, do you? You had to give up your apartment in Bucerias and move in with your mother and your brother's family. None of your past jobs have gone well for you – you've always been 'misunderstood' by employers. Even your own business, the restaurant, is failing. You're getting older, and whatever looks you once had are fading…and this was one way you could reassure yourself you were a real man – not in a sexual way, but by showing you had power over people. You are your mother's 'pretty baby'. She and your brother have unwittingly enabled you to remain free of responsibilities…they've backed you up when you've said that past misfortunes have not been 'your fault'. You display a classic inability to take responsibility for any of your own failures."

Finally, there was a gasp from Miguel. "No!"

"Yes," I replied. "When I saw Rutilio from the condo window, just after the discovery of Margarita's body, he was standing against a white wall, holding a glass of water and what I thought were two chopsticks in his hands, at exactly the time that Bud was trying to save Margarita's life. I could just about spot his white chef hat against the white stucco wall."

I looked at the killer and saw his mask slip even further as I spoke, a snarl beginning to twitch at his lips.

Nearly done, Cait…

"Initially, it was difficult for me to spot that you were wearing a chef hat, because it took a few moments for me to make out the white shape against the white wall. For the same reason, I can say that now I know that what I thought at the time were two 'sticks' that you were holding were not chopsticks – my initial belief – but were, in fact, two red roses; I could only see the long stems, but couldn't make out the red of the flower heads because they'd disappeared against the red of your chef jacket – just like poor Margarita's blood, which must have been all over it at the time. You put on a clean jacket in your kitchen before you joined the crowd in the street outside Margarita's shop. And the knife found at the scene? You might have had one in your pocket when you went to her shop, but I think it might be discovered that the knife used to kill her was Margarita's own. Florists have all sorts of cutting implements to hand; all you had to do was reach out and make one swift slashing motion."

The men with guns were now even more alert. Rutilio's bravado had completely evaporated, but he still seemed to have his toothy grin, because his dry lips had stuck to his teeth.

Al and Miguel were on their feet. But I wasn't done. "You sauntered into Margarita's shop on Sunday morning, Rutilio, needing two red roses, because you knew it was your time to kill again. But she wouldn't sell them to you; she'd collected a special order for a wedding, and they were all spoken for. When I was in her shop with Al, I noticed that she had two buckets with red roses in them, and one with yellow…and spotted that she had twenty-two red roses and twelve yellow. I think it unlikely that a florist would buy fancy roses in less than a full dozen, so I reckoned that two red roses from a full two dozen were gone…which wasn't so unusual, as a single observation. However, when I returned to the shop with Miguel, I saw a newspaper that must have belonged to Margarita on the floor, warning girls to be careful because it was Rose Killer time. She'd worked out that her van was being used without her knowledge…and I believe she'd spotted that she'd actually photographed it in use. Then there you were, urging her to sell you two red roses. And I believe that's when the penny dropped for poor Margrita. Did she accuse you of being the Rose Killer?"

Miguel hadn't taken his eyes off his brother for a second; he let out a little whimper.

I pressed on. "I can also say, with certainty, that Margarita mentioned to you that Callie Booth had raised the issue of the amount of mileage she was getting when compared with her gas receipts...because that's the only reason why you'd have gone after the Booths, which you did. When it comes to their drugging, Rutilio, I suspect it went much as Al suggested, but with you, not me, getting Tony to accept a drugged drink, waiting until he went to bed, then getting Callie to accept a drink from you in her already hazy state. But you got your doses wrong, didn't you? You see, you're only used to drugging young women who are small in stature; Callie Booth is a healthy, fit woman, as I saw from her wedding photographs, and she has a bigger body mass than you were used to dealing with...so your usual dose – which you believed would be sufficient to kill her – didn't work on her, did it? However, Tony was a fit, muscular man, so I'm betting you gave him some extra...just to make sure it did its job. You certainly meant to kill them both, because you couldn't risk anyone hearing about the problem with gas mileage that Margarita had told you that Callie had spotted. It was you who headed to the flower shop to search for photographic evidence. Knowing that Margarita had photographs of her van being driven without her permission, you didn't want to take any chances; might they show your face? That's why you checked through all her photographs, then took all her equipment. We wouldn't have the photos that we do if Al hadn't known about Margarita's secret stash of equipment in her glove box. I'm sure that the time and date stamp in the digital data will prove that Margarita's van was being used by someone other than herself at a...critical time."

There were stirrings around the room.

I was almost done. "The 'long hours' Rutilio worked at the restaurant, Miguel? They were great cover. For example, on

Sunday night, all he had to do was quickly scrape down his grill…then wait until the coast was clear at the Booths', drug them, and head back to search Margarita's store. He still had time to drive off, kill another poor young woman, dump her body, return the van to its usual spot, and come home to bed. Al, you know that Bud was in your cell on Sunday night and couldn't have been out there killing this latest poor young woman. If the medical examiner knows about the use of a refrigerated van, I'm sure they'll be able to determine her actual time of death. In any case, Bud was in Canada on Saturday, and in prison on Sunday, so clearly he didn't kill this poor woman. And – if you're still in any doubt about Bud not being the Rose Killer – my phone is in my bag, and it contains photos of an event Bud and I attended in Vancouver last year, with a giant dated banner in the background, proving he wasn't here for the killing on December 7th either. Captain Soto, I promise you, Rutilio is your man. He is the Rose Killer. He is the man who slashed Margarita's throat. He is the man who drugged both Tony and Callie Booth."

I sat down and waited for it all to kick off…which it did.

Miguel was up on his feet, as were Al and Juan. All three made for Rutilio, who fell to the floor and curled up into a ball.

The chef started to cry and wail. "It was an accident, my brother, an accident. Angélica Rosa drank too much. I couldn't get her to breathe. I did my best. It was an accident! But, brother, when I saw how you felt – that she was pure and safe with God, that you were celebrating that she was with her Maker, at peace – I knew it was alright to take the others. I saved them, my brother. Like your daughter, Juan, all of them were saved."

Is Rutilio really trying to make it sound as though his multiple murders had been some sort of sacrificial act? I wonder how that'll play out in a courtroom.

Captain Soto instructed his guards to break up the melee, which they did, quite quickly. It's amazing what a few automatic weapons can achieve when pointed at a person.

In a matter of moments, Bud's handcuffs were off, and he was being addressed, very formally, by Captain Soto.

At last…thanks heavens.

Rutilio was being hauled away by the *Federales*.

That smile of yours has gone forever, I reckon.

Dean and Jean George were heading toward me, smiling.

"I'm sorry," I said to them quietly. "I didn't know you were 'the operative' that Jack White had referred to until we were here. Dean, when you threw me that challenging look, the penny dropped. But who do you work for?" I still didn't know who they really were, only that they weren't who they said they were.

"US government," said Dean quietly, and conspiratorially. "Let's leave it at that. Working with Mexican authorities, multiple border authorities, and US officials. I got a call from some 'friends' in Ottawa – I've been watching your back. I informed them of your arrest, and I'd been cleared to take action before the *Federales* took you two away. And, like I said earlier, don't beat yourself up about it…we were pretty well ready to move on this group. We might have lost a few drivers in the wind, but I just heard from my superior that we've got everyone important – on both sides of the border – in custody."

I turned to find Bud at my shoulder.

I smiled, and hugged him.

Oh Bud…you stink.

When I released my grip, he asked, "So, will someone tell me what's been going on here?"

I explained. "The *Hacienda Soleado* is selling more bottles of aged tequila than they could possibly produce…because they don't have enough barrels for the job. Tequila starts life as a clear liquid, but the longer it's aged in barrels, the higher the price it can be sold for. Callie Booth spotted the discrepancy between the number of bottles of the older stuff being sold and the number of barrels owned by the FOGTTs in which the tequila needed to be aged. I'm guessing they're coloring young tequila and selling it as *añejo*?"

Dean nodded. "They're breaking any number of the very strict laws governing the production of tequila on this side of the border, and because so much of it is sold in the US, it's creating all types of fraud cases over there. We were sent in because it's the Americans who are running the show down here."

"Greg's not Australian, is he?" I asked, knowing the answer. He couldn't be – he was too Australian to be real. Dean shook his head. "It's him, Dorothea, and Juan?" I asked.

Dean nodded. "Juan's the one with all the local contacts; he knows which palms to grease to get the right certification. Of course, once it's off the hacienda it's a lot safer to transport than drugs: you get caught with a truckload of tequila that's been incorrectly labeled, there's deniability…not the case when you're talking about drugs."

"It's why we're here as a team," Jean said. "They wanted a couple on the case, so we could get to know what systems they were using, which locals were involved. And when poor Margarita was killed, and the *Federales* were bound to be called in, I just knew that something would happen to spoil our set up. They interfere. I guess that's their job, to be fair. We'd tried to build an atmosphere where everyone here supported Al as much as possible in everything he did, so outside forces were rarely called upon. I was angry when I first met you – not with you, yourself, but because of the situation. I'm sorry I was hostile. We've been at it a long time, on both sides of the border. It's not just these guys, and it's not just this plant, you see. It's big.

Big money. At least the call from Ottawa gave us a chance to get everything sorted out." She gave me a huge hug.

I asked, "The Taylors – do they even know what's going on?"

Dean smiled and shook his head. "They don't have a clue. They're in their own little world. We'll protect them. Henry Douglas – the guy whose house you've been staying in? He's away in LA too often to have noticed anything. It's just Greg, Dorothea, and Juan…plus the officials who've been on the take. In a way, I'll be sorry to leave this place. We've liked it here. By the way, Cait, the reason I couldn't tell you where we were when Margarita was killed was because we were having a meeting with a local…resource…down on the beach at that exact time. Sorry that I," he squeezed his wife's hand, "that *we* must have seemed suspicious. I didn't dare break cover sooner than today – Al locking you up last night gave us just enough time to get things all lined up in case this happened." He gave an embarrassed smile.

At least I better understood what had been going on with the "Georges".

As I looked around, I could see Captain Soto, Al, and a weeping Miguel moving toward Al's office. I turned to Bud and whispered, "Just one more minute, and I'm all yours, okay?"

He shrugged.

I waggled a hand at Al and gestured for him to come to me for a moment, which he did, carrying my purse. "Here's all your stuff, Cait. Mr. Anderson's things are in there too."

I took the bag and thanked him. "Sorry to butt in, Al, but one quick thing?" He nodded. "When are you going to tell the people around here about your rights to the García land?"

He stammered, "I…I don't know what you mean."

I sighed. "Your Gram Beselleu? Her maiden name was Dubois. I looked it up. Juan Carlos García García, or should I say García Dubois, is not just 'the father of *Punta de las Rocas*' as you put it so passionately yesterday, he's also your great-grandfather, right?" Al nodded. "Is your family due to inherit a lot of land around here?"

"I believe we might have a better claim than Juan does to the land that Margarita inherited from her mother's side of the family. Not that Margarita and I were closely related – it goes way back, and…well, it's complicated. The charter is clear – every child has their right. And I am one of those children."

"So it wasn't just fate that brought you here?"

"Not exactly. I didn't know at first, but I researched the area, and, of course, I knew my gram's maiden name, so I did a bit more digging. I was always pretty good at research." Al studied his shoes. "I don't think this is the time to make myself known as a García Dubois. I'm not even sure I'll stay. You know, maybe I'm not cut out to be a cop. Given everything that was going on in *Punta de las Rocas*, right under my nose, and I…knew nothing. I'm feeling pretty useless right now, Professor Morgan."

I smiled. The poor guy looked pretty sorry for himself. "It's still Cait, okay?" He nodded. "Listen, I've learned in my life that not everything's for everyone. With Juan Martinez out of the picture, you might get your hands on that beautiful shoreline and save it for posterity…and there's likely to be an opening for mayor around here too. You'd make a good mayor. You should think about it. You love history, art, and literature – who knows, with time, maybe this wonderful old hall could become some sort of cultural center for the tourists who are thirsty for a taste of the real Mexico."

Al nodded, though he didn't look convinced. He said quietly, "I'm sorry about accusing you."

I cut him short. "It's alright. I understand." And I did. I didn't like it, but I understood it. "I'm off. We're off, okay?"

Al held up his hands. "Go. Stay. Do as you please. It's been a pleasure to meet you, Cait, but I wish it could have been…"

"You don't have to say it, Al, I know. Different circumstances? Context, right?" Al nodded. "Good luck, and goodbye," I called as I waved.

Now I need to…escape…

I grabbed Bud by the arm and we both, finally, stepped out into the sunlight together and walked away from the strange building.

Bud threw his arms around me and held me tight. "I am so glad to be out of that place," was all he said, then he kissed me. It was a very bristly experience, but it was wonderful.

As we finally pulled apart I said, "Who are you?"

Bud chuckled. It was a wonderful sound. "What, not used to the beard?"

I hit him on the arm – not too hard. "You know what I mean, Bud…if that's your name at all. *Who* are you?"

Bud stepped back, holding on to my arms as he looked into my eyes. "When I was born in Sweden, which is where I grew up until I was all of ten months old, I was named Börje Ulf Dyggve Anderson."

"That's quite a mouthful," I replied.

Bud smiled. "Exactly. In my first Canadian school I was known as Bud, using my three initials, and I've always thought of myself as Bud. But it's not my real name."

"And what about the work you've been doing for CSIS since you 'retired'? Jack, with Sheila's help, let the cat out of the bag."

Bud paused. "I can tell you that CSIS sees me as a resource. I've got a lot of knowledge in this old noggin of mine," he said, patting his messy hair. "Of course, I'm not the brainbox that you are, but they do like to keep using what I know. But as for the details? I…I can't tell you. Sorry."

"Is it over? Are they done with you? Or will you keep running off to foreign countries without me knowing about it?"

"Maybe, after this, they'll take more notice when I tell them I want to stop."

I nodded. "Bud, we need to talk. Not today, maybe, but soon. There's a lot I don't know about you. In fact…right…I just have to say it: you've deceived me. And you've done an alarmingly good job of it. And that doesn't feel good. Understand?"

Bud nodded. "Cait, we will talk…I promise. You need to know that my professional responsibilities to my country have become an even heavier burden because of what you mean to me, and because of what I can't tell you. And, yes, we'll talk about it all – properly – very soon. But, right now, I need to clean myself up and decompress a bit. Maybe we can start over, and have the holiday we've been looking forward to for weeks?"

We hugged again. It felt like I was home.

"Want a ride, you two? Then we can tell you some more background on our case against ingratiating Greg, domineering Dorothea, and slippery Juan." It was Dean George's unmistakable voice; he and his wife joined us as we stood in the sunlight and enjoyed our freedom.

I didn't wait for Bud to answer. "Yes, please. Could you drive us back to Henry's place, so we can check on how Jack is doing back at home, allow Bud – and me – to clean up, and collect our stuff? Then I'm going to suggest we take ourselves to one of those big hotels on the seafront in Puerto Vallarta for the next few days, get some sun, drink lots of cocktails with little umbrellas in them, and feast our faces off. I think we should leave this area – lovely though it is. I want to find some good food to eat – because I know there must be a lot of it in the area; I want local snapper, fresh salsa, chicken with a light mole sauce…"

Bud smiled. "Hey, hold your horses, Cait…getting clean to start with sounds great, and, of course, I'm anxious to know how Jack's coming along." He hugged me tight. "And, as for your suggestion about staying in Puerto Vallarta and hunting down some excellent food, I'm all for that, too; my diet since we arrived has been…'bland'? So, okay then…let's do it, Cait…let's indulge for the time we have left before our flight home."

It was only as we were being driven toward the shimmering sea at the bottom of the hill that I remembered the promises I'd made to my mirror-self that morning about everything I'd give up if only Bud and I managed to survive our ordeal.

I told myself that what happens through a looking glass doesn't really count, especially if it happens in a world that's full of fake…everything. So I'd allow myself to indulge for the next few days, then I'd make a fresh start when we got home.

I'd make a list of things about myself that I could work on.

I like lists.

Acknowledgments abridged from the First Edition (2014)

My thanks to everyone I met on my travels in Bucerias, Mismaloya, and Puerto Vallarta who took the time to share their fascinating insights about life in their beautiful part of the world. To my mum and my sister, who, as ever, were the first to read and give feedback on my writing, as well as the sort of encouragement that can only come from those who truly love you. To my husband, who supports me in every way, through every day. Thanks to the TouchWood Team.

Acknowledgments: Second Edition (2025)

It sounds as though editing a book that's already been published would be a straightforward task, but it turns out that it's not.

I've lost count of the hours I've struggled with this task; my husband has been my rock during what people euphemistically call "a journey", when they mean "a nightmare". Without his patience and wise counsel, I might have thrown in the towel…but perseverance is easier when you have a cheerleader. Thank you.

Sue Vincent, my proofer, has also been a stalwart: she and I have done our best to ensure that not one single error gets past us…but, if you spot anything we missed, please let me know. (My email address can be found at my website.) I hope that anything we didn't manage to catch didn't pull you out of the story too much. We're only human (no AI interference here) and, apparently, to err *is* human; please forgive us our humanity.

Thanks to the Four Tails Publishing team: you were patient with me, and that means a great deal.

Thanks, finally, to all the printers, distributors, booksellers, librarians, reviewers, and bloggers who played a part in getting this book into your hands and, of course, my thanks to you, for choosing to enter Cait's world: I hope you enjoy your time with her. I know I always do.

Cathy Ace, February 2025

About the Author

CATHY ACE was born and raised in Swansea, Wales, and migrated to British Columbia, Canada aged forty. She is the author of The Cait Morgan Mysteries, The WISE Enquiries Agency Mysteries, the standalone novel of psychological suspense, The Wrong Boy, and collections of short stories and novellas. As well as being passionate about writing crime fiction, she's also a keen gardener.

You can find out more about Cathy and all her works at her website: www.cathyace.com

www.ingramcontent.com/pod-product-compliance
Lightning Source LLC
Chambersburg PA
CBHW030339310726
48979CB00001B/107

* 9 7 8 1 9 9 0 5 5 0 3 7 9 *